Portrait of Mme René de Gas, née Estelle Musson
1872-73
Oil on canvas
39 ³⁄₈ x 54 inches
New Orleans Museum of Art: Museum Purchase
through Public Subscription

Estelle

Estelle

A Novel

LINDA STEWART HENLEY

SHE WRITES PRESS

Published 2020
Printed in the United States of America
Print ISBN: 978-1-63152-791-3
E-ISBN: 978-1-63152-792-0
Library of Congress Control Number: 2020905898

For information, address:
She Writes Press
1569 Solano Ave #546
Berkeley, CA 94707

Interior design by Tabitha Lahr

She Writes Press is a division of SparkPoint Studio, LLC.

Cover: detail of a painting by Edgar Degas, *Woman with a Vase of Flowers* (Estelle De Gas née Musson), 1872-73. Oil on canvas, Musée d'Orsay, Paris

For Vince

De Gas–Musson Family in New Orleans

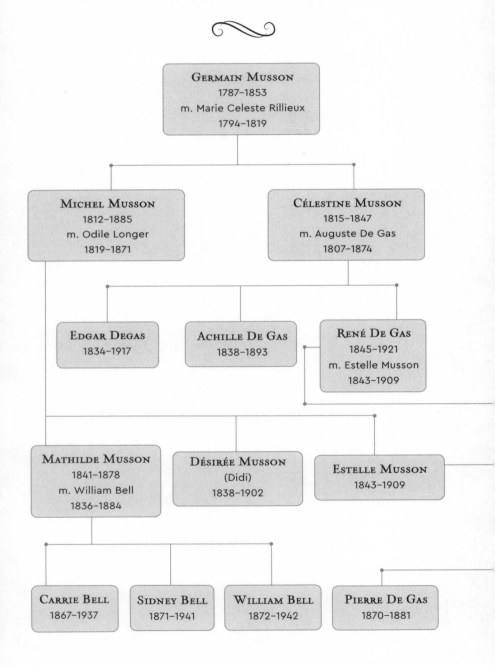

Germain Musson
1787–1853
m. Marie Celeste Rillieux
1794–1819

Michel Musson
1812–1885
m. Odile Longer
1819–1871

Célestine Musson
1815–1847
m. Auguste De Gas
1807–1874

Edgar Degas
1834–1917

Achille De Gas
1838–1893

René De Gas
1845–1921
m. Estelle Musson
1843–1909

Mathilde Musson
1841–1878
m. William Bell
1836–1884

Désirée Musson
(Didi)
1838–1902

Estelle Musson
1843–1909

Carrie Bell
1867–1937

Sidney Bell
1871–1941

William Bell
1872–1942

Pierre De Gas
1870–1881

FONTENOT FAMILY

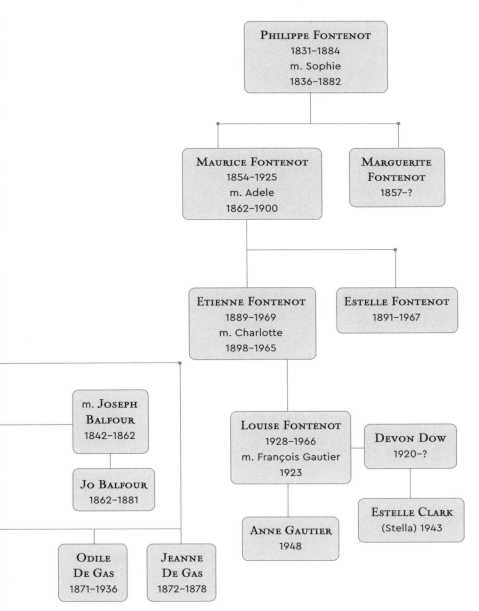

"A man is an artist only at certain moments, by an effort of will."

—EDGAR DEGAS

Chapter 1

September 1970

At ten o'clock on the first cool morning of late summer, Anne Gautier threw on a pair of shorts and a T-shirt, laced her running shoes, and stepped into the street. She hummed as she jogged the few blocks along Esplanade Avenue under spreading oaks and magnolias until she arrived at the house with the rusting wrought iron gate. As she kicked empty beer cans from the pathway leading to the porch, she noticed that the front door stood ajar. A thread of anxiety twisted down her spine. Surely the contractors weren't working on this day, a Saturday.

The raspy voice of the neighbor next door startled her.

"Mornin', Miss Anne." He smiled, showing his yellow teeth. "Makin' progress in there, is they?"

"Yes. They finished repairing the roof last week. Now they're working on the inside. They'll treat the termites first."

"Uh-huh. Nasty little critters. My place must be full of 'em. Them and the roaches make a nice pair." He cackled with laughter.

"You're right there, Mr. Jackson," she said, waving to him as she pushed her front door farther open. She didn't want to engage him in conversation about insects—or anything else, for that matter. He was old, and strange.

She stood for a few moments on the threshold and peered inside. "Hello. Anyone there?" she yelled.

Only the rustle of palm fronds in the breeze responded. *No need to panic*, she scolded herself. *The contractors just forgot to lock up.* Treading with care, she crept in.

The interior of the house looked worse than it had the first time she'd seen it. Paper hung in strips from walls still standing, and grimy windows obscured the view of trees in the garden. Dust covered every horizontal surface. It had once been an elegant house on one of the finest streets in New Orleans, and the high ceilings, moldings, and decorative woodwork served as reminders, but in its present state she could hardly imagine the place as an habitable dwelling. It was her dearest wish to bring it back to its former state of grace and beauty, shining with fresh paint and spotless windows. She noticed nothing unusual on the first floor.

She mounted the stairs, taking care not to trip on any loose boards. When she reached the attic on the third floor, she turned her eyes to the ceiling. The roof appeared solid, and she could no longer see the sky. *Progress at last.* But dust motes dancing in the sunlight told her that months of work remained before she could entertain any sense of pride about the place or consider moving in. She caught an image of herself in a wall mirror. The reflection of her long brown hair, almost gray in the dull glass, relayed a ghostly impression of her pale face and dark eyes. She held her breath. *This place feels creepy, sometimes.*

On her way down from the attic, she glanced into the bedrooms on the second floor. No work completed there yet. The bathroom door swung idly on the hinges, its toe dragging on the floor. Stepping back, Anne almost lost her balance as she surveyed the scene. Utter chaos lay before her. She pressed her hand to her chest to calm her galloping heartbeat. The clawfoot bathtub and pedestal sink she had admired and wanted to preserve sat in fragments on the floor. The toilet kneeled before her, ripped from its foothold like a fallen idol. They would have to replace the fixtures, smashed almost beyond recognition. Then she noticed a note taped to the remnants of the sink. She moved closer.

The sign, scrawled in black letters said, *Stop Fixing What Don't Need Fixing. Remember Section C. Death to HANO.*

She slumped against the wall. *Who did this? Who wrote this note?* Not the workers. *What does it mean, and who is Hano?* She felt sick. Someone had come into the house, someone who didn't like what she was doing. Heart still racing, she dashed downstairs and out the front door, slamming it behind her. She needed to do something. She would report the vandalism to the police at once. On her way back to the boarding house where she rented a room, she almost tripped over the cracks in the sidewalk. "Stay calm," she said aloud as she retreated up the stairs to her room to make the call. She collapsed on her bed and called the police.

The dispatcher took her statement. In a sleepy voice he said an officer would stop by to look at the damage within the next few hours. Anne groaned. That meant waiting until the police arrived. She wasn't good at waiting. To pass the time, she'd talk to her friend Andrea, who rented room number six, next to hers. She knocked. Silence. *Damn it all.* Well, it would help to call Sam, her boyfriend. No answer. *On weekends he's often out and about,* she remembered. More waiting—she'd have to wait until she saw him that evening. After pacing the room for several minutes her legs felt limp. She lay on the bed and stared up at the ceiling. She could use a drink but remembered she had finished the last of the wine. Her thoughts whirled as images of the shattered fixtures spun around, images now etched in her mind. Her enthusiasm for the renovation project at the house had taken a sinister turn for the worse. It was as she had feared all along: one long, hopeless hassle.

At noon, the front doorbell rang. Anne roused herself and clattered down the stairs. A burly policeman stood outside.

"Miss Gautier? Officer Hammond," he said, showing his badge. "You reported a case of vandalism, right? What's the location?"

"On Esplanade, number 2310, down the street," she said.

"Okay. Get in the car and we'll drive there."

"Place is in bad shape," he said as they entered. "This your house, miss?"

"Yes. I inherited it from my grandfather," she said. "Work's in progress," she added.

She stood aside to let him into the bathroom. He swept his eyes around and strode over to the note on the sink.

"Have you talked to the construction guys to find out if they know anything about this?" he asked.

"No, but they would have told me. They're working on the walls and they've finished the roofing. Anyway, they wouldn't have written the note."

"Any idea who did?" he asked. "Any people you know who aren't friends, if you see what I mean?"

"No one. Some of my friends say I'm crazy to renovate the house, but no one would have left a message like this. I don't know what section C is, or anyone called Hano."

"Don't you read the papers?"

She shook her head. "Afraid not," she said.

"They're full of the story. Section C is an area in town that's planned for redevelopment. It's a slum, not just rundown like Esplanade Avenue. The houses there, more like shacks really, are in terrible condition. HANO stands for Housing Authority of New Orleans. It's the government agency that has responsibility for providing housing for low-income residents. They plan to demolish the buildings. My guess is someone who knows about that is trying to send you a warning. Question is, is this personal, or is it just an attempt to make a point?"

Anne blanched.

"If it's making a point, they've got my attention. If it's personal, I guess I should worry about my safety," she said, her voice rising.

"I don't want to scare you, but you might want to think about someone you know who bears a grudge. Could anyone have seen the perpetrator?"

"The workers, but that's unlikely. They finished work yesterday evening, so whoever did this must have come into the house between then and this morning, when I found this mess."

"How about neighbors?"

"Hm. Well, there's Homer Jackson, next door. The house on the other side is empty. I guess I could talk to Mr. Jackson, but he's a bit funny in the head, I think."

"You do that. In the meantime, I want to find out how they got in. I take it you keep the house locked. Do the workers have a key?"

"Yes, but only to the front door. The back stays locked. It's off the kitchen. Someone left the front door open, though."

"So perhaps the vandals didn't break in, then."

Downstairs in the kitchen, the breeze floated through a jagged hole in the windowpane.

"Here's how they got in," he said. "They may have left the front door open when they left."

She took a step back to avoid the broken glass on the floor.

"Damn. We'd better fix that," she said. "What else should I do? Do you have any advice?"

"I'd advise you to install a burglar alarm as soon as possible. This isn't a good part of town. We'll have a report on file, and if you find any further problems or clues concerning the culprit, give us a call. I'll dust the doorknobs for fingerprints, and if we come up with any suspects I'll be in touch. Here's my contact information."

He handed her a card and finished his inspection. After he drove away, she stood for several minutes on the porch. The shock had left her weak-kneed, and she sat on the top step and tried to drive the ugly scene from her mind. She propped her elbows on her knees and rested her head on her hands to think. *Better to talk to Homer now, while the incident is fresh, than wait until later.* She held onto the railing and stumbled down the steps through the gate into Homer's front garden.

His house looked like hers, but in slightly better condition. Sitting in a rickety chair on the porch, he rubbed his stubby beard.

"Someone dead in there?" he asked.

"No. Why would you think so?" she replied, blinking.

"Thought I heard gunshots. Middle o' the night. Saw the police car."

"That's what I want to talk to you about. Did you see anyone at my house last night?"

"Didn't see no one. Didn't wanna. There's bad things goin' on around here, you know. Drugs and stuff. It's not good to have empty houses. Squatters come in, maybe ghosts."

"That's probably true. Well, thank you anyway, Mr. Jackson. Oh, and do you think you could call the police next time you hear signs of intruders next door?"

Homer nodded and gave her a yellow-toothed smile. *He really is a batty old man,* she mused, *useless as a good neighbor.* She sauntered back to the rooming house wondering about the wisdom of living in a crime-ridden neighborhood and restoring the old home. Her grandfather had expected it, and her father had argued that they needed an urban renewal program to improve the street rather than allow it to fall into further decline. Whoever had vandalized the bathroom didn't agree with that concept. But who?

It was only at that moment that she remembered Estelle: Stella, her half-sister.

Chapter 2

October 1872

*T*he Musson family stood on the platform waiting for the midday arrival of the steam train. Six children, all cousins, ranged in age from one-year-old Odile, wriggling in Estelle's arms, to ten-year-old Josephine, called Jo. The smaller children ran around the benches, chasing each other, jumping up and down, and squealing. Patriarch Michel Musson, wearing a top hat and glasses, and his adult daughters, Matilde and Estelle, stood craning their necks, peering down the railroad tracks that disappeared into the horizon.

"Here it comes, *Maman*, see the smoke!" two-year-old Pierre said to Estelle. "Is Papa on the train?"

"Yes, and *Oncle* Edgar, too," she said.

Edgar Degas had arrived from France. Estelle looked forward with excitement to his first visit to New Orleans. The entire family turned up to greet him at the station, honoring him as a great celebrity, although in fact he was almost a stranger to them all.

The train, enveloped in clouds of smoke and steam, puffed its way closer to the platform. Straining with the weight, the platform shook, and the locomotive arrived at the station hissing and screeching as the brakes caught. The monstrous black engine came to a stop. Whistles sounded, and a man in a blue uniform descended from a carriage waving a flag.

"All of y'all for N'Orleans, step right down. This here's the Pontchartrain Lake End station," he said.

Pierre coughed as the wet steam clouds descended on the platform, and Estelle bent to pat his back and wipe the smut off his small face. After the engine's rustling ceased and the air cleared, the Musson family moved with the crowd along the platform toward the passenger coaches at the back of the train. Travelers descended, many holding trunks that they passed down to porters with waiting arms. Achille De Gas, dressed formally in a frock coat and cravat, identified his brothers Edgar and René as they disembarked and strode quickly to meet them. He shook hands with the younger one.

"René, welcome home," he said.

He wrapped his arms around his older brother. "Edgar, *bienvenue à* la Nouvelle-Orléans. You're here at last! Let the porter take your luggage and come meet the family."

René rushed over to his family and stooped to pick up Pierre. Estelle smiled as their son's initial shyness vanished, and he put his arms around his father's neck. It had been three months since René's departure for France, and she saw that her husband looked well. He set Pierre on the ground, hugged Jo, and kissed baby Odile.

"It's good to be home," he said, placing both hands on Estelle's shoulders.

"You've been away too long, dear, but I'm glad you brought Edgar back with you," she said, smiling up at him.

Estelle, though eager to hug Edgar, her brother-in-law and cousin, had stayed behind when the other family members surged forward to meet him. She wanted first to observe, to find evidence of change, for it had been almost ten years since she had last seen him in Paris, and she had been fond of him then. Now twenty-nine, a mother of three, and in her second marriage, she still appeared youthful, and her walnut-colored hair showed no sign of gray. She had gained some weight, however, and moved with trepidation, as though she might fall.

Edgar Degas, at thirty-eight, was shorter than his younger siblings, and wore a long dark jacket, white shirt, black cravat, and a white peaked cap, which gave him a rakish appearance. He had a clipped, slightly graying beard, a mustache, and small brown eyes. He was slim, and if it were not for the cap, he would have had the air of a Parisian gentleman of refinement and taste. In fact, he was an artist, the only one in his family, but so far had achieved little recognition.

His face broke into a smile as he took in the large gathering of family members, and he greeted them in broken English, "I thank you. . . ." Then he continued in French, ". . . for coming. I'm thrilled to see you all . . . but I haven't had the pleasure of meeting so many of you." The adults stepped forward, and as he recognized each one, he shook hands or kissed them on both cheeks.

"*Bonjour, oncle* Michel, *ma chère* Estelle! Always lovely to see you. It's marvelous that the whole family is here to welcome me!" Edgar said, smiling.

Michel grinned as he shook hands with his nephew. Estelle embraced Edgar warmly, with a rush of emotion. The children giggled and held their arms out, and Edgar bent and hugged each one. Then he recognized Jo.

"But how you have grown! When I met you in Paris, you were no bigger than this little one," he said, pointing to Odile.

As he straightened and glanced around at the assembled family, a young woman, fashionably dressed in a purple silk dress with black trim around the waist and hem, rushed along the platform toward him.

"*Mon cher* Edgar!" she cried, giving him a kiss on each cheek.

"Désirée! Delighted to see you again!" he said, beaming.

She was his cousin, four years younger than he. They had met when she, Estelle, their mother, and Jo had visited Paris ten years earlier. Désirée took his arm, and they strolled together to the horse-drawn carriages that waited outside the station.

"I trust your journey was not too difficult," she said.

"Long, but not difficult. We set out from Paris and crossed the channel to England to catch the steamer. I disliked the ocean voyage from Liverpool to New York on an English boat. That took ten days. The train from New York took four, and I liked it, especially the sleeping car, very comfortable."

Estelle regarded the couple as they walked together, thinking they looked well matched. It would be delightful to see her older sister Désirée married at last. She had missed many opportunities, though not from a lack of attractiveness or attention from suitors, and Edgar had still not married.

"You will come to our house for lunch, then I suspect you'll need a rest," Estelle said to Edgar. "You'll have plenty of time to paint tomorrow, and every day after that, if you wish."

"Estelle, thank you, but I didn't bring my paints and canvases. Without these, I am helpless."

Estelle gazed at him, her eyebrows raised. Before she could speak, five-year-old Carrie pulled at her uncle's sleeve and said, "You can use my paints. I have lots of colors, and paper, too."

Edgar mussed the top of her head.

"Good. We can paint together, then," he said.

"Come, children, let's go home. It's almost lunch time," Estelle said.

As they left the station, she couldn't help wondering why he hadn't brought his paints. Had he given up his dream of becoming an artist? Surely not. She would find out soon enough.

The family members dispersed and climbed into the carriages. The route would take them through the old part of the city, and the drivers knew the way. René sat beside Estelle and their two children in one vehicle, and Edgar rode with Désirée and Achille in another. When they came to the Rue Royale, Désirée sat forward.

"Edgar, this is the Vieux Carré, the French Quarter. Look at the rows of houses built by the Spanish and the lacy ironwork balconies. Beautiful, yes? If you look into the courtyards, you can admire the fountains surrounded by orange and banana trees."

Edgar nodded and smiled. "So exotic."

"This house should have special meaning to you," Désirée said, pointing to a large two-story house with an archway over a gated courtyard, "This is where your mother's family lived, before they all moved to Paris."

"A piece of my past! Could we stop the carriage for a minute?" Edgar asked, his eyes shining.

Achille tapped the driver on the shoulder, who brought the carriage to a halt. Edgar alighted and stood for a few minutes, seeming to absorb every detail of the house, then peeked through the wrought iron gates to gain a better view of the courtyard. He returned to his seat wearing a thoughtful expression. He exchanged glances with Désirée, his eyes moist.

"I am thrilled to visit this lovely home. I wonder how *Maman* felt when she went to Paris, never to return," he said.

Achille answered, "I wondered about that too. I was nine when she died and never asked her about New Orleans, but you were older. Did she speak to you about her birthplace, Edgar?"

"I was thirteen when she passed away. I only remember that she missed this place and her brother, Uncle Michel. He moved back to New Orleans to establish the cotton business, and she married our father and stayed in France. She spoke often of the warm nights here, and how cold Paris was. I know she longed for the masked balls and lively Creole society."

The horse pulling their carriage clip-clopped slowly through the streets and turned onto Esplanade Avenue. There the houses became individual grand dwellings. Carvings of classical figures and flowers adorned their facades, and long verandas stretched over front porches. A double row of live oaks, palm trees, and magnolias in the neutral ground in the middle of the street flung mottled shadows onto the grass, and a streetcar rumbled its way between the columns of tall trees.

"Most impressive," Edgar said.

"This is our neighborhood, where all the best French Creole families live," Désirée replied.

"What is that heavenly fragrance?" he asked.

"Magnolia; see the big white flowers on the trees?"

"Ah, yes. It reminds me of the south of France, all this lush vegetation—and the sun," Edgar said, shielding his eyes from the glare. "Is it always so warm at this time of year?"

His face had turned red, and he loosened his necktie.

"No, it's unusually warm for October," she said.

The carriage stopped in front of the Musson residence.

"*Mon Dieu*, what a large house! *Magnifique!*" Edgar exclaimed.

A cast-iron fence surrounded it, and high gates for coaches stood to the right. The mansion towered above, white columns supporting a two-story veranda. Dark green shutters offset the sash windows, and large trees and shrubbery provided shade on all sides. At least one other building was visible from the street behind the main house. The coachmen pulled the reins to pause the horses, and the riders stepped down. Two manservants came out of the house and between them carried the trunks inside.

René, whose carriage had arrived first, ushered his brother up the front steps and through the grand door.

"I'll show you to your room," he said. "Normally Estelle would do that, but as you know, she's expecting a child soon, and we don't want her to go upstairs any more than necessary. Her eyesight is not good, and she doesn't want to risk a fall."

"*Naturellement*, and I look forward to being a godfather for the first time," Edgar replied.

Désirée stepped forward. "Let me do the honor of taking him upstairs," she said to René. "This is my father's home, Edgar, but as you can observe, it's big enough to accommodate all thirteen of us and the servants."

"I've noticed that all of them are Negroes. Is that unusual? From the little that I know about the recent war, the Negroes are free now."

"They are not slaves," Désirée said. "They choose to work for us. But yes—many people who choose to work in the households of Creole families of means are former slaves."

She led Edgar through the tall-ceilinged foyer and up the curving staircase to the second floor, opening the door to a bedroom. A four-poster bed and a wooden desk and chair comprised the furnishings, and sunlight poured through the windows. He squinted and held a hand to his forehead to shade his eyes.

"You will be comfortable here, we hope. You can step outside onto the balcony and enjoy the view and cool breezes. We've set aside the gallery next door for your use as a painting studio. I hope you like it."

"Thank you for your kindness," Edgar said, turning his back to the windows. "I know my brothers have sung the praises of your life here in New Orleans, but I didn't expect it to be this grand. I'll be happy here, I'm sure."

"We all want you to stay for as long as you wish. Lunch will be ready momentarily. Please come down when you have freshened up a little."

As soon as Désirée had taken Edgar upstairs, Estelle sank into an embroidered chair in the large parlor on the first floor. The heavy-set wet nurse, Flora, took the child from her arms.

"Madame, shall I feed her now?" she asked.

"Please do. Would you mind asking Clarice for a jug of water as well? It's so hot today," Estelle said, wiping her forehead with one hand and fanning herself with the other.

She felt cooler after her first glass of water, and René came into the room and sat down on a chair beside her. He grinned, displaying his gleaming white teeth.

"Well, our great *artiste* has arrived at last," he said.

"I'm glad, but I wish you would stop making fun of his chosen profession," Estelle said. "Edgar works hard to improve his skills, and I hope he finds an interesting subject to paint. It'll be wonderful if he can achieve some success and recognition as an artist while he's here."

"I agree, but don't expect too much of him. Edgar is hard to please. He pouts when things don't suit him. He can be very abrupt in his manner and has quite a reputation for rudeness in Paris. But perhaps here, among family, he'll make an effort to be agreeable."

Estelle met his gaze in surprise.

"I've never seen that side of him. He has always treated me with nothing but kindness."

Glancing at Désirée, who had come into the room, Estelle said, "Did he like the studio?"

"He didn't look at it, but said he expects to be happy here. That's a start, at least. I'll make sure Clarice has set a place for him at the table," Désirée said as she left.

Turning to René, Estelle said, "I'm pleased that all your persuasive letters and talks resulted in this visit, my dear. We'll try to make him comfortable. New Orleans is an unusual town, and there's much to admire, though it's not Paris. It's part of his heritage, even if he chooses not to live here. Your mother would have been gratified to find him settled in the city of her birth."

"You're right. We're all French Creoles—Edgar, as much as the rest of us. As you are."

He touched his wife's arm and met her dark eyes. "How are you, my dear?" he asked.

"Just tired, probably from the heat. Lunch is almost ready."

"All right. I hope the new cook does us proud."

"Clarice seems very competent. She's making shrimp remoulade, soft shell crab meunière, and bread pudding with cognac."

"Very good. The menu should please him, especially after all the dishes they called food that we have been eating for weeks now,"

René said, grimacing. "The meals on the ship were the worst—you know about the *Anglais* and their cooking . . . *horrible!*"

Estelle laughed. "I've missed you. I'm glad you're home," she said, reaching for his hand.

He went into the dining room, and she poured herself another glass of water. The baby was due before Christmas, and she felt as round as a pumpkin. She would have preferred more time between babies, three in as many years. Everything was fine, though. She loved children, there were plenty of cousins for hers to play with, and her daughter Jo, whose father had died before she was born, had proven herself a good older sister. She wanted Edgar to enjoy her new child and to take seriously his role as godfather. It would be even better if he decided to stay in New Orleans, she thought, as the image of him and her sister promenading together flashed through her mind. She wanted the best for him, for them both really. *Why hadn't he brought his paints?* She blinked. If only her eyes didn't hurt so much. . . . She turned away from the floor-to-ceiling windows so the light wouldn't shine so intensely on her face.

Chapter 3

September 1970

*H*ow could I have forgotten about Stella? Anne asked herself. That was the only person who might hold a grudge against her. She had tried not to think about the whole complicated and uncomfortable situation. Anne knew Stella felt slighted, and deservedly so: as a grandchild of Etienne Fontenot, she wanted her share of his former house. As recently as last week, Stella had written Anne a letter asking her to discuss the matter. Anne had put the note aside. While not against it, she didn't favor the idea of giving up part of her own share to a half-sister she barely knew. She considered calling the police officer to tell him about Stella as a person of interest in the vandalism case, but she wasn't sure she wanted to arouse suspicion about someone whom she wanted to get to know and who, apart from her father, was her only living relative. In her heart, she couldn't believe Stella capable of such an act of violence, and it would hardly be in her sister's best interest to destroy the property that might someday be her home. She settled her mind. She would hold off on calling the police until she'd talked things over with Sam. After a shower, she chose a dress to wear for her date that evening.

Sam arrived at Anne's promptly at seven, rang the bell for her room, and waited on the front step. Thirty-two, ten years older than she, he looked good: tall, dark, and broad-shouldered. He wore a gray suit. Anne greeted him with a quick hug, but he held her in a tight embrace.

"It's great to see you. Are you hungry? I thought we'd go to the Court of the Two Sisters. We have a reservation for seven thirty."

"That sounds nice," she said, forcing a smile.

"Hey, what's wrong?" he asked, holding her at arm's distance and searching her face.

"I'll tell you at dinner. Tried to call, but you weren't home. I'm calmer now, but I need some advice."

"I'm all ears," he said, pulling on hers and hugging her to his chest.

She relaxed into his arms, and he took her hand as they walked to his black Mercedes. They parked in the French Quarter, then strolled past old houses graced by shutters and iron latticework. Some had sagging balconies extending over the street, and laughter and the clink of glasses rang out from above. A spicy fragrance of jasmine infused the night air, and strains of jazz floated from open windows. The mismatched French Quarter houses always reminded Anne of charming but unruly children. She squeezed Sam's hand and couldn't help the smile playing across her face.

The restaurant, on Royal Street in a stucco building enclosed by a vine-covered courtyard, had once been a fine private residence. They headed straight for the bar, and Sam ordered two glasses of chardonnay.

"Okay, out with it. What's biting you?" he asked.

Anne's heart skipped a beat, and she took a sip of her wine before replying.

"Someone broke into the house and tore the place apart," she said.

"What? Tore what apart?"

"Actually, just the bathroom. Destroyed the tub, sink, and toilet. Whoever did it left a note."

She told him about the sign and the police officer's suggestions.

"Well, I'll be damned. You need to put in a burglar alarm. I'll do that for you right away. You should have done it sooner—the neighborhood's not the best. You must be scared out of your wits. Any idea who the vandal could be?"

As he put his arm around her, she raised her head, her throat taut.

"The policeman asked if I knew anyone who might bear me ill will, who might hold a grudge," she said haltingly. "The only person I can think of, but I didn't at the time, is my sister, Estelle Clark. Stella, as she prefers to be called."

"You have a sister?" he asked.

"Half-sister, five years older. I've only recently met her. My mother told me about her during my freshman year of college. Turns out she had the baby out of wedlock at fifteen. The father claimed to be an artist. Her own father, our grandfather, threw her out of the house when he learned she was pregnant."

"Not unusual in those days. What did your mother do then?" Sam asked.

Anne grimaced, then went on in her softly Southern-accented voice, "Well, the baby's father didn't stick around, and she put Stella up for adoption. About a year afterward she married my father. Dad was in graduate school at Tulane when they met. After finishing his doctorate, he got a job teaching at Ole Miss, and they moved to Oxford, Mississippi. I was born there. Mama never talked to us about her family in New Orleans, or about her childhood home—the house I now own—or about my sister, until shortly before she died."

"Quite a story," Sam said. "So you never got to know your grandfather while growing up?"

"Right. I wasn't aware he knew about me, either. But he left me the house and lived there until he died last spring. My half-sister Stella has no part in the inheritance . . . you see, she's of mixed race. He wanted nothing to do with her and didn't recognize her as his heir."

Sam nodded. "I understand a little about the law in that regard. If they adopted her, the parents had to sign away all rights to the child, and the child would have no legal claim to the property."

"Yes. But that doesn't make it right. Stella would like to claim what she considers her birthright. She wants me to sign over half of the house, or at least to have the right to live there."

"I can understand that, too. But are you saying that she might be angry enough to commit a crime? That she might have broken into the house?"

"No, I don't believe she would do that, but she's the only one I can think of who might have a motive. What I'm not sure about is if I should mention this to the police."

"Why not? If she's innocent, she only has to say so. I'd think they can't convict her without proof."

"True, but I worry that she'll be upset if she's considered a suspect, particularly if she knows I'm the one who reported her. I don't want to destroy my fragile relationship with her. I'm considering either giving her a share in the house, or allowing her to live there, rent free."

"I applaud your good instincts," Sam said, "but this is a difficult situation. You want my advice?"

She nodded.

"I'd say talk to her yourself. Tell her what happened and watch for her response. If she's guilty, she may lash out at you and tell you that in her opinion the house is her true birthright, or some such thing. Then you can report her to the police. If she's innocent, you may know by her choice of words, and you can say you want her to consider the dangerous neighborhood and reasons for the need to take time before making any decisions."

"You're right. I'll talk to her myself first. Darn it all. Why did this have to happen? Owning a house is a big responsibility, and restoring one is even worse. I just want to get on with my life."

He looked at her, suppressing a smile.

"Welcome to the world of adulthood. That's a problem for many new college graduates. They spend so many years studying and partying that they have no idea how the real world works. It comes as a shock, doesn't it?"

She puckered her lips.

"I resent that. I worked hard in school. Art majors spend many hours painting, trying to improve. But it's true that I'm finding a degree in studio art doesn't qualify me for much of anything, especially not for renovating houses."

"Well, that's your choice. You could always let the old place go."

"*Never*. It's my heritage. And, thanks to you, I have the money to pay for it."

"Okay, okay. But you need to figure out who's working against you here."

"I agree. I'll start with Stella."

"To change the subject, how do you like it so far, interning at the museum?"

"Now come on, how am I supposed to answer honestly, when you have a vested interest in the response, *Mister curator?*"

"True."

"Well, I'm grateful for the opportunity. I do want to earn a living and not rely on an MRS degree."

"MRS? Oh. . . ." He broke into a grin. "You don't want to resort to marriage."

Anne's dimples deepened as she smiled at him and slowly nodded her head.

"Most of my friends do, including Isabelle, whom I want you to meet. But paid work has to be meaningful. I'd much rather be an artist, but I realize that's not an easy way to make a living."

Her face resumed its worried expression, and he put his hand on hers.

"Look, these are big questions, but let's not let them spoil our evening. You're looking none the worse for wear," he said, "and that green dress suits you."

"Thanks," Anne said, smoothing her brow. "It's new. I decided I needed new clothes for dates with you."

"Good decision. I've noticed that you don't dress up for work, though."

"That's because I want to be comfortable. It's the student in me, still. I can think better when I'm wearing blue jeans."

She didn't tell him the whole story. When she'd been overweight, the casual clothes had hidden her large abdomen and wide hips.

"What? You can think better?" he exclaimed. "I never heard that theory before."

"Just teasing. Are you trying to say I should dress better at the museum?"

"Well, since I sponsored you for your internship, I guess that entitles me to give you some advice about how you present yourself professionally."

"Oh. Well, I'll give it some thought. I know how to dress. I learned that at Newcomb. We used to wear dresses to class, but things changed during my senior year. The women who went to Newcomb could afford to—and did—dress well, but the anti-war movement took hold in a big way. Demonstrators shut down classes and burned flags. Everyone began wearing blue jeans, including the debutantes, who wore bellbottoms under their fur coats to class that winter. I wore blue jeans, but not a fur coat, which I didn't have."

He smiled. "All right. But you're not in college now. To change the subject, I'm concerned about you living in such a dangerous area. Where you're living now is bad enough, but you're renting, and it's temporary. Are you sure it's wise to move into your house? You could lease it or sell it. I don't like the possibility of more vandalism, either."

"It's not so simple. You don't understand the terms of the inheritance. My grandfather stipulated that if I don't restore the property, ownership will revert to the city. They may tear it down."

"I see. That does complicate things," Sam said.

"We need to find out more about who might resent what I'm doing to improve the house," Anne said. "Do you know anything about HANO?"

"A little. There's been a lot of news in the papers about the redevelopment that's going on in poor neighborhoods. They're planning to raze whole areas and build a cultural center."

"Well, I ought to learn more about that. You see, I've been so preoccupied, what with the house, the job, you. . . ."

"As you should be," he said, "but you might talk to the people at the city to learn more."

"I'll do that, of course," she replied. After a pause she continued, "I won't give up easily on the house. I want to restore and live in the place that's been my family's home for five generations. It's worth preserving. As a museum curator, you must understand that. And as for my rental, it's convenient, within easy reach of the big house."

"Okay, okay. I've said enough."

A waiter alerted them that their table was ready, and they followed him into the dining area. They ordered Cajun food, crawfish and gumbo, and stopped talking while they enjoyed their meal. Then Anne put her fork down and looked up. Sam's gray eyes met hers, and she felt the thrill up her spine that had become a familiar sensation lately. She reached for his hand.

"I didn't see you at the museum yesterday. Were you there?" she asked.

"I had meetings downtown and only stopped by my office briefly. I went to the gym for a swim at lunch."

"You went swimming? I've been meaning to ask you to tell me more about your athletic career in college," she said.

"I wouldn't call it a career exactly, but I trained for the biathlon, and I love running and skiing."

"Doesn't biathlon training involve target shooting?"

"Yes, using a rifle. And yes, target shooting is part of the course."

"Maybe that's why I feel so safe when I'm with you," Anne said, grinning. "I'd be a terrible shot, myself."

"You can never guess when you may need someone to protect you, especially in New Orleans. There's a long history of duels here, fought about matters so trivial you can hardly imagine a person risking his life for them, but there it is. There were plenty of duals fought over women, you know, to preserve their honor."

"Goodness. This is all news to me. Where?"

"Oddly enough, in City Park, near the museum," Sam said with a twisted grin. "There's a tree called the dueling oak. Seriously, safety is not a joking matter, Anne, but I guess you don't want to talk about that again tonight."

"True. Let's have crème brûlée."

"You're impossible!" Sam said, shaking his head and tucking a stray lock of her hair behind her ear. "It's part of your charm, refusing to look at the practical realities of life, always wanting to make things beautiful, or in this case, tasty. All right. Crème brûlée it is."

They finished their dessert, and Sam drove Anne home. The rooming house stood cloaked in darkness except for a light on the porch. "This place is like a tomb," he said as he escorted her to the door. "Does anyone else live here?"

"Sure. Hospital workers in four of the six rooms, but they work night shifts and sleep during the day. I rarely see them. Andrea, the woman in room six, next to mine, is studying architecture at Tulane. She's becoming a friend, and we sometimes make dinners together in the shared kitchen. Do you want to stay over?"

"I wish I could, but not tonight. I'm running with a friend early tomorrow morning."

He kissed her goodnight.

After he had gone, Anne sat for a while in her room in a chair by the window and gazed at the faint sliver of a pale moon. Her head felt light and woozy from the wine. Despite the incident at the house and the worry about Stella, her young life now seemed charmed, full of mystery and magic. She appreciated having Sam in her life, her first serious relationship, and she didn't analyze her feelings for him. He made her sing inside. Although she wanted to be independent, she enjoyed soliciting his advice and talking to him about her choices. She reveled in the new sensation of being an heiress, having a job and her own money to spend as she wanted. If she couldn't make a life for herself as an artist, at least she could make the historic house beautiful again.

In addition, she wanted to become familiar with the lives of ancestors who had lived in the old house, to preserve and honor her family's past. The connection with Edgar Degas had turned out to be the spectacular icing on the cake—or ginger-bread on the house, in this case. She had only scratched the surface by the exciting discovery in the attic of Degas's notebook, old letters, and the painting by an unknown artist of her great-great-grandmother Sophie, and she anticipated unearthing much more history soon.

She had met Sam when she'd taken the notebook to the museum for authentication during her senior year of college. He had sold it to a library in Paris for a great deal of money, enough to pay for the renovations to the house. It amused her that Degas had indirectly paid for the work, making the association more vital. Shivering despite the warm night, she remembered that she resembled Sophie, her attractive ancestor in the painting. What secrets did that young woman hold in the steady gaze of those brown eyes? Had she known Degas? She was impatient to learn more about Sophie, and herself, along the way.

She stared again at the slender moon, now obscured by clouds. The troubling matter of the vandalism and decisions about Stella were hard to ignore. She needed time. Perhaps, if Sam proposed, it would be easier to marry and let him help navigate her future. He had an established career, and if they married, she could more easily paint and be an artist. She soon dismissed the idea. As she had told him that evening, marriage wasn't her only goal in life. She wanted to work things out for herself and make her own way in the world.

Chapter 4

October 1872

Estelle watched Edgar descend the long staircase carrying a heavy bag. Seeing her in the front room, he sat beside her, putting the bag on the floor. As he did so, she admired his delicate hands and long fingers. Artist's hands.

"I brought presents for the little ones," he said. "Bonbons and toys. Shall I pass them out now?"

"How kind. Best to wait until after they've eaten."

"Will they dine with us?" he asked.

"No. The children are having lunch now in the kitchen. The adults and Jo will eat in the dining room. Jo is becoming quite the young lady, as you've no doubt noticed."

"I have. I wonder if girls her age look as grown-up in France, but then I'm not acquainted with many young people there."

"Why is that? Don't you visit other families in Paris?"

"Not much. As you know, my sisters have no children, and most of my acquaintances and friends are artists. We paint together sometimes and talk to each other about exhibitions, but we don't socialize much with our families, or at any rate, I don't. I like my own company and prefer to work alone."

Estelle settled her eyes on him. "Well, I should warn you that you'll not find much peace here," she said. "The children keep us all amused, but family life is boisterous sometimes with so many young ones in the house."

"I'll manage. The family is delightful, and I could not wish for a better welcome. I'm at home already."

She clapped her hands together. "I am glad."

The lunch bell sounded.

"Time to eat. I've seated you between my sister Mathilde and her husband, William, because they're the ones you haven't met before."

Edgar offered his hand to Estelle to help her rise from the chair. She leaned on his arm, and he escorted her to the dining room. Furnished with a long table and tall windows, it faced the garden landscaped with lawns, shrubs, and mature trees. The afternoon sun cast rays onto the waxed wooden floor, lighting a porcelain figure on the mantle that stood below a gilt-edged mirror. Dark-green velvet curtains framed the windows, giving the room an elegant and expensive appearance. The table, set for eight, displayed crystal wine glasses at each setting and a large vase of flowers in the middle. The family members seated themselves, and Beulah, the housemaid, brought out the first course.

"Before we start, I'd like to welcome Edgar to our home," René said, standing up. "Let's drink a toast to his health and thank him for coming—at long last."

The family members clapped, and Edgar stood up.

"I would like to thank you for inviting me—at least seventeen times," he said, "and I want to say what a good thing family is."

Everyone smiled as the brothers sat down, and for a while no one spoke while the rapid tinkling of silverware on plates showed the diners' enjoyable consumption of the shrimp. After Beulah removed the dishes, René addressed Jo at the opposite end of the table.

"*Et toi,* Josephine, *est-ce que tu parles toujours le français?*" Do you speak French now?

"*Mais oui*," she replied, with a shy grin.

"I told her to practice while I was away," René explained to Edgar. "Perhaps you can talk to her every day to help her improve. We can't abide children in this house who speak only English!"

"I'll be glad to. Perhaps in exchange she could teach me the language of America. The only two words I can pronounce well are 'turkey buzzard.'"

"Turkey buzzard? Why those? They're hardly everyday terms," William said.

Edgar shrugged. "The sounds please me. Turkey buzzard. *Bon, n'est-ce pas?*"

Everyone laughed.

The second course, crab, arrived, accompanied by chilled white French Burgundy wine.

"The food, it's delicious," Edgar said to Estelle.

"I'm glad you like it. We have a new cook."

"Edgar has an excellent cook in Paris," René offered. "He wanted to bring her here, but I think she would have run off with some rich gentleman if she had come—"

"I'm not sure I agree," Edgar broke in. "Clothilde works hard for me, and I would not want to lose her, but then, I don't yet understand the temptations of this new place, and of the opportunities I hear are so readily available."

"Opportunities are what you're here to discover, we hope," Estelle said, "and while we're on that subject, we need to get you some painting materials."

"In time, in time. Let him first become familiar with our city and our family business," Michel said. "I'd like to invite him to come to the office tomorrow morning and learn something about the cotton industry."

"Happy to oblige. I agree the paints can wait," Edgar said.

Dessert arrived, and coffee, and the meal ended. Estelle motioned to Edgar.

"You can catch the children now, before they take their afternoon naps. Go through to the parlor," she said.

Edgar picked up his bag of gifts and joined his nephews and nieces sitting on the floor. The children had surrounded themselves with building blocks and dolls. Carrie shouted out, "*Oncle* Edgar, do you want to paint now? I can get my colors and brushes."

"Later, my child," he said. "I've brought treats for you all."

He passed sweets around to the four older children. Then he produced colorful balls and wooden toys in the shapes of animals and birds.

"This one's very pretty," Carrie said, picking up a pink flamingo. "I like pink. Do you like pink, Uncle?"

"Very much," he replied.

Each holding a ball, the two-year-olds, Sidney and Pierre, chased one other.

"It's a big ball," Sidney said.

"No, it's a small one. I've got a big one," Pierre said.

"I want it!"

"It's mine!"

"Now, boys, be nice to each other. Say thank you to your uncle," Flora, the nurse said, touching them on their shoulders and urging them forward.

A smile played on Edgar's face as the children thanked him in their wispy voices. Passing Estelle in the living room he said, "The children are delightful. You know, my eyes are opened. I have not married, but a good woman, a few children of my own, would that be excessive?"

Estelle turned toward him, widening her eyes,

"Not at all. These words please me, my dear cousin."

"I'll rest now. Thank you again for your hospitality, for the lovely meal."

After he had gone upstairs, Estelle recalled Edgar's behavior in Paris, where he had lived in the style of a confirmed bachelor. *Had she heard him correctly? Had he talked about marrying, settling down, and having children?* Perhaps the city had already bewitched him, enticing him to explore new opportunities. She had never witnessed such words from him before, nor known of any important women in his life. Or any woman, for that matter. Yet she knew he enjoyed the company of ladies, and he loved having them sit for portraits. Perhaps he would find the women of New Orleans irresistible, perhaps even—or perhaps especially—Désirée. She hoped so; oh, she hoped so. She resolved to do all she could to encourage the match. *But why hasn't he brought his paints, and why does he seem so resistant to the idea of painting here?* She would ask him more about that tomorrow.

Chapter 5

September 1970

*A*nne took up the letter she'd received from Stella the week before. She admired the handwriting, even and artistic, much better than her own. *Where had she learned to write like that?* Anne knew so little about her. They'd met twice before in the spring, during Anne's senior year of college. Stella worked as a sous-chef at Commander's Palace, one of the best restaurants in the city, and she had invited Anne to dinner there. Her roommate, Isabelle, had gone with her. Stella, an accomplished cook, had recommended entrees she had prepared, and the two friends had enjoyed the sumptuous meal. It was so rich that Anne needed to watch her calories for the next several days.

She picked up the phone. After several rings, Stella's soft voice came on the line. She had only the slightest trace of a Southern accent.

"Hello," she said.

"Stella, it's Anne. Sorry I've been out of touch for so long, but I've been busy, and work at the house has been slow."

"I wondered when you would call. Any idea when the house will be ready?"

"Hard to say. Spring, maybe."

"*Spring*? But that's months away," Stella said.

"'Fraid so. So, you're still interested in living there, then?"

"Definitely. I drove past the other day, and it looks fine. Has a new roof. Still needs painting, I guess."

"That, and a lot more work inside. You might want to see it before you think any more about moving in. I should warn you that the neighborhood's not safe."

"Couldn't be any worse than the one I'm in now," Stella said. "And I do have to move."

"We should talk about that. Let's meet for coffee. How about at the Café du Monde at ten tomorrow morning?"

"Perfect, see you then."

Anne hung up the phone. It might be awkward, but meeting Stella again was the right thing to do. Meanwhile, she had the whole of Saturday to herself. Perhaps she should check the house again. The raw ravages of the vandalism remained, but she wanted to make sure nothing else was amiss. And she needed to learn more about HANO, the Housing Authority.

Wearing exercise clothes, Anne jogged to the Café du Monde near the French Market. She stopped for coffee before turning onto Esplanade Avenue, passing number 2306 on the way. That had been Degas's family residence, the one where he'd stayed while visiting New Orleans in 1872 and '73. She always admired it when passing, though she had learned that only part of the historic mansion still survived. Her imagination caught fire whenever she considered the painter's connection to her family. *Had a friendship developed? Or a romance?*

When she reached her house, she unlocked the front door and disconnected the alarm. She appreciated Sam's keeping his word and installing it. The contractors had replaced the glass in the kitchen door, but upstairs the bathroom looked the same, still a disaster. She bounded up the staircase that led to the attic. Nothing seemed out of order. Before leaving, she swept her eyes around the room to be sure she had overlooked no items of interest. As she turned to go, she caught her shoe on the uneven floor. Regaining her balance, she noticed a loose floorboard. She kneeled and pried it up. Squinting into the dark space underneath, she could make out the red cover of a book under the spider webs. Heart pounding, she reached and pulled it out. With a shudder, she brushed the spiders off, hugged it to her chest, and rushed down the stairs.

Once outside she gently opened the book. The old pages crackled in her fingers, and the sepia ink had faded, but the name Marguerite Fontenot appeared in capital letters at the top of the first page. She almost shouted out loud. *Marguerite!* Her mother was a Fontenot, so Marguerite must be a relative. A series of journal entries followed, each one written in neat handwriting under a date. She eagerly turned the pages. The first entry, dated November 3, 1872 and written in French, read:

> Papa gave me this as an early Christmas present for the new year, but I don't wish to wait until then to write. So much excitement! We heard that René De Gas's brother Edgar arrived from Paris this week. I can't wait to meet him. Maman says we're invited for dinner on Saturday. What fun.

She had seen the name Marguerite before, as a signature on one of the original letters to Degas she'd discovered a few months before in the same room. The young Marguerite had apparently liked him—perhaps more than liked him. This discovery might fill in an important piece of the puzzle about her ancestors' connection with Degas. But why hide the book in the floor? Had Marguerite put it there, wanting to keep it from prying eyes?

The intriguing discovery distracted her from her plan to inspect the house. Now she wanted to read the journal. Setting the alarm and locking the front door behind her, she hurried home holding the precious book. She would relish reading every word.

When she had read the letter earlier, its significance had paled compared with the exciting discovery of the notebook containing sketches and comments by the artist. Now it commanded her attention. After rummaging through several drawers, she located the envelope addressed to Monsieur E. Degas. She presumed it had never been sent because it bore no postmark or address. Had Degas even read it? She unfolded the letter and saw that the handwriting on it and the journal matched. Good! Just as she'd thought.

> March 12, 1873
> Dearest Edgar,
> It broke my heart yesterday when I learned you left so suddenly without saying good-bye. Will I ever see your dear face again? Papa said you would leave soon for Paris. How will I bear it? I have become so used to your visits these past few months, and I dared to hope for more so we could dance together again. Please write as soon as you can.
> With great affection,
> Marguerite

Who was Marguerite? Had she changed her mind about sending the letter? What had happened? Anne couldn't wait to learn more about Marguerite's relationship with Degas. Lost in her reading, she realized that time had passed, and she was hungry for dinner.

The following day Anne strolled to the café to meet Stella. She had dressed in bellbottoms and a muslin blouse and was relieved to note that her sister, who had a better dress sense, wore similarly casual clothing, though with accessories: large hoop earrings dangled from her ears. Stella appeared slender, as Anne did now, thanks to years of dieting and exercise, and Stella's almost-black hair lay flat, smoothed into a clip at the back of her head. Her light brown skin glowed in the sunlight. She displayed an even-toothed smile as she caught sight of Anne.

They claimed their seats outdoors and ordered coffee and beignets. Around them people chatted as they downed coffee from white cups and brushed confectioner's sugar off their clothes. The beignets, still warm, made eating a messy business.

"How've you been?" Stella asked.

"Fine. Working, and trying to keep things moving along at the house. How's work at the restaurant?"

"Going well, thanks. I'm grateful I fell into a career I enjoy. I love cooking. It's fantastic to get paid for something you would want to do even without compensation."

"True," Anne said, suppressing a pang of envy. She would love to earn her living doing what she loved, as an artist. "How did you get into the restaurant business?"

"It's a good story. You know that our mother put me up for adoption when I was a baby. Her father, our grandfather Etienne, disowned her, and wanted nothing more to do with her. I understand that after he kicked her out of the Esplanade house, she never saw him again. I never saw her again either. Well, Etienne had a sister called Estelle. A good soul, she didn't resemble him, and took pity on our mother. She continued to stay in touch with her for a while and had an interest in me, too. Estelle went to some trouble to find me, as you did. She made sure I got a decent education and, when she learned of my interest in cooking, sent me to France to cooking school."

"Fascinating. So that explains your accent. You almost sound as though you're French."

Stella nodded and grinned. "I lost my drawl. But you sound like other educated New Orleanians, with only the slightest Southern twang."

"Interesting, isn't it? We don't sound like people from other parts of the South. Must be the French influence. You've done well for yourself. Did our mother name you Estelle after the aunt who helped you?"

"Just so."

Anne narrowed her eyes as she took in the information. Stella knew more about the family than she did.

"And that accounts for your bringing flowers to the Fontenot mausoleum," she said. "If I hadn't been painting there that day, we might never have met."

"Right. I have much to thank Estelle for. Not so much other family members, though . . . anyway, that's the story."

Anne bit her lip. She'd caught the slight insinuation that other family members, herself included, hadn't been helpful. Stella smiled brightly at her.

"Tell me more about our mother. I heard about her from Estelle, of course, but that's a different perspective. What was she like?"

Anne waited a few moments before answering. She still missed her mother after her death four years ago. Freshman year had been difficult, and she had gained a lot of weight while grieving. She had a special desire to develop a relationship with this estranged sister and chose her words carefully.

"She had a reputation as a beauty when young."

"No surprise there," Stella said. "That's where we get our looks."

She smiled again, easily, with the assurance of a woman who's aware of her own attractiveness. Anne smiled weakly and pushed her hair out of her eyes. She had never considered herself a beauty.

"Anyway, she became a bit of a rebel," Anne continued. "You probably know that she was an artist, like your father. She resisted Southern ways and expectations for young women to fit into society. She had talent, too. We have some of her paintings back home."

"Where's home?"

"I grew up in Oxford, Mississippi, but I'd like to make New Orleans my permanent home. I got to know the city while in college, and I love the place, and now there's the house. Mama never talked about her hometown, a sore point between her and my dad, somehow. He only told me he didn't want to hear about her past, and as you said, she never saw her Fontenot relatives again after our grandfather kicked her out."

"I know some of this, but tell me how you liked her as a mother."

"She was a wonderful mother. Real supportive. She encouraged my art and took a lively interest in everything I did. Like you, she could cook. Seems to run in the family, though I didn't inherit that skill. Actually, that's not quite true—I like making pastry and pies. And eating them. She planned to take me to Europe as a graduation present, but she got sick. Cancer."

Anne gulped and twisted her hands.

"I wish I'd known her," Stella said, "though I can't complain about my adoptive parents. They're good folk."

Anne stared across the table at her. How unfortunate, to have lost both her natural parents. Stella had as much to gain as she did by reuniting with her lost kinfolk.

"We must talk a lot more about the family," Anne said gently. "Do you have any interest in learning more about our ancestors?"

"Sure. What's to know?"

"Well, you're aware that the artist Degas stayed on Esplanade Avenue when he visited New Orleans. It seems that he became acquainted with our relatives. I've come across a journal belonging to Marguerite Fontenot. It's fascinating. She describes how she met him in 1872."

"Wow. Can I see it?"

"Sure, once I've finished reading it."

"You were an art major, I remember," Stella said. "Have you given up your goal of making a living as an artist?"

"For now, I have. It's not very practical. I'm working at the art museum."

"Well, what's wrong with that? You're employed in the art world, at least."

"Yes, but I think to enjoy the work and have opportunities for advancement, I'll need to go back to school and earn my master's degree," Anne said. "They don't normally hire curators without more education."

"Wouldn't you like to go back to school?"

"School would be fine, but I'm not sure about the field, and I want to finish the house first."

"Right. How's that coming along?" Stella asked.

"Slowly, as I mentioned. I want to be sure things are done correctly, and that takes a while."

"Sure. Aren't you enjoying it all? Making improvements, I mean?"

"Sort of." Anne drained her coffee cup. This would be the time to ask Stella about obstructions to the progress. She shifted in her chair.

"Actually, we've had a setback."

"Oh? What do you mean?"

"Someone doesn't like the work I'm doing."

Her sister frowned. "Why would anyone object to improvements to a beautiful, historic house?"

"Exactly."

"Who's complaining?" Stella asked.

"No one's complaining, but someone trashed the bathroom. They left a note referring to Section C."

"Section C? That's where I live. They're tearing homes down, and I'm being evicted. Didn't you know?" Stella raised her eyebrows as she stared at Anne.

"No . . . oh, so that's why you're eager to move. Well, I understand that, and I'm sorry. We should talk more about this."

Stella reached across the table and touched Anne on the arm. "It's cool. I have a few more months."

"Right," Anne said with relief, and a sudden feeling of warmth toward her sister flowed through her. Stella sounded as though she didn't care about the morality of either demolishing or restoring old houses. She continued speaking. "As I've said, there's much to do yet before the house is fit to live in. Let's meet again in a few weeks."

"Good idea. Shall I call you?"

"Sure. Perhaps you can take a tour of the house, too, when it's more presentable."

Anne left, thinking their talk successful. They weren't friends yet, but Stella seemed innocent of any wrongdoing regarding the vandalism, and if she faced eviction, that was another reason for offering her a home. Anne felt sorry for her; perhaps after another meeting and learning more about her plans for the future, she would extend an offer. One fact remained painfully clear to her: unlike herself so far, Stella had begun a career that she loved, and appeared successful. They had not discussed boyfriends, though. That much more personal discussion could wait until later.

Chapter 6

November 1872

*E*stelle had slept poorly. The day after Edgar's arrival, though pleased by his positive reaction to the family and New Orleans so far, she could not ignore her sense that all was not well with him. Now in the last two months of her pregnancy, sleeping and getting around were uncomfortable. She stayed in bed in longer than usual that morning and arose unsteadily.

Her maid knocked, then entered the bedroom. "*Bonjour, madame. Voulez-vous le petit déjeuner ce matin?*"

"No, thank you, Beulah, no breakfast, just coffee," Estelle replied. "I'll wear my blue dress today. All my clothes are becoming too tight, I fear."

Beulah opened the armoire, removed a deep blue dress, and laid it on the bed.

"I'll bring your coffee and then help you dress," she said.

Estelle padded her way to the washbasin and pitcher of water that stood on the dresser. Removing her white nightgown, she splashed water on her face and arms. She stood on her toes as she tried to observe the image of her swollen belly in the mirror above the washbasin and rubbed it tenderly. Not too much longer, she thought, and soon it will be winter, and the weather cooler.

By the time Beulah had returned with the steaming coffee, Estelle had finished brushing her long tresses. Her black hair and eyes were her best features, but when she peeked in the glass in the dim light, she could hardly see her reflection anymore. Shoving the thought aside, she reached for the cup of coffee that Beulah had placed on a nearby table. As her hand grasped for the handle, she knocked the cup over. It crashed to the floor, spilling the liquid and smashing into pieces.

"Oh, Beulah. I am so clumsy," she said, tears springing from her eyes.

The maid put her hand under Estelle's elbow and guided her to an armchair.

"Do not concern yourself, madame. It is nothing. I will bring another cup."

After taking some deep breaths, Estelle grew calmer. A few minutes later, Beulah handed her a new drink. She sipped the coffee slowly and gratefully. She valued early morning, the quietest and coolest part of the day, but wished that René would spend more time with her. He had only recently returned from his long trip abroad, and though he had written often telling her about the success of his business there, she wanted to hear more about her cousins in France and about the costumes he had bought there for Mardi Gras. And most of all, she wanted to talk to him about the new baby.

An hour later, dressed and coiffed, Estelle went downstairs. She wanted to be a good host for Edgar and wished she had more strength. Her pregnancy and widening girth made her clumsy, and her poor eyesight required care to avoid bumping into the furniture. Luckily, she knew the house well. She found Edgar sitting in the front room perusing *L'Abeille*, the French newspaper published in New Orleans for the Creole community.

"Good morning," she said. "Did you sleep well? Have you breakfasted?"

Edgar stood up as she came in and replied, "*Mais oui, merci.* The coffee's rich and dark, with chicory, exactly how I like it, the bedroom is most satisfactory, and I'm ready for new adventures."

At that moment, René rattled down the stairs and entered the room. He flashed his white-toothed smile.

"Edgar, are you ready? I need to get to the office now. You will come with me. We'll take the carriage."

"As you wish," Edgar replied.

"My dear, we'll have lunch out and be back for dinner," René said, looking at Estelle. "Edgar must become acquainted with our business, and the sooner the better."

He escorted his brother out of the house and to the carriage waiting outside. As Edgar left, he glanced back at Estelle with a shallow smile, almost apologetic, she thought.

I don't think my cousin is very interested in cotton, she mused. It would be best to get him some art materials. He would surely enjoy his stay more if he completed some paintings. She could ask her friend and neighbor Sophie Fontenot about where to purchase supplies. Sophie's husband, Philippe, an artist, would know. She penned a brief note to her friend inviting her for tea that afternoon, sent it by courier, and busied herself by perusing the dinner menu while she waited for a reply.

Désirée burst in through the front door. Hearing the door slam, Estelle called out, "Who's there?"

"It's only me," Désirée said, coming into the room where Estelle sat. Pink-cheeked and out of breath, with loose strands of hair, she appeared unkempt.

"It's so warm outside, more like summer than autumn," she said, fanning her face with her hands. "I walked to the French Market and back. Now I'm already hungry for lunch."

"It's too early," Estelle said. "You can ask Clarice to make you up a plate in the meantime. We'll eat at one. There will only be four of us: you, Matilde, Jo, and me.

"What about Edgar? Won't he join us?" Désirée asked, tidying the loose locks of hair out of her eyes.

"He's gone with René to the office. Papa's there already, and William is at the racecourse."

"I see. I hoped to show Edgar more of our city today, and I thought he might like coffee at the French Market."

Observing the disappointment in her sister's face, Estelle said, "Don't concern yourself, Didi. He'll be here for several months, I hope. There will be plenty of time for you to show him everything, and perhaps he'll even find some subject matter for painting. That will keep him here longer."

"I'm not so sure," Désirée said. "I think your husband has better things in mind for our guest. He would love another partner in the cotton business."

Estelle said nothing. She understood better than her sister how much René and Achille wanted Edgar's help financially, if not otherwise.

Beulah had set the table for lunch, and the three adults and Jo took their places at one o'clock. They started eating their crab-meat salads.

"When do you return to Alabama for school, Jo?" Mathilde asked.

"Next week. *Maman* has ordered the carriage for me. I'm not looking forward to going."

"Why is that?" Désirée asked.

"They call me 'The French Girl,' and tease me."

"Are there no other Creole girls there?"

"Not many. Most are Americans, and they all speak English. That's why it's hard for me to speak French here."

"It's a very fine school," Estelle said. "We want only the best for our daughter, and a good education is important."

"Quite so," Matilde said. "William and I plan to send Carrie to boarding school, too, when the time comes."

"You'll be home before Christmas," Estelle said, placing her hand on the girl's thin arm.

"But that seems like a long time away," Jo replied tearfully.

"We promise to write often," Estelle said.

Estelle knew that Jo dreaded leaving, but like other good Creole families, she wanted her daughter brought up reading French literature, studying music and dancing, and learning the social skills and etiquette that would ensure a good marriage for her. She herself had many advantages and had gone to France before her marriage at eighteen. French culture was important to well-bred Creoles in New Orleans, and, like René, she wanted their children to speak French as fluently as English.

When lunch ended, she and her daughter inspected the clothes she would need for school.

"*Maman*, I don't want to go. I want to be here when the new baby comes," Jo said.

"You will be, I'm sure," Estelle said, giving her daughter a hug.

René and Edgar alighted from the carriage in front of a four-story building on Carondelet Street. Edgar followed his brother upstairs through the humid heat trapped in the stairwell. Panting and mopping his forehead, Edgar asked, "Will I be underdressed if I take my coat off?"

"Yes. In the office you'll look like a worker standing around in shirt-sleeves, rather than one of the owners, which our family members are," his brother replied.

"I would think dressing less formally makes good sense. How can anyone work in this appalling heat?"

Edgar took off his coat. René stared at him in obvious disapproval but held his tongue.

A door with a glass pane confronted them on the landing in gold lettering: Musson, Prestidge, & Company: Cotton Factors and Commission Merchants. Inside they encountered a buzz of male voices. Clouds of tobacco smoke filled the air, and mounds of white cotton lay on a long table in the middle of the room. Several gentlemen sporting bowler hats bent to examine the wares, and one grabbed a handful, held it up to his nose, and scrupulously picked the wad of cotton apart, opening his palm as if to weigh it. A man in the corner poured over a set of ledgers, making notes on the pages.

"Welcome to the world of cotton," Achille said, coming forward to Edgar. Dressed in a tan jacket and a bowler hat, he pumped his brother's hand vigorously.

"Let me show you around," René said, guiding Edgar to the far side of the room. Michel Musson sat at a desk wearing a top hat. He rose to greet his nephew.

"*Eh bien*, Edgar, wonderful stuff, this cotton, as you can see. It's of the best quality. Here, touch it."

Edgar reached onto the table loaded with raw cotton and grasped a handful.

"It's soft like snow and has the scent of dry grass, I think. Where does it come from?"

"From plantations on the River Road," Michel said. "Some belong to friends of ours—the Millaudon family, for example. You must visit their property."

"It would be my pleasure. I've never seen a cotton plant before. Is it large? All I know of the material is what I see in a shirt," he said, pointing to the white one he was wearing.

"The plants are not large, only about waist-high," René said. "Now let me explain to you about the cycle of cotton production."

"I understand that they tend the plants at the plantations, but who picks the cotton?" Edgar asked.

"Uh . . . that's a slight problem, perhaps our biggest one these days." René said.

"What do you mean?"

"Before the war, the one they call the Civil War, we used Negro slaves, but since the war ended seven years ago, we can no longer rely on them for labor. As you've learned, slavery is outlawed, and few of the freed slaves are willing to work now in the fields. That has affected production along with prices. Still, as cotton factors, we manage, and do our best."

"What are cotton factors?" Edgar asked.

"That is what we do; we buy, sell, receive, and forward goods from planters to buyers. For this, we receive a commission, called factorage. We work with others, brokers and agents of buyers as well as sellers. Our company represents several growers, and we keep books and records of credit and other transactions for them. We're a sort of bank, similar to Father's in Paris."

"Is there, then, an element of risk?"

René, ignoring the question, said, "This is not a country for people with faint hearts. It's a land of opportunity for people with nerve."

"All right, but nerve shouldn't imply risk taking," his brother said.

"Spoken like a true son of bankers," René said, frowning.

"Oh, please don't accuse me of understanding money. I only know about paint, and I've no intention of asserting myself here. I can tell that you're running the business successfully. Good for you," Edgar said, smiling.

"Don't rule out the charms of cotton. How can you resist appreciating the magic of turning plant fibers into cloth? It's amazing," René said.

"I *would* like to see the plants growing,"

"Very well, but not today. That's enough business talk for now. We can discuss more about this later. You know a little about our work, and I hope you'll come here every day to learn more."

"I'll come as often as possible, but so far I can't see that I can be of much help," Edgar said.

"Well then, there is one reason for coming that may interest you." René said. "We receive and send letters from here."

"Now, that does indeed interest me; is the mail delivered every day?"

"Yes, every day. Now, let's go to lunch. You'll have to put your coat on to eat at Antoine's. They require formal dress there."

Edgar complied, and the brothers went back down the stairwell and into the street. They crossed wide Canal Street, took

Bourbon Street to St. Louis, and turned right. As they walked, a pungent smell of frying chicken filled the air, causing Edgar to wrinkle his nose in obvious disgust.

"Is this the food we're about to eat?" he asked.

René laughed. "No, don't worry. That's American food. We'll eat Creole-style. You'll love it."

Antoine's stood in the middle of the block. As they entered the restaurant, they stopped for a few minutes, allowing their eyes to adjust to the dim interior.

"I fear my eyes will not take kindly to your New Orleans sunlight," Edgar said. "You see, mine are sensitive and I must take pains to protect them for the sake of my art."

René looked at his brother. "Don't concern yourself. I'm sure you will become used to our climate in due course. It's always a shock at first, coming to America from France. Even I notice it, still."

The maître d' approached them. "Monsieur De Gas, you will sit at your usual table, *je suppose?*"

"*Mais certainement,*" René replied.

They passed through a large room crowded by diners sitting at many small tables and proceeded to a nook in the back. As in the outer room, dark wood panels covered the walls, and white linen cloths adorned the tables. A crystal chandelier gleamed overhead.

"You're about to experience some of the finer cooking in this food-loving city," René said as he sat down. "I'll order for both of us. We'll start with oysters, then have redfish for the main course, and finish with banana pudding. Would you prefer red or white wine?"

"I prefer white for this meal, which sounds delicious."

They ate their meal, savoring every course. When they had finished, Edgar sat back, a look of satisfaction on his face.

"I understand now that I did not need to bring Clothilde to ensure I would have excellent food," he said, "though I miss her arms."

"Her arms?" René asked, winking at Edgar.

"Oh, I see what you're thinking." Edgar frowned. "I mean

arms for painting. Clothilde used to be a laundress, and I've taken great pleasure in drawing the bare arms of such women as they go about the task of ironing."

René looked again at his brother and smirked. "Only an artist would find such things interesting. Now cotton, that's the stuff of life, don't you agree?"

Edgar made no reply. René raised his glass, drained the last drop of wine, and set it down with a thump.

Estelle received a response to her invitation. Sophie would come at four o'clock. After leaving instructions for Clarice about dinner, she refreshed the flower arrangement on the dining room table. She liked flowers, particularly the brightly colored gladioli. Tiring easily, she wanted to take a nap before her friend arrived. To her distress, she spent less time among her children these days. With a sigh, she reminded herself that she needed to preserve her strength for the new baby, and she could not take care of everyone else at the expense of herself.

Sophie arrived on foot from her house a few blocks away on Esplanade Avenue. Beulah opened the door and brought her into the parlor where Estelle awaited her. Sophie, seven years older than Estelle, was still a beautiful woman. She wore a pale green dress with flounces around the hem, and her shiny dark hair was piled stylishly on top of her head.

"Don't get up," Sophie said, bending to grasp Estelle's hands. "How are you feeling?"

"I'm well, a little tired, that's all. You remember how it is, or have you forgotten? Your youngest, Marguerite, is almost sixteen now, isn't she?"

"She is, but I remember my confinement well," Sophie said.

"Please sit down. Tea will be here in a minute. How's your family? How are Philippe and Maurice?"

"Maurice is away at school. His latest interest at eighteen is travel. He wants to go to Europe, perhaps in the spring. Philippe spends most of his time painting."

"That is what I wanted to talk to you about, Sophie. Could you tell me where your husband buys his painting materials?"

"I don't know; why do you ask?"

"My cousin and brother-in-law Edgar is visiting from Paris. He's an artist and has no paints here. I would like to introduce him to you and your family. Would you and Philippe like to come to dinner on Saturday?"

"Thank you. That would be lovely," Sophie said. "I've been meaning to inquire, how's your family's business coming along?"

Estelle looked away and avoided meeting her friend's eyes as she replied, "Going well, so I understand."

"I only ask because of all the gossip these days about the difficulty for businesses in the city trying to recover after the war. Of course, your family is well respected, and you have many members to help."

Estelle smiled. "Of course."

Clarice brought a plate of madeleines and a pot of tea on a tray and placed it on a low table between the two women. Estelle poured a cup for each of them.

"You're fortunate to have such an accomplished cook," Sophie said. "I need to hire a new one. We don't entertain as much as you, but I'd like to introduce Marguerite to some eligible young men. She's old enough to attend dinner parties alongside adults now and to learn some manners."

"Well, then, you're welcome to bring her with you to dinner this weekend. I'll include her in the invitation."

"That's very kind," Sophie said.

At five Sophie rose to leave. "I look forward to seeing you on Saturday and to meeting your cousin," she said, giving Estelle a hug. "Thank you for the tea."

Estelle went upstairs to dress for dinner. Although she considered Sophie a good friend, she did not want her or any of their other neighbors prying into the family's business. She wondered how Edgar's first visit to the cotton office had gone, and if the industry had awakened any interest in him. She would find out soon enough.

Chapter 7

October 1970

At five o'clock on a Thursday in late October, Anne completed her project cataloging drawings at the museum. Three months into her internship, she still didn't know her career's direction. She strongly believed in the importance of preserving works of art and figured her time at the New Orleans museum might serve as a stepping-stone to work in the field. Now she wasn't so sure. She acknowledged that Sam's presence made the job more attractive to her, but that was not a good reason for staying. Anne dawdled on her way from the museum to the car. At home, yet another letter from Stella awaited her, asking when renovations at the house would be complete.

She needed to talk to Stella again. In fact, the guilt she experienced about her half-sister's lost inheritance haunted her day and night: like a dull drumbeat, ignore it as she might, it never went away, and she would have to deal with it or go crazy from the constant throbbing in her head. Besides, she ought to inform herself about the urban redevelopment project that might deprive Stella of her present home. There were so many questions to answer.

Too many. She slid into the car's front seat and drove slowly home.

It was a warm evening, and despite her gloomy mood, she looked forward to her date with Sam the following weekend. When she was with him, she forgot about decisions that weighed upon her conscience. The second-floor room that she rented faced a garden, and the late afternoon sun crept into the window. The golden light cheered her, and she wished she could capture it in a painting.

On the easel sat the beginnings of her last painting, started months earlier, an oil study of horses. It needed more work, but she had little time these days, and besides, she wasn't satisfied with the results. It lacked life and hope, like fallen leaves. She'd paint over it and start again. Lifting the canvas from the easel, she turned its face to the wall.

She remembered that horses had been a favorite subject for Degas. Perhaps he had gone to the racetrack at the end of Esplanade Avenue to sketch. She'd never seen any paintings he'd completed in New Orleans and wondered if other obligations or interests had interfered with his artistic career while here. *Had the great artist given up on any paintings, before he had finished them? Had he perhaps loved someone, someone who kept him from painting? Or become stultified by some deep disappointment?*

She wondered if Marguerite had anything to say on the subject and picked up the red-covered journal that sat on her nightstand. She hadn't opened it since she'd put it aside the month before.

November 7, 1872
We met Monsieur Edgar De Gas at the Mussons' house last weekend. Maman, Papa, and I were invited to dine. All the Musson and De Gas family members were there. I wore my new white tulle dress. It's a little too big for me, but it looks stylish, and I like the lace trim. My satin slippers were too tight, but we sat down for aperitifs in the lounge before dining, and I could kick my shoes off under the table in the dining room with no one noticing.

I must remember to ask Maman for some new dressy shoes. I did not have an opportunity to speak much to Monsieur De Gas because he sat at the other end of the table and talked to Papa, but I liked what I saw of him—he dresses well and has nice manners, and I hope we see him again soon.

November 10, 1872

Today Maman and I shopped at the Gentilhomme department store for shoes. We bought a pair of white ones suitable for dancing. The Mardi Gras balls will start in January, and it's not too soon to be choosing gowns. Last year's pink dress, my favorite, is much worn and only suitable for children's parties. I'm older this year, and I'll attend a ball. I would like a new dress with ruffles around the neck and low enough to show some decolletage. Maman says that is fine for evening wear. I hope we are invited to some of the best balls this year; the invitations should arrive soon. Very exciting!

November 12, 1872

Maman has invited the Musson family and M. De Gas to take tea soon. I hope I can talk to him this time. Maman is having the floors polished and the chandeliers shined especially for the occasion. The Musson home is so grand! Ours is fine, but not nearly as large or splendid.

November 14, 1872

Today we entertained the Musson and De Gas families for tea. Maman worried about the petits fours, but the cook made them well: tender and sweet, with colored icing and small flower decorations on top. They were much admired. M. Degas (we discovered that is how he spells his last name) was not familiar with these patisseries.

The people who came were René De Gas and his wife, Estelle; Mathilde and her husband, William; and their uncle Michel Musson. I talked to Estelle. She has a very pleasing manner but did not eat much. Her baby is due next month. She asked me if I have any suitors. I told her not yet, and she said that surprised her, since I am such a pretty young woman. I said I expected to meet some eligible young men at the carnival events next year, and that last year I could not attend many because of my illness. I am better now.

P.S. Maman explained to me that the name De Gas is pretentious, and Edgar (she uses his Christian name now, and he calls her Sophie) doesn't approve, since his family origins are humble. That's why he uses the last name Degas. I like him even more now that I've learned this.

Anne put the journal down, fascinated as she read the girl's thoughts. Marguerite struggled with the desire to join the adult world, just as she, Anne had, and in some ways still did. Marguerite's relationship to Anne's family wasn't clear, but she seemed to be the teenage daughter of her own great-great-grandparents, Philippe and Sophie. Of course, Sophie was the woman in the painting Anne had discovered in the attic, and whom she resembled. Anne had heard nothing about a child from that marriage, but the journal detailed the connection between the families. Impatient to learn more about Marguerite's relationship with Degas, even though she bore some guilt at reading the girl's private diary, she turned the page.

The telephone rang several times before Anne, caught up in her thoughts, picked it up.

"Hello, Anne dear," her father François's voice rumbled over the line, "I've been thinking about the termites."

"Termites? Oh, right, the termites in the house. What about them?"

"I realize you're planning to call an exterminator, but I have a different idea. One of my colleagues in the Entomology Department has been experimenting with ants."

"With ants? You mean, using ants to kill the termites?"

"Exactly. Ants of the *Megaponera* genus are one of the few predators known to prey on this species of termites. How would it be if I ordered some? They would be less invasive and probably less expensive than the conventional treatment using tenting and gas."

Anne suppressed a smile. "I don't know, Dad. It's all very well, experimenting and so on, but what if it doesn't work, and I'll have thousands of invading ants as well as—or instead of—the termites."

"That's a possibility, I suppose. Hadn't considered that. Well, it's up to you. I wanted to present an alternative, and you have a perfect setup there, with all those termites."

"I'm sure there are plenty of other cases like mine around," she said, "but I'll keep the ants in mind. I need to call an exterminator for an estimate first."

"All right. Let me know if you need any help."

Anne hung up, smiling. Her father meant well, but sometimes he had very strange ideas. She did not like the thought of millions of ants crawling around her house feasting on termites. A wake-up call: she needed to attend to the pests. The vandalism had sent her a message, and mixed emotions about moving in with her sister had dulled her enthusiasm. But her father's call inspired her. After looking at names she had scribbled on a pad of paper, she called an exterminator and set up an appointment.

Later that week Anne drove downtown to where HANO, the Housing Authority of New Orleans, kept offices. The imposing building on Touro Street looked nothing like the houses the agency supposedly planned to demolish. Several men in suits entered and left by the front doors. Glad she'd made an appointment and had dressed appropriately in a skirt and blouse, she inhaled deeply as she pushed the door open and stepped inside. The attendant at the front desk directed her to Mr. Lyon's office on the second floor. She mentally rehearsed her questions and knocked on the door.

"Come in," a man's voice drawled.

"I'm Anne Gautier."

"Aw, yeah, you wanted to see me," he said, making an effort to stand up and offering his hand. He had graying hair and wore a suit that seemed too tight. His tie hung loosely around the collar.

"Denis Lyon. What can I do for you, young lady?" he asked in a slow Southern drawl. He took a sip of water from a glass on his desk as he settled back into his chair.

"I'd like to learn more about your programs, the ones concerning the deteriorating neighborhoods in Section C," she said.

"Well, yes. Reckon I can talk to you some about those. May I ask why you have an interest?"

"I've become aware that some people are against the destruction of homes in the area, and I wondered why."

"Well, some folks can't accept change," he said, looking at her and taking off his glasses.

"But if the changes are for the better, why would they object?"

"Just so. Don't ask me to understand the workings of some minds. Those houses are slums, you know. Terrible places to live. No plumbing, no running water, high crime, a blight on the city."

"Really? No plumbing or water? I didn't realize. . . ."

"So we think it's best to take 'em down."

"Oh, I see. And you'll rehouse the people who live there in better accommodations, is that right?"

"That's the plan, of course, in time."

"In time? You mean, there's no new housing for the displaced people to go to?"

"Now listen here, ma'am. We're workin' on it. Public housing, it's called. Now if you don't mind, I have work to do."

He put his glasses on and straightened some papers on his desk.

"Well, thanks for seeing me," Anne said.

She left the office, beginning to understand. People were losing their homes, poor people, who now had nowhere to live. It made her wonder all the more who had come into her house and destroyed the bathroom. Could that person have been a friend of Stella's? She didn't know where she lived. Perhaps she'd drive to the area and see for herself.

Anne returned to her car. As she pulled the keys out of her purse, she saw a man carrying a sign that read DEATH TO HANO. Her body tensed. Could this be the person responsible for the damage? About her age, he had intense blue eyes, a tie-dyed T-shirt, and hair pulled back in a ponytail. She clenched her hands. She should talk to him. Bracing herself, she approached him.

"Hi," she said.

"Hey," he replied. "Do I know you?"

"No, but I'm curious to find out what your sign means."

"Don't you listen to the news? Don't you read about what's goin' on in this town?"

"I'm familiar with the work that HANO's doing."

"So you're aware of the disgraceful way they're treatin' people. They're bein' evicted and have nowhere to go. We're tryin' to get people like yourself to get involved and to stop the destruction of their homes. Wanna help? There's a meetin' tonight."

"I'll think about it. I may know someone who's being evicted. Do you know Estelle Clark?"

"Stella, you mean? Yeah, I know her. She's got two months before she has to get out of her place. Friend of mine got really bent out of shape about it. She's got rich relatives who won't lift a finger to help. Outright discrimination."

"A friend of yours got upset? Did that person destroy property to protest? Could you tell me who?"

The guy opened his eyes wide.

"Hey . . . you know somethin' about this, don't you? You related to Stella? *Bitch! You should be ashamed of yourself!*" He spat on the ground.

Anne turned to leave. Sensing a deep gnawing in her stomach, she unlocked her car and sat in the driver's seat, too shaky to drive. The young man glared after her, shouting. She yanked the key in the ignition, pressed her foot hard on the accelerator, and squealed away from the curb.

Back in her room, she poured herself a glass of wine. Now what should she do? She had stumbled upon evidence that might lead to the identity of the person who destroyed her bathroom. Should she report the protester to the police so they could investigate further? After her second glass of wine she began to think she no longer wished to find the culprit. She now understood the vandal's possible motives and even sympathized with the notion of protesting property renovation when a short distance away homes were being demolished. *Homes without plumbing, in 1970? How appalling!* Occupants like Stella were being displaced and had nowhere to go. The accusation that she behaved like a rich relative who cared nothing about her less fortunate sister disturbed her. She wanted to do the right thing. She would talk to Stella again, and soon.

Chapter 8

November 1872

$\mathcal{S}$aturday arrived, the day of the dinner party. Estelle had prepared carefully, instructing Clarice about the menu and ensuring that she purchased the freshest ingredients from the market. While accustomed to giving dinner parties, this was the first one with the new cook. She hoped that Edgar would enjoy meeting her friends. They were mostly her friends, after all. René, the businessman, had little in common with Philippe, the artist, who came from an aristocratic French family and did not need to work.

Earlier that afternoon, Beulah had set the long, polished table for eleven. Estelle inspected it with a practiced eye. Silverware surrounded the plates edged in gold with a pattern of exotic birds. Two sizes of glasses sat to the right of each plate beside a white linen napkin. Candelabras holding ivory candles stood at intervals in the middle, and a large vase of pink camellias and white calla lilies adorned the center. The room and its tall windows and paintings provided an inviting setting for the formal dinner. Everything seemed satisfactory.

She wanted to spend some time with the children before dressing for dinner, and crossed the room to the back parlor to see them. Sidney and Pierre were playing with a wooden train on the floor.

"Look, *Maman*, it goes fast," Pierre said, pushing the toy across the room.

"It's like the one *Oncle* Edgar came on, but small, and this one is red," said Sidney.

"I see that. Where is it going?" Estelle asked as she sat down.

"To France, where *Oncle* Edgar lives."

"But France is across the sea, and trains can't go in water," Estelle said, smiling.

"Then it can go on a ship," Pierre said, taking a model boat from a box.

"Yes; perhaps Flora can read you a story about a ship," she said, looking at the nurse. The baby, William, slept in a crib in the corner, and his five-year old sister, Carrie, sat holding a drawing of a long-eared animal. Estelle pulled herself up and moseyed to the crib. She gazed at her nephew's small face and stroked his hair. Soon she would have a little one like him. She touched her round stomach, full of love for her unborn child. Then she bent over Carrie, peering at her drawing.

"*C'est un lapin*, a rabbit. When will *Oncle* Edgar paint with me?" she asked.

"Soon. He's been busy, but he will, soon."

Estelle gave her niece a kiss and left to go upstairs to dress for dinner.

Marguerite, dressed in her white gown and matching satin slippers, cast her eyes around her. She had not been to the Musson residence before and thought it very grand. She stood fluttering her fan in the foyer beside her parents. Beulah motioned to them to come through. The family had assembled in the front room, and Michel Musson stepped forward to welcome the guests.

"*Bienvenue* Monsieur et Madame Fontenot, Mademoiselle Marguerite; may I introduce my nephew Edgar? You already know my other nephews, René and Achille, my daughter Mathilde, son-in-law William, and Estelle. And this is my daughter Désirée."

The adults smiled, and Marguerite took pains to make her best curtsey. She turned her attention to the men. Michel's spectacles and graying hair gave him a distinguished air, while Edgar Degas, dressed in a black coat and cravat, appeared uncomfortable. *Perhaps he is shy like me,* she thought, trying not to stare at him. *I wish my shoes fit better. They are pretty but hurt my feet. I would go to him and talk, but I am afraid I would limp and look foolish.*

"Please sit down," Estelle said. "We'll have drinks before dinner."

The guests took seats in the overstuffed chairs.

A servant appeared beside her holding a tray, and Marguerite accepted a cold drink, a mint julep in a silver cup. Taking a sip, she suddenly felt as if she belonged in this grown-up dinner party. She could hardly keep from beaming. Her mother and Estelle sat together laughing, and René and her father talked quietly in the corner.

Estelle soon announced that dinner was served, and everyone rose to go into the dining room. Cards beside the plates identified each person's seat at the table. Michel presided at the head, and Marguerite's card placed her near the end between her mother and Achille. Edgar sat on the other side near her father, Estelle, and René, and opposite Désirée. She could hear none of the conversation between those people and turned to her mother.

"*Maman,* I would so like to talk to Monsieur Degas about Paris," she said.

"You will, I'm sure, but perhaps not tonight. He's an artist like your father, and they will have much to discuss. He's the guest of honor, and you will have to wait for your turn to speak to him," Sophie replied, patting her hand.

Marguerite turned to Achille and tried to think of something to say, but noticing that he was staring at his plate, she gave up. She slipped her shoes off under the table and looked at Edgar. Désirée was talking to him with animation from across the table, and they were laughing. With a flash of envy, she wished she were more skilled at making polite conversation.

The maid entered the room to serve the first course, shrimp on a bed of greens with a slice of lemon. She carried the small plates on a tray and now placed one before each guest. Conversation died as each person picked up a silver fork and began to eat. A servant came around pouring white wine. Marguerite wasn't sure he would offer her any, but he filled her glass, and she decided not to say anything. She took a sip, but set the glass down, as she saw that no one else had touched theirs. Michel stood up, wine in hand.

"I'd like to propose a toast to our guests, all of you. Thank you for coming and for sharing this meal," he said. "We're happy to welcome everyone from France to our Creole society, and we're especially glad to have Edgar here."

Edgar smiled, a shy smile, Marguerite observed. The company raised their glasses and drank. Marguerite thought the wine bitter, not as sweet as the pale color suggested. She puckered her lips and took another bite of shrimp, which was plump and succulent. She observed the diners. Everyone ate with gusto except Edgar, who seemed to be staring at Désirée. She wondered what he was thinking. Désirée did not seem to be aware of him as she delicately moved morsels of shrimp into her mouth. She looked lovely in a yellow dress with small flowers embroidered on the bodice, a yellow flower tucked over her right ear. At that moment Marguerite would have given anything to change places with her, but then she remembered she had no idea how to engage him, to make him watch her every move, as Désirée obviously knew how to do.

During the next course, filet of catfish topped by a garlic-butter sauce, the servant again filled the wine glasses. Marguerite had finished her first glass, and began to feel lightheaded, pleasantly so. As she looked around, the room took on a magical atmosphere, reminding her of the moment when the house lights dimmed, minutes before the curtain rose at the opera. Candlelight suffused the colors, bathing the diners and walls in an amber glow. Even Achille, sitting next to her, looked more cheerful.

Dessert arrived, the best part of all: pecan pralines, Marguerite's favorite. By the time she had taken the last bite, she no longer cared about the lack of conversation on her part. She sat content and drowsy, and more grown-up than when she'd arrived.

Dinner over, the men retired to the front room for cigars. Marguerite sat with the women in the parlor drinking coffee and listening to Estelle and Mathilde talking about their children and how well they played together. Finally, it was time to leave, and her father and mother thanked their hosts for the excellent dinner before they walked the short distance home.

Once there, Sophie turned to her daughter.

"You were very quiet tonight, *chérie*. Did you enjoy yourself?"

"Well enough, but I need some new slippers. I wish I knew how to converse better. I have nothing to say sometimes."

"You are young, and those people were all older than you. You'll gain confidence in time, you'll see."

Marguerite felt her mother's arm around her. "We'll go shopping soon."

Hugging her back, Marguerite replied, "*Oui, Maman, bientôt*, soon."

After the guests had departed, Estelle sank into a chair in the front room.

"Well, my dear, the dinner party exceeded expectations, and I think our guests enjoyed themselves. It's important to keep up appearances. Are you pleased?" René asked.

"I think so. Monsieur Fontenot asked to send his compliments to the cook, and I heard Edgar talking to him about art. It seemed they understood one another."

"I noticed that Sophie's daughter Marguerite has inherited her mother's good looks. She will be a beauty, someday. Achille sat next to her, but he's such a boor he scarcely paid her any attention at all. *Idiot!*"

Estelle blew out the candles, and they went upstairs to bed.

Next morning, Estelle found Edgar in the front room nursing a cup of coffee.

"*Eh bien*, how did you like the dinner last night?" she asked.

"*Magnifique*," he said. "I was happy to meet Philippe. He told me where to buy painting materials, and we plan to spend some time painting together."

"Very good. I hoped you would meet a companion, someone you could see eye-to-eye with," she said, then hesitated. After a moment she continued, "I mean someone who shares your artistic inclinations."

He nodded. "Estelle, I don't mean to pry, but how is your vision these days?" he asked, looking at her sadly.

She averted her gaze. "I've lost sight altogether in my left eye; in my right, I can still see, vaguely. But don't concern yourself; I get along well enough. I'd rather talk about you: how are your eyes? Far more important, since you are a painter."

"We're *both* cursed with this affliction. I won't deny that the light here is strong, too strong. But I can paint indoors, and I now intend to do that, as soon as I can buy supplies," he said.

"But since you're here, in a different environment, don't you intend to paint New Orleans?"

"No. Exotic as it is, I prefer to paint what is familiar, and the light hurts my eyes," Edgar said.

"Then why not paint portraits of the family?"

"Why not, indeed? Who would you suggest?"

"You could start with Désirée. She was one of your favorite models in France."

"True, but there I enjoyed drawing her hands, so beautiful," he said.

"I'm sure she would sit for you again; have you asked her?"

"No. Perhaps I will."

"Anyway, the children will enjoy posing for you. How about doing a series of family portraits? Carrie, at least, will sit. She has been asking about you, and when you will paint with her, for some days now."

"I'll be delighted to do so, perhaps even tomorrow, after I've been to the merchant. But Estelle, I'd much rather do a portrait of you. Would you be willing to sit?"

"Me, in my present state?" she asked, putting her hands on her belly. "Only if I would inspire you, which is unlikely. There are so many others, far more attractive."

"Estelle, it would give me the greatest pleasure to paint you," he said. Gently he added, "You embody new life; what could be more affecting?"

She glowed inside. Smiling up at him, she said, "All right, I agree, but only after you have finished at least one painting of the children. You see, I drive a hard bargain. But I've been meaning to ask, why didn't you bring your paints from France?"

"Ah. That's difficult to answer." Edgar hesitated before continuing, "I admit, I've not had the success I hoped for in Paris. Other friends have done better and have sold their work. I've been wondering if I should continue in this so-called profession. It is competitive, you see. And then, there was the problem with Manet."

"Manet? Who is that?"

"Edouard Manet, my friend, a fellow artist. I offered to paint his wife, and did so, a portrait of her playing the piano—he appeared in the picture, as well. It turned out to be a disaster."

"What do you mean? Wasn't the portrait a good likeness?"

Edgar sighed. "He didn't like it, said I had not portrayed his wife as an attractive woman. He was so displeased, he cut the canvas where her face was, cut her right out of the painting. Ruined it."

"*Mon Dieu!* Terrible. Then what happened?"

"We have not spoken since. I was angry. The thing is, I cannot paint what is not realistic. I paint what I see, the truth without adornment. Not all artists do that. They often want to flatter their subjects, particularly women. Not me. That is one reason for my lack of success, I think. There are other reasons, of course, including my resistance to painting scenes out of doors, as my colleagues do in France."

Estelle gazed at him and asked slowly, "Let me be sure I understand. Are you saying that you plan to give up painting?"

"I've considered it. Anyway, I had no thoughts of painting here. I intended to visit New Orleans and the family, nothing more."

Estelle took a deep breath.

"Well, it wouldn't hurt you to do a few domestic scenes while you're here, and it would please all of us," she said.

Edgar stood up to leave, took her hand, and kissed it tenderly.

She sat thinking for a while after Edgar left. Now she understood why he hadn't brought his paints along: his uncertainty of his future as an artist. Sympathetic, but sure of his talent, she hoped he would not give up. *What would he do with his life, if he didn't paint?* She had always enjoyed her close connection with Edgar and wanted only the best for him. Perhaps he could find a similar connection with Désirée. She had been so lively and pretty ten years ago, and Degas had painted her often. She had been one of his favorite models, in fact. *What has changed?* she asked herself. *Didi herself seems as fond of him as before . . . but then she is older now and has lost the freshness that youth offered in such abundance. If he paints her again, maybe he will rediscover her virtues.* Désirée should meet someone to marry: if the family's business should continue to struggle financially, she would then have some security. But at thirty-four, she will not have many opportunities for marriage. These two people, both so dear to her, had their problems, she knew all too well, and try as she might, Estelle could not stop herself from worrying.

The clock chimed eleven. She roused herself and went into the kitchen to talk to Beulah about the leftover food from the dinner party. The maid approached her as she entered the room.

"Madame, I found this among Monsieur René's clothes in the laundry basket yesterday. It looks new. I expect he planned to give it to you."

Beulah held it out, and Estelle took it. Edged in fine lace, it was a woman's handkerchief. Perhaps he had bought it in Paris.

"Thank you, Beulah. I expect you're right. What a fine gift."

She would thank her husband later.

Chapter 9

November 1970

The phone rang. It was Isabelle, Anne's best friend, now pregnant.

"We need to get together. How are you doing?"

"Fine. More to the point, how are you?"

"Some morning sickness. As you're aware, this baby is a surprise, but it's exciting. Since Paul's in school, I'm not sure how we'll manage, but Mama's thrilled to be a young grandmother, and she may help us out. And you? How are things with Sam?"

"Fine. I'm seeing him tonight. He's been away all week."

"Oh. Where?"

"He didn't say. I wanted to ask but didn't have a chance before he left. He's often away on business. Why do you ask?"

"Just curious. Actually, I've been meaning to talk to you about him. It would be nice to get to know him. Where's he taking you?"

"No idea. He's picking me up at seven, so we'll go to dinner, I guess."

"Well, how about coming over here? I'll be glad to cook."

"Thank you, I'll ask him. If not today, let's get together next week."

Anne opened the closet to choose an outfit for her date. She needed to do laundry. She hated going to the Laundromat, something she wouldn't have to do once she moved into her own house. After throwing a pile of dirty clothes into a bag, she set off down the street.

She sat in the stuffy shop listening to the dryer whirling her clothes around. Her heart skipped a beat as she anticipated her date. She wanted to tell Sam about her visit to the HANO office and hear his thoughts. It would be pleasant to drink wine with him and forget all about her upsetting encounter with the activist. She understood that Sam liked her to dress well and always felt deeply pleased when he admired her. He had such mysterious eyes, watery and mesmerizing. She had no idea where he planned to take her, and surmised he wouldn't want to spend the evening at Isabelle and Paul's, but she could ask him. When she arrived home with her folded laundry, she picked up the phone to call him.

"Hi Sam, just wondering, do you have a plan for our date tonight?"

"No," he said; then, after a pause, added, "dinner, but I haven't made a reservation. Anywhere special you want to go?"

She told him about Isabelle's invitation.

"Who's Isabelle?"

"My college roommate. She's married to Paul, who I grew up with in Mississippi."

"Well, not today. I've not seen you for over a week, and I'd like to have you to myself."

She smiled. "I feel the same way."

"See you at seven," he said.

Anne showered, brushed her long hair, parting it in the middle, and chose the green, form-fitting dress to wear. Since she had lost weight, she could now wear flattering clothes. Green, her favorite color, suited her. She looked all right, fitting for a date with a man who cared perhaps too much about her appearance. Would Sam be interested in her if she was fat? She doubted it. She dabbed perfume on her neck and wrists. As she dressed, she recalled her young relative Marguerite's desire for a new dress, one that would make her look older, more alluring, and perhaps marriageable. She, Anne, living in 1970, had more choices about her life, both about whether to marry and about whether to pursue a career. All the same, she enjoyed the experience of dressing up to please a good-looking man. She and Marguerite had that in common, despite all the years separating them.

Anne heard the bell ring and ran down to meet Sam. He held a bouquet of red roses. She smiled, took the flowers, and held her face up to his as she murmured her thanks. He kissed her.

"You look great." he said, "Let's go. There are no parking spots on the street, and I don't want to leave my Mercedes on the curb."

"Wait a minute, while I put the flowers in water," she said.

Ignoring his impatient frown, she stepped inside while he waited on the porch. He took her hand on their way to the car.

"It's not the best neighborhood," Sam said. "I still worry about you living here, more than ever after the intruder's sabotage."

"It's not your concern," she said, her face tightening. "If it was good enough for Degas, it's good enough for me. He stayed a few hundred yards down the street from here."

"So what? He lived here almost a hundred years ago! You're such a romantic!"

"Don't kill my dream. The house is the most important thing in my life right now—other than you, of course."

"Glad to find I'm in the running, at least. I'd hate to lose out to old ghosts."

"Right now, there aren't any, unless you count termites," she said. "Where are we going for dinner? If you don't have anywhere in mind, how about going to your place? We could pick something up. I've never seen your house."

"Uh, I don't think so. I'd need to clean up first. Some other time."

"All right, but let's go somewhere quiet. I want to talk to you."

"How about Napoleon House?"

Sam parked the car in a public garage in the French Quarter, and they strolled along Chartres Street to the bar in an old house, rumored to be one where Napoleon would have lived if he had escaped from prison. Inside, peeling paint held the disheveled walls together, and strains of classical music resonated from the ceiling. Liquor bottles gleamed on narrow shelves, adding sparkle to the otherwise dark room. Anne considered the place quirky but romantic. Sam guided her to a corner table, and they squinted like bats as they read the menu by candlelight and ordered the house specialties: Pimm's Cups and muffulettas.

"So what is it you want to tell me?" he asked, covering her hand with his.

She met his eyes. "I stopped by the HANO office to find out more about the urban renewal projects they're running. The guy there was a jerk. Doesn't care about displacing people from their homes. Then I ran into a demonstrator who knows my sister Stella. He cursed me, said I'm a rich bitch for not giving her a place to live when her housing is being torn down."

"Poor baby! Not fun. You got a shot of reality, my dear. So what are you going to do about this? Are you getting rid of this ridiculous notion that you have to offer a home to your half-sister?"

Anne scowled. "I don't know that Stella has anything to do with this man. Anyway, I'm sympathetic to the cause. If anything, I'm more inclined now to let her move in, perhaps even to share ownership."

He took his hand away. "Okay, it's your decision. Aren't you afraid of more vandalism? Those guys are vindictive."

"I refuse to be driven away from a good cause. If I let her move in, they'll have no reason to complain. Anyway, there's a burglar alarm now, thanks to you."

Sam regarded her, his eyebrows raised.

"Maybe I should give you a gun for self-defense," he said. "If I were you, I'd wait until I knew a lot more about her before asking her to move in. Let's change the subject. The evening's young, and you like jazz. Let's get out of here and go listen to some."

She assented, straightened her shoulders, and said nothing. She didn't want a gun in her house, but she understood that he was trying to be protective, and she liked him for that. He paid the bill, and they ambled along Bourbon Street, passing bars with flashing neon lights. Not a charming street like others in the French Quarter, it was the home of several venues offering good music. A couple slurping pink Hurricane drinks from Pat O'Brien's, swaying dangerously, almost bumped into them.

"Tourists," Anne said, and Sam laughed.

They entered Pete Fountain's. Anne sat back, sipped her drink, and enjoyed the sultry sounds of the jazz. She became drowsy. She had wanted to ask him about his business trip, but the music was too loud for talking. Sam shouted in her ear that he had missed her and put his arm round her shoulders.

"Love your perfume," he said.

A shiver crept up her back. "Want to stay overnight?" she asked.

"I do. Let's leave the car where it is and take a taxi."

Next morning, Anne woke up and stretched luxuriously as she recalled Sam's ardent lovemaking. He lay face down in her bed, his arms flung around the pillow. She noticed a scar on his left shoulder. He really was a most attractive man. She brushed her hair and threw on a robe as she went into the bathroom down the hall. Suddenly she remembered: she had wanted to ask him about his trip and had still not talked to him about her discovery of Marguerite's journal. Perhaps they could eat breakfast together. She jumped into the shower and came back to her room wrapped in a towel.

The bed lay rumpled and empty. On the pillow rested a scribbled note:

Had to go. Forgot about an early meeting. Thanks for last night. Call you later. Sam.

Anne sat down on the edge of the bed. *He wouldn't be so inconsiderate*, she thought. He must have a good reason for not waiting to say good-bye in person: he has deadlines, he had told her his concerns about his job. After all, it was Monday, a workday. For that matter, she had to get to work herself. Downhearted, she dressed and drove to the museum, feeling loved, left, and used.

With good reason.

Chapter 10

November 1872

*B*y the end of Edgar's first week in New Orleans, he had established a daily pattern: he rose early, had black coffee and sourdough bread spread with butter and jam for breakfast, then headed to the cotton office for his mail. Some days he traipsed the several blocks through the Vieux Carré; on other days, he took the horse-drawn streetcar.

Estelle sat in her usual comfortable chair in the front room as Edgar prepared to leave the house one morning.

"What's your opinion of our city, Edgar, now that you've seen more of it?" she asked.

"*C'est très intéressant*," he said, "everything here attracts me. I enjoy seeing the Vieux Carré buildings, their courtyards and fountains surrounded by orange and banana trees, and the red and magenta flowers. There's an air of mystery, and it's almost like spying, looking into those private spaces. The trees have delicious scents! I find it all to my liking—particularly the women in white muslin dresses sitting on porches, and white children in the arms of black women."

Estelle smiled as she listened to his complimentary remarks.

"What about the sunlight, and the heat? Are you adjusting to our climate yet?"

"Not really. I don't believe I will ever think that the ghastly weather and white light here suit me."

She swallowed her disappointment and tried to keep her face calm.

"You must see other sights," she said. "We will arrange a visit to a plantation soon. You will enjoy seeing the cotton growing in the fields, I'm sure."

"I will," he said.

"Désirée wants to show you the steamboats on the river, too, and William would like to take you to the race course."

"Wonderful! I like race horses. I painted them often in Paris."

"So they might be subject matter for you here. That reminds me: today the children are dressing up for a birthday party. Carrie looks very nice in her white dress and blue sash. Perhaps this would be a good time to do her portrait."

"Certainly. I'll come back from the office early. I have paints now." He smiled. "Philippe Fontenot kindly took me to the merchant so I could buy them. He lent me some of his canvases, too. What are you doing today, yourself?"

"Only my usual things, planning the day's meals, and seeing to the children. Will you be home for lunch?"

"Yes, and afterward, I'll paint. I have you to thank for that. I've said this before, but I realize I enjoy being in New Orleans among the family. Somehow seeing you all here brings me closer to my dear *maman*. But now I must go. À *bientôt, ma chère cousine,*" he said, bending to hug her before putting on his hat and going out.

Estelle would need to talk to the nurse that day to arrange time in the afternoon for Carrie to pose. She could keep her party dress on all day; that would please her. Estelle still hoped that Edgar would discover other subjects worthy of painting, but at least he could do some family portraits now that he had the materials.

He had a reason as well: to bring back memories of his mother. Though he suffered from the heat and strong sunlight, she believed his mood would improve once he began painting. She got up and felt her way into the parlor to find the nurse.

Edgar walked along Esplanade Avenue to Canal Street, then turned onto Carondelet, to the building where his family had established their cotton business. He opened the door.

"*Bonjour,* Edgar. *Est-ce que tu veux parler anglais aujourd'hui?*" René asked.

"*Mais oui; aujourd'hui* I will say turkey buzzard," Edgar replied.

It was a joke, of course. Edgar had not yet learned English, and while in New Orleans had no need to.

"The cotton sales are magnificent," René said, "and we have new customers and shipments of the highest quality materials."

"Very good, I'm sure. Are there any letters for me today?" Edgar asked. "I'm always eager for news from home. I worry sometimes that my friends forget me, now that I'm here."

Achille handed him an envelope. Edgar grasped it and removed his hat, then broke the seal and took out a sheet of paper.

"A letter from my friend Dihau, at last!" he said, and settled down to read it.

René and Achille resumed showing customers samples of new cotton. Michel held a long conversation with an accountant. When Edgar finished reading his letter, he called to René.

"May I have some paper and a pen? I need to write a reply."

"You may, but first come here and learn about the quality of the cotton. This shipment is top of the line! We'll be able to command the highest prices for it, I'm sure."

Edgar stood up next to his brother, who placed a strand of cotton in his hands.

"Pull it like this, to test the threads and texture," René said.

Edgar took the wad, but soon threw it down. "The color

pleases me more than anything else," he said. "It's pure and white like the magnolia trees outside."

"I think it's hopeless, trying to inspire you to like our business," René said, shaking his head and handing him the paper and pen.

"I respect your knowledge of the trade, but I agree, my passion lies elsewhere."

A knock at the door interrupted the conversation.

"*Entrez*, come in," René said.

The tapping continued, and Michel opened the door.

"Désirée, what a surprise! What brings you here? This is no place for a lady," he said.

"I came for Edgar," she replied, looking past her father into the office.

Edgar stood up and rushed across the room to where she stood.

"Is something the matter?" he asked.

"Not at all." She lowered her voice. "I thought you might like to be rescued from all the cotton talk," she smiled.

"You're an angel," he whispered. "I'll come right away."

Edgar jammed his hat on his head and waved to René.

"I have to go back to the house now," he said. "See you at dinner."

René, looking annoyed by his brother's sudden departure, spoke to his uncle.

"We shouldn't waste any more of our time on Edgar; he clearly has no interest in working here. Let him paint his heart out. Maybe he will even be good enough someday to sell his work . . . and help us out."

Outside on the street, Désirée took Edgar's arm.

"Where shall we go?" she asked.

"Anywhere you like. I'm glad to have some time with you. I've always enjoyed your company—it reminds me of Paris!"

She smiled, and he patted her arm.

"I thought we could see the steamboats by the river," Désirée said. "They're unlike anything you see in France. I remember they designed the ships there for sailing across the sea, not down rivers like ours."

"We have boats on the Seine, but I expect you are right; they are different. Those you saw on the Mediterranean were similar to the one that took you across the Atlantic, only smaller."

"It's wonderful that you came all this way to visit us, Edgar. I expect everyone has already asked you a hundred times, but how do you like la Nouvelle-Orléans so far?"

"It's true. Everyone wants to know, and I want to say good things. In particular I do not wish to disappoint your sister Estelle. She wants so much for me to be happy, and to make this place my home. . . ."

"Yes. She worries about everyone except herself, and she should pay more attention to her own needs. Her eyesight is getting worse by the day, it seems," Désirée said sorrowfully.

"She makes light of it, but I can tell she has trouble. Is there nothing to be done?"

"The doctors say nothing, but she never complains."

"I know. That's one of the most endearing qualities about her. As René says, there's so much sweetness in her sadness that she makes us all sympathetic. She looks always on the good side, to the horizon where the sun is rising, and finds color when there is none . . . I intend to paint her portrait. She has already agreed."

"That would be wonderful," Désirée beamed.

"And yours, too, if you don't object."

"Of course not, but I'm no longer the young woman you knew in Paris. There you painted my hands."

"Beautiful hands," he said, as he held one of hers up to his face.

She let him hold her hand, her face showing obvious enjoyment at his touch. Then, dropping her hand abruptly, he said, "I am not fond of painting outdoors. Now, my friend Manet, he would see lovely things here, even more than I do. I promised Estelle I would paint the family, and I will content myself with that."

Désirée's face fell, and she turned away from him. They walked down Canal Street to the river, and soon the steamboats were in full view. Désirée held her handkerchief to her nose as they neared the docks. Open sewage ran in streams along the streets there, leaving green slime in its wake.

"*Mon Dieu, les bateaux!* They have chimneys!" Edgar said, looking at the smoke stacks. "And huge wheels!"

The multi-tiered boats towered above them on the dock, black smoke belching from their funnels. One boat was leaving, and the huge wheel at the back churned the water into foam as it propelled the ship into the middle of the river. A strong smell of salt and fish filled the air, and seagulls wheeled overhead. Throbbing crowds clustered by the waterfront, many waving at passengers standing by the rails on the vessels as gruff horns warned of their imminent departure.

"The riverboats are like the houses in the Vieux Carré, with their balconies and ironwork. Where do you imagine they're going?" Edgar asked.

"Perhaps up the river to Memphis, where I've never been," she said, "but that doesn't matter. I'd like to go back to Paris. Now that's a fine city."

"It is, but not as fine as it was . . . the war with Prussia has destroyed many buildings, and it will take time to rebuild." He stopped, and focused dreamily on the departing boat. "I miss it already," he said.

Désirée said cheerfully, "Well, you never answered my question. How do you like this city?"

"It's satisfactory, but I wonder what there is besides cotton. I am becoming weary of the climate of cotton. Isn't there any music here? I love to go to the opera and am used to going often."

"Oh yes, Edgar. We love the opera. Sadly, there is no program this season, but we attend recitals sometimes. Estelle sings beautifully. I could ask her to arrange a musical evening, if that would amuse you."

"That would give me much pleasure, thank you," he said. "Let's follow the river a little. It's so wide, and so muddy. The color is like my paints, a mix of ochre and sepia, much browner than the Seine."

"It is a slow, serpentine thing, the Mississippi, and for me, full of mystery. It stretches far to the north and flows many miles south before it empties into the Gulf of Mexico. Small communities nestle on its banks, homes of Cajuns, who live by fishing."

"Cajuns? What are they?"

"They are French speaking, but their language is not like our French Creole," Désirée said, wrinkling her nose. "They come down from Canada, from a place called Acadia."

"Do you know any of them? Are they friendly?"

"We don't socialize at all."

He looked at her. "Oh. What else do you do here, yourself? You have no connection to the cotton business, I see."

"It's not an appropriate pastime for women. We have Mardi Gras to look forward to in February."

"Ah, yes. Are balls and parties part of the carnival?"

"They are. Didn't René talk to you about them? He traveled to Paris to obtain ideas for costumes. This year there's a special theme: Darwin's *Origin of Species.* He brought back insect masks to wear."

"So he did. I had forgotten."

"It's all great fun, one of our best Creole traditions here. I love the costumes and dancing. Do you like to dance?"

"No. I've never been fond of dancing, though I love painting ballet dancers. Ballet—now, that's the art of dance that I can appreciate."

She glanced at him and started to speak, but he stepped ahead of her. The intensifying morning heat bore down on them like a wool blanket. He slowed down and dabbed at the back of his neck with a handkerchief.

"Would it offend you if I loosened my necktie?" he asked.

No . . . as long as you keep your shirt buttons fastened. It would be improper for you to escort me in a state of undress," she teased.

He cleared his throat. "Is it time for lunch? I find I have an appetite. It must be your company, Didi, and the walk."

"Or the heat." She laughed. "But we have always been friends." She turned sideways to meet his eyes.

"Perhaps we should be more . . ." Edgar began.

She waited for him to continue, but he again strode ahead of her, and said, "It's almost noon. Shall we turn back?"

"Yes. Edgar . . . I've enjoyed our talk," she said, bowing her head.

"Thank you, Désirée, for the tour. As always, I am charmed by your company, and I cannot thank you enough for rescuing me."

She nodded.

They strolled toward the Vieux Carré and soon arrived back at the house. Estelle was giving last-minute instructions to Clarice about drinks to serve with lunch. They didn't drink wine every day with the noontime meal, but since Edgar would be joining them, she wanted to have it available. The table was set for four: Edgar and the three women, Désirée, Mathilde, and herself.

"How did you spend your morning, Edgar?" Estelle asked

"Didi met me at the office, and we visited the dockyard. I liked the riverboats, their funnels like factory chimneys, and the river—so wide, so brown." He smiled.

"It is. Did you see the bales of cotton waiting for shipment?"

"No. I didn't notice those."

"We send much of our cotton all over the world, and New Orleans has one of the largest ports in the country. Well, please sit down. Lunch is ready."

The women took their places at the table, and Clarice served the first course.

"What's this soup? I'm not familiar with the ingredients," Edgar said.

"It's shrimp gumbo, with okra and filé. The filé is sassafras leaf powder, and okra is a vegetable from Africa that grows well in this area because of the heat."

"Delicious," said Edgar, eating with relish and taking small sips of white wine.

"Edgar, William would like to take you to the racecourse soon. You'll like the horses, won't you?" Mathilde asked.

"I like race horses, yes, and I've painted them. Their legs are elegant, much like dancers, you know. Both appear fragile, but in fact have enormous strength. They are active, too; I love the sense of movement that's always present, even when they're not in motion."

"William works at the racecourse sometimes. He admires the animals and knows them by name. But I understand you want to paint Carrie today. She's excited. This morning she did a drawing of our dog," said Mathilde.

"Ah yes, I must ask to see it," he said. "A mother is always proud of a child's efforts, but an uncle can be as well, I think."

The meal progressed with a fish entrée, followed by fried plantains.

"How will you approach your painting?" Mathilde asked.

"I always start by sketching. Sometimes I begin painting while the subject is right in front of me, but I usually complete work in my studio. I'm able to manage very well from my notes and drawings."

"Let me see if Carrie has finished lunch. If so, she can sit for you now."

Estelle watched Edgar's face for any sign of enthusiasm about painting her niece. She had pushed the idea and did not want to imagine he was merely trying to oblige her. He seemed relaxed, but she had to admit he had expressed more excitement about painting horses and dancers.

Désirée touched Estelle's shoulder as the diners stood up after the meal.

"Do you have a minute to talk to me in private?" she whispered.

"I do. Let's go to my room."

The sisters mounted the stairs, Estelle holding onto the banister. They sat on her chintz-covered couch.

"Estelle, what do you think about Edgar as a suitor?" Désirée asked.

"He would be an excellent prospect for a husband. Has something happened? Has he talked of marriage?"

"Not exactly, but he often seems on the verge of saying something and then stops. What can I do to encourage him?"

"I'm not sure. Edgar is not like most men of my acquaintance. René was always interested in me and told me so right away. I don't know why Edgar has never married, but he did say it might be a good idea."

Désirée's eyes widened.

"He did? When?"

"Soon after he arrived. He even spoke of having children."

"Well, that's a good sign," Désirée said, her face lighting up. "We get along, and he has always told me he enjoys my company."

"That's surely a good beginning. You've got charm, my dear. He was quite taken with you in Paris. I would say, continue to amuse him and flatter him. Take an interest in his painting. You already have an advantage because you don't talk endlessly about cotton."

"And I haven't entirely forgotten how to flirt."

They both laughed.

"He also likes music," Désirée said. "I told him I would ask you to arrange a recital, since there's no opera this season."

"It would please me to do that. Let's pick a date."

❦

Edgar kept his promise to paint his niece. He began a preliminary sketch in his leather-bound notebook. She sat down, her back toward him, her head slightly bowed, her dark, shoulder-length hair contrasting with her white dress. The full skirt billowed out around her. The curve of her childlike cheek was the only visible part of her face.

"*Oncle* Edgar, I am getting stuck, sitting for so long. Are you done yet?" Carrie asked.

"Not quite, *ma petite*. Please move your arm forward a little. That's right. Now keep it there for a few more minutes, please, and I will be finished."

She moved her arm, and held still for a minute or two, then turned her head to peer at him.

"I've had enough. I'd like to play now," she said.

"All right. I have all that I need."

"May I look?" she asked, standing up and coming around to Edgar's side. "Oh, it's all pencil, black-and-white and no colors," she said.

"I'll add the colors later, when I do the painting. This is only a drawing," he said. "But it already has a title: *Young Girl in a White Dress*. Do you like it?"

She peered at it and nodded. "It does look like me, but I'd like it better if you called it *Carrie in a Party Dress*."

"Good idea. I'll consider it. Your mother tells me you've been drawing, too. I'd like to see what you've done," he said.

She twirled around. "I like my dress. I'm going to a party now. I'll let you see my pictures later."

Edgar gathered his pencils and notebook and disappeared to the gallery designated as his studio.

At dinner time, Estelle knocked on his door.

"Go away! I'm busy," Edgar shouted.

"Edgar, it's Estelle. May I come in?"

She heard his footsteps tap toward her, and he unlocked the door. Holding the doorframe, he spied at her through a narrow crack.

"I must have privacy when I'm working; it's necessary for me to be alone, without interruption," he said. His voice softening, he went on, "But the light is fading, and I need to stop now. I'm working on a painting of Carrie."

"May I see it?" she asked, tentatively.

He inched the door wider. His easel stood in the middle of the room, a small canvas perched on the ledge. The painting featured the girl in her white dress, a sepia background, and the suggestion of a tree outside, beyond the doorway.

"Even though you can't make out her face, that's Carrie," Estelle said. "Nicely done, Edgar. Matilde will be delighted."

"I'll paint her again beside the other children. Today they were playing on the doorstep leading to the back garden. It would make a good family scene. Perhaps I can continue these portraits tomorrow."

"By all means," she said, "but now dinner is ready. Clean yourself up and come down."

Estelle was overjoyed that Edgar had begun painting again. If he derived pleasure from using the family as subjects, that was fine with her. She wanted him to enjoy his stay and to extend it long enough to reestablish a connection with Désirée. Though not talking about her fear, she had become increasingly concerned that Désirée would have no financial security unless she married. Estelle knew the truth that her husband tried to keep from her: the faltering family business. Michel would not be able to support Désirée indefinitely. But would their father approve of her marriage to a cousin, another member of the De Gas family?

She remembered René's long courtship of her. She had been twenty-six, and newly widowed, with a child, when they met. René was two years younger. Her father had sent her, Désirée, and their mother abroad to wait out the terrible Civil War that had already devastated the South. The Musson women soon contacted their De Gas cousins in Paris. René declared his love for her almost immediately, corresponded with her when she returned home, and followed her to New Orleans. He educated himself in the cotton business and accepted a job at her father's cotton office. Upon his arrival in America, he proposed. The fathers on both sides adamantly opposed the marriage at first, but once he understood René's serious intentions and how happy he made her, Michel gave approval. She and René had married in 1869, a short three years ago.

Estelle sighed as she recalled the tender memories. René had been so handsome when they'd met, almost a boy, not a man of the world at all. She reflected that he had changed, and not for the better. Still handsome, he had become worldly and less attentive to her . . . but she must not dwell on such dreary thoughts, she told herself. After all, he had written to her often while away, and had brought her the handkerchief from Paris. Or had he? She hadn't yet thanked him. What mattered most now was Désirée's prospect for marriage. A union with Edgar would be a godsend.

Chapter 11

November 1970

*A*nne had more than an hour to kill before a one o'clock meeting with her boss, Peter Knight, who curated the museum's European paintings. She took a stroll through the galleries to look at the paintings on display. As she climbed the flight of stairs leading to the second-floor gallery, she noticed a large painting on the wall she had not seen before. She stopped in front of it. Why did it remind her of something from her past, as in a *déjà vu* moment? The style—the loose brushstrokes and the asymmetrical composition—looked familiar. The portrait depicted a dark-haired woman dressed in a black dress, almost hidden by a large bouquet. She looked down, concentrating on a red gladiolus as she added it to the arrangement in the vase. Placement of the figure on the left side of the painting beside an expanse of negative space to the right was typical of Degas's Japanese-like compositions. The work showed the hand of a master, and she stepped closer to read the label posted underneath. She collided with a man observing the picture and holding a sketchpad. Excusing herself and moving aside, she read the label: *Portrait of Mme. René De Gas, née Estelle Musson, 1872–73, by Edgar Degas.*

Amazing! This must be the same Estelle that Marguerite had written about in her journal. The dates coincided exactly. The young woman had been represented with feeling by the artist, and it was a subdued, domestic scene, perhaps painted in New Orleans. Anne's excitement matched her astonishment that Sam, the Impressionist curator at the museum, had never mentioned this important painting to her. He knew about her interest in Degas: he had authenticated the notebook belonging to the painter that she had discovered in her attic and had encouraged her research into her family's connections with him. *Why hasn't he told me about this painting? He'd better have a good excuse.* Now he owed her two explanations. She would stop by his office and confront him right away.

Anne braced herself as she knocked at Sam's office door.

"Come in," he said.

He sat at his large desk in front of a window, pen in hand and a pile of papers in front of him. He glanced at her, smiling.

"Anne, what a nice surprise. What brings you up from the underworld?"

She didn't return his smile. "First, you owe me an apology, and second, you need to explain yourself."

"Oh, my sudden departure this morning. Sorry. I should have told you before, but I forgot about my early meeting. Guess your charms knocked me off my feet. . . ." His voice trailed away.

She glowered at him.

"You could at least have called to me in the shower to tell me you needed to leave. Your rude behavior made me feel awful."

"As I said, I'm sorry. It won't happen again."

She watched him shift uneasily in his chair.

"Another thing. Why didn't you tell me about the portrait of Estelle De Gas?"

His face reddened. "But I planned to—it was to be a surprise. I figured you'd be excited, and I wanted to show it to you myself, today."

"I see. When, exactly, did you expect to do this? We had no

lunch plans, and we don't have a habit of seeing each other at work during the day."

"But as I told you, I was planning to tell you about it today. I was going to ask you to lunch."

"All right. But you knew about the painting. Is it part of the museum's permanent collection?"

"It is, but there's a story behind that as well, too long to go into now. I'll tell you about it when we have more time. How about lunch?"

"Okay, but it will have to be a short one. I'm meeting with Peter at one."

"All right, what about dinner, then?"

"I guess so."

"See you tonight. Don't worry, sweetheart," he said, giving her his most winning smile.

She left his office and returned to her desk. Her head ached and, unconvinced and flustered, she went outside for some fresh air. His explanations were only just plausible. She wanted to trust him but had more than a twinge of doubt. His charm always captivated her, and she took delight in their relationship, but a small voice inside told her that something was wrong. After walking in the grounds around the museum for half an hour, her headache disappeared. Perhaps he had better explanations; she would hear them over dinner.

At one o'clock, Anne met with Peter Knight.

"Let's sit here at the table so we can see what we're doing," he said. "Excuse me a minute while I search for my notes." She sat down at a wooden table in the corner of his spacious office. White-painted bookshelves with thick, hardcover books lined the walls of the light-filled room. Most art history texts are like that, Anne mused, wishing she owned such a collection. Because she had majored in art, she had a few books, but not enough to complete even a shelf. Some paintings hung on the walls, but she didn't recognize any.

Peter was tall and had the bearing of a middle-aged professor, scholarly and comfortable with himself. He wore a wrinkled white shirt, the top button undone, and no tie. She appraised her own attire. Ignoring Sam's advice, she was wearing her usual uniform, blue jeans and a loose blouse. If she'd known she would be meeting with her boss, she might have dressed better—although perhaps not, since Peter seemed to dress informally himself. Or, she thought, as a grin tugged at the corners of her mouth, maybe he could think better when he wore casual clothes, as she'd told Sam she did. Or perhaps he, too, had a weight problem.

After he finished rummaging through papers, Peter left his desk and sat next to her at the table.

"Here's what I'm thinking," he said. "You did a good job of the inventory, but you might like a more challenging project to broaden your skills. Perhaps it's time you learned a bit about planning and organizing an exhibit. We'll have one next year featuring Western American art. It's not my field, so you'll work under Mary Wharton, the American painting curator. Does that appeal to you?"

Anne's spirits sank, partly because she wanted to work with Peter again, and partly because she lacked enthusiasm about most things that day. She had little interest in cowboy paintings. Hiding her thoughts, she said, "Very much, though I'm not familiar with many of the artists."

"You will be once you're done. Good enough. Here are few books to read and a list of artists whose work we might consider showing. Mary is away this week, but you can get going right away. Go through the list, find more names to add, and determine where the works are. You might also give some thought to a theme for the exhibit."

"Thank you. I understand this will be a useful learning experience for me," she said, brightening her voice and standing up to leave.

"Do you have questions before you go?" he asked.

"Will I still be working with you in the future?" she said.

"Yes, and I'll continue to be your mentor. Feel free to talk to me anytime you run into problems."

"That sounds good. But I have another question, on a different matter."

"Sure, fire away."

"I noticed that Degas's painting of Estelle is back on the wall. Where has it been all this time?"

"It was out for cleaning."

"I see. Thanks." She smiled and left the office.

At five o'clock Sam called Anne from his office.

"Hi, sweetie. We have reservations for dinner at six at Brennan's. Want to drive together? I can bring you back afterward to pick up your car."

"Nice offer, but I'm not dressed for dinner at a good restaurant," Anne said, cursing herself for wearing jeans. "And I'd rather take my car, thanks all the same."

"Okay. Want to go for pizza?" he asked.

"How about a drink at the Black Cat?"

"All right. See you there in half an hour."

She put the phone down. Still raw about Sam's early morning departure, she wanted to be able to get home without relying on him if their talk didn't go well. Soberly she realized that she had already distanced herself from him, and she hoped the sentiment didn't last. She wanted the relationship to work out, or at least to continue for a long time, and she hoped his explanations would bring them closer again.

She encountered Sam reclining in the bar drinking bourbon on the rocks. He pulled out a chair for her.

"What'll you have?" he asked.

"A gin fizz, please," she said.

He searched her face, creasing his brow. "That's not your usual drink. What's going on?"

"Perhaps I'm hoping all this nonsense between us is just that—a lot of fizz," she said, wishing he didn't always charm her into saying frivolous things.

He called to the waiter and ordered the cocktail.

"How did your meeting with Peter go?" he asked.

"Not much to it. He's given me a new project, and a new boss."

"Really? Who?"

"Mary Wharton. Do you know her?"

She saw him blink and take a gulp of his drink before replying.

"Yes. I know her."

"Well? What's she like?"

"She's an expert in American art. Very smart." He hesitated. "And quite beautiful, in a cold sort of way."

She studied him again, but his face showed only an expression of mild amusement.

"You'll learn a lot about Frederic Remington and others, anyway. I understand there's to be an exhibit soon."

"Yes. I'll be working on that."

He beamed at her. "Good experience for you. Congratulations! Let's have another drink."

"Not for me, but go ahead," she said.

He ordered another bourbon, and she watched as he gulped it down, swirling the last drops around the ice in the glass. It made a low clinking sound, like muffled bells.

She sat forward and looked him in the eye.

"Sam, what the hell was going on this morning?" she asked.

"Nothing. I guess I overreacted, realized it was late, and needed to get to that early meeting."

"All the same, you could have called to me while I was in the shower before you left. I felt used, as though I'd been a one-night stand, or something."

"Sorry about that," he said. "I should probably tell you more about the pressure I'm under at work right now. This has to do with the Estelle painting, as well."

She sat back and watched his hands clench and then unclench as they rested on the table.

"After I graduated from Yale with my art history degree, and before I got this job, the museum began a public campaign to raise funds to buy Degas's painting of Estelle. It had come on the market in the early sixties, and they gave the campaign a name: 'Bringing Estelle Home.' You may have read about it in the papers. . . ." He paused.

"No, I was in high school in Oxford, Mississippi, and didn't pay attention to the news in those days."

"Anyway, the campaign had a deadline. If they hadn't raised enough funds by then, the painting would be sold elsewhere. The museum really wanted it, since Degas painted it in New Orleans, and Estelle was a member of his family who lived here, as you've no doubt learned by now. I needed a job and wanted to work for the museum, but since I only had a bachelor's degree, the most I could hope for was an internship like yours. My family has means, and they had already contributed generously to the campaign, but the day before the deadline, funds were still short, many thousands short. Through my family's connections I contacted a donor who came up with the sum of money needed at the last minute. The museum hired me in recognition of my efforts. I planned to pick up my master's degree so I would be better qualified for my job, but so far, I haven't. That means I'm living on borrowed time, so to speak."

Anne listened, wanting to believe him. Then she said, "But I assume you're now an expert in the field of Impressionist painting, so why would your job be in jeopardy?"

"Ah. The problem there is that we already have Peter, the curator of European painting, and we're a relatively small museum. It's overkill to have a specialist in Impressionism, which is largely a European school of painting."

"Okay, I understand; but did they tell you that your job is on the line, or that having a master's degree is essential?"

"Not in so many words, but the memory of the story of 'Bringing Estelle Home' is fading, and I admit I've not worked as hard as I should have in my job."

"That's hard to believe," Anne said.

"True, all the same. My meeting this morning was with Tom McDermott, the museum director. It went all right. By the way, and keep this to yourself, they're planning an exhibit of Degas's work next year."

"Oh, how wonderful! Now that's something I'd love to help with," Anne said, her eyes lighting up, and enjoying the surge of excitement that rose whenever they talked about art together.

"Maybe you will. Now, does my explanation excuse me for my bad behavior?" he asked.

"Pretty much, though I still wonder why you didn't tell me earlier about the rehanging of the Estelle painting. I guess I'll accept that you wanted it to be a surprise, which it certainly was." She sat quietly for a few minutes, allowing her pent-up feelings to subside. Then she said, "I'm hungry. Let's eat. Do you want me to dress up so I'll be presentable at the restaurant?"

"Nah. It's getting late, and tomorrow's a workday. Let's go to Camellia Grill."

This time, relieved that they had resolved their difficulties, she let Sam drive her in his car to the popular restaurant on Carrollton Avenue. Its informal character and the efficient white-uniformed chefs cooking right next to the high counter where Sam and Anne sat had a soothing effect on both of them. Sam ordered a "cannibal special," raw ground hamburger, which caused her to wince but smile, and she chose a salad. She told him about her exciting discovery of Marguerite's journal.

After they had finished their meal, Sam dropped her off at her car and kissed her.

"I love your company, Anne, and I find you devastatingly attractive. Don't give up on me."

"Don't worry. I'm stubborn. My problem is that I don't know when to give up. You won't scare me off that easily."

As she drove home, she decided he had redeemed himself. She hadn't realized that his job was so tenuous. One thought persisted, however: she had been seeing him for five months, and had only now learned about the circumstances surrounding his hiring, his job insecurity, and the Estelle painting. He was clearly capable of withholding information, not only about himself but also about significant things that he must have known were vital to her. What else did she not know about him? How might he still surprise her in ways she didn't like?

When she opened the front door, she heard her phone ringing and dashed inside to answer.

"Hi, Anne, Isabelle here. You're hard to catch—I've been calling and calling. I wanted to ask when we can get together for dinner. Come by yourself, or bring Sam. How about this weekend?"

"I'll ask Sam, but I can come."

"Great. Saturday at six?"

Actually, she wasn't sure she wanted Sam to get to know her friends, but she couldn't hide him from them forever, and perhaps it would be useful to listen to their impressions of him and whether they considered him a good match for her. She'd grown up with Paul in Oxford, they had dated in high school, and she had depended upon his friendship almost all her life. Isabelle had advised her often about men in college. She was annoyed she wanted reassurance about her boyfriend, but after what had happened, that was exactly what she needed, and from people she could trust.

Chapter 12

November 1872

*E*stelle made plans for the music recital she promised to organize. Her guest list included the Fontenot family as well as the Oliviers, whose house stood behind her garden. Edgar had used the house as a background for his most recent painting of the children on the back doorstep. Madame America Olivier taught music and would be a welcome addition to the gathering. She had given Jo a few piano lessons, and the families were friends. Estelle spoke to Désirée about her plans.

"I have the scores for some popular French songs," she told her. "I haven't sung in a while, so I'll ask America to join me, and René can accompany us on the piano. Do you think that will amuse Edgar?"

"I'm sure it will. You sing beautifully, and it will cheer him up and give us all an evening of music."

"All right. I'll send out the invitations and start practicing," Estelle said. "It will be fun, I agree, and a change from children's play—not that the little ones aren't entertaining, but Edgar says they can't sit still, so it's difficult to paint them."

Désirée smiled. "I've heard him complain. Perhaps he doesn't understand that children are not ideal models."

Estelle's excitement mounted. Besides amusing Edgar, the event would please her husband, also a musician. He and she had often performed together in the past, and he had complimented her on her voice, but not recently. The recital would be good for both of them.

Estelle chose the songs and arranged for a rehearsal with René and America. Her neighbor was several years younger, and pretty. As they began to sing, their voices rang out loud and clear, enticing Degas down from his studio to listen, notebook in hand. He sketched as he watched them. They sang through the repertoire with gusto. America extended an arm toward Estelle in a threatening motion, and Estelle responded, holding her hand stiffly in front of her face.

"I haven't had this much fun in ages," Estelle said as the songs ended.

"Great drama, and you both sound glorious," Degas said, "I can't wait for the recital. Please keep your poses a few minutes longer so I can capture them in my drawing. I assume you will dress up for the performance."

"We will, yes. Why do you ask?" Estelle said.

"Only because when I finish the painting, I'll change what you're wearing. I can work from my sketch but I'll detail your fine clothes in the final one. I enjoy portraying beautiful dresses."

"Well, then. We won't disappoint you," Estelle said.

René, seated at the piano behind Estelle, banged some chords, descending the scale. "You see Edgar, we're not entirely without culture," he said. "I think sometimes that you under estimate us here in *le nouveau monde.*"

Estelle had scheduled the event for the following Sunday in the parlor. She surveyed the room. The piano stood in the corner of the spacious area, and the music would resound there, soaring to its high ceilings. The white slipcovered sofas and chairs would provide comfortable seating for the guests, and potted plants standing out against the dark yellow walls added a decorative touch.

Estelle dressed carefully. She asked Beulah to help with her hair, which she wanted piled on top of her head.

"But first, please bring me my good yellow dress, the one that has frills around the sleeves and ruffles on the hem—you know the one. It's loose, and will still fit me. I'm tired of wearing black clothes—and of being pregnant," she said. "Besides, America will dress up, and I don't wish to appear matronly next to her."

"Madame, you are carrying a baby. No one expects you to look your best . . . you're almost there; the baby will come in a month. Are you sure you wish to exert yourself, so close to your confinement?"

"I've already promised to sing, and this might be the last chance to have company for a while."

Beulah brought the lacy dress out of the armoire and laid it on the bed.

"It is a beautiful garment," she said, as she helped Estelle to stand up and put it on. "Now let me see what I can do with your hair."

Half an hour later, Estelle was ready. Stylish and fragrant, she descended the stairs to greet the guests.

The family members had assembled in the parlor. When she came into the room, the men stood up.

"*Ma chère* Estelle, *très élégante ce soir*," Degas said advancing toward her and kissing her on both cheeks.

Moments later the guests arrived, Philippe and Sophie Fontenot first, followed by Madame and Monsieur Olivier. René immediately took America's hand and, raising it to his lips, kissed it slowly.

"*Bonsoir*," he said to her. "You look divine. I expect your singing to be just as heavenly."

Overhearing René's greeting, Estelle managed a half smile. She thought her husband's welcome was effusive and felt thankful she had dressed with such care.

"Welcome and please have a seat. Beulah will serve you drinks," she said, strengthening her voice.

After Beulah handed iced drinks to everyone and the company had exchanged greetings, René struck some chords on the piano. Estelle moved in front of the instrument.

"We will sing some short French songs for you tonight. They're not opera, but they have an element of drama. We'll try to act our parts," she said, smiling.

America smiled too—a dazzling, flirtatious smile, Estelle observed.

"Yes, we'll do our best to entertain you," America added.

The two women sang several songs, first solo, then in unison, acting like divas with dramatic gestures and hands held to their hearts. America's soaring soprano voice contrasted well with Estelle's contralto. As they warbled the words of their last piece Estelle turned to René. He was looking straight past her to America, his eyes blazing. *She has bewitched him*, she thought. Her voice broke as the song ended, and she forced a smile. The audience applauded, and the performers curtsied. Estelle stumbled to a chair while America acknowledged René, the pianist.

The audience clapped again.

"Wonderful!" Degas said. "Encore!"

"Yes, yes, encore," said Désirée.

"I must decline," Estelle said in a hoarse voice, "but America may wish to sing again."

America giggled, a high, girlish giggle. "If it would please you all," she said.

She sashayed to the piano and whispered in René's ear. He gave a quick nod and a wink.

"I'll sing some folk songs," she announced.

She gathered her skirts, pulled them up above her ankles, and assumed a coquettish pose. René played the opening bars, and America began to sing.

Estelle watched in amazement, her heart beating wildly. The baby kicked in her womb and she sat straighter, trying to relieve the tightness inside, hoping the turmoil in her body wouldn't show on her face. She had no idea that this woman could behave in such an unconstrained manner. Her singing was bold, just like a gypsy. She noticed that René could hardly keep his eyes on the keyboard. With a stab of envy, she wished she were not older than her husband, almost thirty, and pregnant. Torn between her duty as a hostess and the strong desire to disappear and retreat to the safety of her room, she held her head high and maintained her composure until the ordeal ended.

When America had trilled the last note, she fluttered her eyes, took a curtsey and sat down, her cheeks flushed. The audience clapped.

"A grand success! What a lovely evening. Thank you so much for entertaining us," Degas said, glancing at both women.

America acknowledged the compliment with a smile and a flick of her fan. Estelle bowed her head but said nothing. Désirée came to her sister and gave her a hug.

"Thank you for arranging this musical evening," she said. "Edgar already told me he enjoyed it, and he looks happier than I've seen him for some days now. We must do this again . . ." She lowered her voice, ". . . but without America next time."

"Yes, yes, again. . . ." Estelle said, feeling lightheaded and more than a little dispirited.

She swept her eyes around the assembled company, who smiled and talked among themselves with animation. The evening had been a success. Edgar was pleased. While glad about that, she couldn't avoid the truth: for her the recital had taken on an unreal, nightmarish character. She fervently wished that America had behaved more modestly. How had she learned to sing like that? Worse, how did René know precisely how to accompany her? They must have practiced . . . but she had never been aware of it. Pushing the disturbing thoughts aside, she rose to accept thanks from the guests for the evening as they gathered coats and moved toward the front door.

When all the visitors had gone and the house had become quiet again, she shuffled to the staircase. René caught her arm.

"I think everything went well, don't you?" he asked.

"Yes, but I'm tired now. I'm off to bed."

"You sang well, my dear," he said.

"Thank you. So did America, I'm sure you agree," she said narrowing her eyes in the poor light as she tried to read his expression.

"She, too, yes. She's quite an accomplished performer," he said, avoiding her eyes.

"Her last songs surprised me. How did you know how to accompany her, playing all those unusual rhythms? Did you practice together?"

"I'm familiar with gypsy music. It wasn't hard, once she hummed a few bars," he said.

"And by the way, René, I want to thank you for the beautiful lace handkerchief," she said.

He knitted his brows. "What handkerchief? Oh, of course! From Paris!"

Estelle's pulse raced, and her face burned in anger. The handkerchief had not been intended for her.

She resisted his attempt to take her arm to help her. Shocked and exhausted, she climbed up the stairs to bed alone.

Chapter 13

November 1970

Anne spent the week researching cowboy painters and arranging for termite treatments, both projects that she would have happily passed on to someone else. On Friday, the house would be covered in a tent and chemical gas applied, guaranteed to rid the building of the pests for several years. On Tuesday, Anne lifted the parrot-shaped knocker on her neighbor Homer's door and released it. It fell from her hand with a thud.

"Hello there, missy," Homer greeted her, as he cracked the door open, came out, and shut it behind him. "I won't ask you in, if you don't mind. Cane is loose inside."

"Cane? Is that your dog?" she asked.

"Parrot. Short for Hurricane. She's flyin' around. Can't risk 'er gettin' out, if you know what I mean."

"Sure. I came to tell you that the termite treatment will begin at my house on Friday. It won't affect you, but the tent will remain over the house for a few days. Are you interested in having your house treated at the same time?"

"What? The fumes would kill the parrot, not to mention me. It's meddlin' with nature, that's what. Unnecessary assault, that is."

"All right," Anne said, turning to leave. "Just wanted to let you know."

"Yer folks have always taken the life out of things," he said.

Anne stopped and stared back at him with a flash of anger. "What do you mean?"

"That Etienne, yer grandfather, I believe, took my favorite chicken, Henrietta. Hen, for short. Had a rooster and said he wanted to use my chicken for breedin'. Had good feathers, she did, and was a good layer, at least one egg a day. Never gave her back. Killed 'er, I think."

"Sorry about that," Anne said, moving fast to get away. She did not like the direction the conversation was taking. The crazy old man was almost shaking his fist at her as she left.

Back in her room, she gratefully picked up Marguerite's journal. She needed distraction, and sanity.

November 20, 1872

Papa has been meeting with Monsieur Degas often. They talk about painting, and a few times M. Degas has come to the studio at our house. Papa is painting Maman. She says M. Degas would like to paint her, too, but so far Papa has not agreed. He says M. Degas has been painting the Musson family. Meanwhile, I practice my drawing and wish I could see one of M. Degas's paintings.

Now Anne understood how Degas's notebook might have ended up in her house. He had visited Philippe Fontenot, her great-great-grandfather, often. Marguerite was the daughter of Philippe and Sophie. So was Marguerite her great-grandmother? She too had apparently inherited some talent, or at least interest, in painting. Anne wondered what her family members had achieved artistically. She herself would love to create a work of great artistic merit, whether that be a painting or the beautiful renovation of an historic building. For now, the house would satisfy her need for art in her life, and she looked forward to the day when she could turn her attention to the finer aesthetic details.

What does it take for a painter to become an artist of significance, as Degas had been? she wondered. He'd shown promise, worked hard to improve his skills, and had still not achieved any recognition at thirty-eight. She could hardly compare herself to Degas, but she shared some goals with Marguerite: wanting to learn, eager to create something of artistic value, and distracted by the desire for a relationship with an older, accomplished man. Had Degas been different? Single-minded, wanting to pursue art at any cost, regardless of his lack of success or desire for marriage?

A knock interrupted her musings. Andrea, her housemate, stood in the hallway.

"Nice to see you," Anne greeted her. "We never seem to be here at the same time. Come in."

Andrea took a seat in a chair by the table.

"I saw a man here ringing your doorbell recently," she said. "Was that your boyfriend?"

"Probably. No other men come looking for me, other than the occasional policeman," Anne said with a wry grin.

"Nice looking guy," Andrea said.

Anne made no comment and, despite her displeasure with Sam, couldn't help her sense of pride. She knew he made a good impression, especially on women.

"Listen, I want to talk to you about the house," Andrea continued, running her hand through her honey-blond hair. She wore a diamond ring that flashed as it caught the light. "How are the renovations coming along?"

"I'm thinking about the next steps. Reconstruction's slower than molasses, but so far, so good. I'd be grateful for some advice about the interior design. Since you're studying architecture, you may have some ideas. I'd like to create more open space and combine two smaller rooms on the first floor. The architect has drawn up some plans, but I could use a second opinion."

"I need to see the place first. Might be exciting. Most of those old Creole houses have great bones, as they say."

"I'd describe mine that way. It was built in 1853."

"It's a classic, then. Name the day."

"Sometime after Friday. I'll be in touch."

Anne had accepted Isabelle and Paul's invitation for dinner on Saturday. Sam had declined, claiming he had work to do. She wanted to buy flowers for Isabelle at the French Market and set off on foot. Turning onto Esplanade, she passed several large houses, all in a dilapidated condition like hers. Most stood three stories high and bore balconies supported by pillars. Blackened with age, they no longer looked grand, and piles of trash obscured neglected palmettos and shrubs in their gardens. The neutral ground in the middle of the avenue hadn't changed since Degas's time, and tall palms, magnolias, and a double row of spreading live oaks provided an arc of shade. She had heard that a streetcar drawn by horses used to run there. It was easy to imagine Sophie and Marguerite strolling along the avenue wearing long flowing gowns and holding parasols. In those days, the clapboard and stucco houses were painted white. *Faded beauties, like the old Creoles.* How sad that the neighborhood had declined, along with the gracious way of life that Marguerite described in her journal. Anne reaffirmed her wish to bring life back to the one house that was hers.

She pushed her way through the crowds at the market. Musicians stood on street corners, and she paused to listen. A juggler threw colored balls, causing a small dog to bark. Anne feared dogs and kept a distance from the yapping animal. She bought a bouquet from a street vendor and retraced her steps.

Back in her car, she took St. Charles Avenue to her friends' shotgun house on Cherokee Street. A small, one-story building, it had a hallway that ran from front to back that would allow someone to shoot a gun all the way through the house, though Anne didn't know anyone who had ever wanted to do that.

"Come in, so glad to see you," Isabelle said, giving her friend a hug and taking the flowers. "White roses, my favorites. Thanks."

Isabelle Attwood was tall and slender with green eyes, but not the proverbial eyes of envy. She had been popular in college and, unlike Anne, had always attracted many boyfriends.

"What will you have to drink?" Isabelle asked.

"The usual, please," Anne said as she watched her friend go to the kitchen to mix a gin and tonic.

She took a seat on the sofa. Barely noticing the sparse furnishings, she focused on a photograph in a silver frame of Isabelle and Paul on their wedding day. They appeared joyful, a perfect couple, he with his dark good looks, and she with her red hair flaming under a veil crowned with a headdress of gardenias. They were laughing, almost obscured by showers of rice, as they came out of the church. Anne had introduced them earlier that year and attended the wedding as maid of honor. It all seemed such a long time ago, and they were already living such different lives.

"Whatever happened to your appetite for Sazeracs?" Isabelle called to her.

"Only for very special occasions now," Anne said, "and lately, there haven't been any." Isabelle stuck her head out of the kitchen, and, noticing her friend's look of concern, Anne added, "I didn't mean that really—everything's fine. I have to make some decisions, that's all, and you know me. I don't always make the right ones."

Isabelle laughed. "Yeah, I remember," she said.

Paul came into the room. His face broke into a smile as he removed his glasses. "Hi, Annie. Haven't seen you for weeks." he said. "How are you doing? What've you been up to?"

"Working, mostly."

"So are you finally digging into the relics of your long-lost Creole ancestors?"

"Yes, but not literally," she said, making a face at Paul. "The house is in chaos, still. I'm especially pleased to unearth the family's connections with Degas."

He sat down next to her on the couch.

Isabelle's voice rang out. "Paul, please come and get the cocktails. I made one for you, too."

He disappeared into the kitchen and reappeared moments later with the drinks.

"Cheers," he said. "So tell me more about the house."

"I'm sick of all the dust, but soon we'll get to the interesting part. I'm looking forward to choosing paint colors and flooring and deciding whether to keep the fine moldings and medallions in the ceiling."

"Good for you," he said. "I remember how reluctant you were to accept your inheritance. You considered it a burden, an impossible dream."

"I did. I thought I was too young for all the responsibility, and at first I couldn't afford to pay for the work or imagine the outcome . . . but you helped me to look beyond the broken-down facade."

"Let's just say I'm more practical."

"Okay, and now there's no stopping me. But restoring the house isn't easy. Someone broke in and vandalized the bathroom, possibly an activist, someone who doesn't like my project and who's fighting the city over displacement of people resulting from urban renewal work."

"That sounds serious. Are the police investigating?"

"I reported the incident, but no, they're not doing much. It's complicated."

"Dinner's almost ready," Isabelle said as she joined them carrying the dishes. "We're having fried chicken, mashed potatoes, and collard greens. Good Southern food, not Creole. My tradition, not yours, Annie."

"Nothing wrong with that," Anne said. "Can I help?"

"You can bring out the wine, if you like. Bottle's open in the fridge."

Anne fetched the wine, and Isabelle set the food on the dining room table. Paul filled glasses for Anne and himself, and they sat down to eat.

"How's work?" Isabelle asked Anne.

"It's okay. My latest project concerns art of the American West."

"Rather you than me on that one," Isabelle said, "but at least you'll be learning something new."

"True, and so will you. You'll be learning about babies and diapers and motherhood."

"Yes. Babies are intriguing."

"Intriguing, yes, but frankly, I have no idea how I'd manage if I had one."

"You would, but you've never had motherhood as a goal, if I remember correctly. It's hard to be an artist and a mother, or a mother and anything else for that matter, and I guess you still have artistic aspirations, don't you?"

"I'm not sure anymore. I'm seeing Sam. A relationship takes time, and because of the work at the museum and the house, I have little free time to paint," she said, "and no inspiration."

"No inspiration? Come on, you did some amazing paintings in college and won awards. You can't suddenly lose your talent."

"It takes more than talent. Many artists struggle."

"I have confidence in you. You'll figure it out."

"Thanks. Work isn't bad, but the museum staff aren't artists. They love art, but most have little understanding of the people who make it."

"I'm not sure anyone understands artists. You've always been independent, Annie. It's one of the things I admire about you. You sure resisted your father's influence while we were in college. He hoped you would get married."

"Yes, he wanted to see me settled and financially secure, but that was before I became an heiress." She chuckled. "Enough about me. I also recall how hard it was for you. Your mother wouldn't allow you to live your life as you wished at all. She wanted you to marry and practically had your wedding planned before you were out of high school."

Isabelle laughed. "You're right. Well, she almost got her wish. I held out until I finished college. But unlike you, I always wanted to get married. Guess I'm traditional."

Anne nodded. The transition from college to adulthood had been easy for her friend.

"Thanks for the great meal," she said. "It's good to taste home cooking for a change."

"You're welcome. Come more often," Isabelle replied.

Addressing Paul, Anne asked, "How do you like your classes at the law school?"

He grimaced. "If you consider case histories worthy of intense study, fine."

Isabelle picked up the plates. "There's no dessert—I thought you'd prefer to skip the calories, Annie—but I can offer coffee," she said.

"No coffee, but I would like another glass of wine," Anne replied. "Need help with the dishes?"

"No, thanks, y'all should visit," Isabelle said, getting up from the table.

Paul and Anne ambled into the living room carrying their wine glasses and sat down. Paul stretched his long legs out from the chair.

"How are things going with Sam?" he asked.

"Okay. Why do you ask?"

"Just curious, as I consider you one of my oldest—and dearest—friends."

"I hoped he would come tonight, but he had to work." Anne said.

"Did he give you a reason, other than that? Is he working on some special project, or deadline, or something?"

"No. Why?"

"I can't help wondering what he does for a living that keeps him busy on a Saturday night."

Anne flushed. "He works at the museum as a curator. He often works on weekends. Look, we're only dating. I don't know what he does all day."

"Why not, when you work at the same place?"

"He has a different job, a higher-level one than mine, and it involves a lot of meetings and travel. He's away a lot . . . wait a minute, what are you trying to get at? I'm beginning to sense this is an inquisition."

"Sorry. It's not meant to be, but Isabelle and I want to be sure you're not getting into any trouble," he said.

Anne quelled her annoyance and attempted to remain calm, reminding herself that Isabelle always had her best interests at heart. She did not want to alienate Paul either, her oldest friend. She took another sip of her drink. After a few minutes Paul spoke again.

"Does Sam like fishing?"

Anne again wondered what he was getting at, and paused before answering, in thinly disguised irritation.

"Not that I'm aware of. Why all the questions?"

"I saw someone running down the levee north of the city in the middle of the night carrying a big package that someone threw to him from a barge in the river. It looked like Sam."

"Only *looked* like Sam? Weren't you sure? How could you tell, if it was dark? What were you doing at night on the levee, anyway? Did you talk to him?"

"I called out, but he didn't answer. There was a full moon. I was out fishing, and my car broke down."

"Oh. Well, why even mention this, if you're not even sure it was Sam?" she said, her voice rising. "You've only met him once before, and that was months ago when you saw us together on campus."

"Anne, I'm not trying to scare you. Izzy and I agreed that

we should talk to you about this and ask if you know anything or can explain it."

"I appreciate your concern, truly." She gulped her wine, and clenched the arm of her chair. "When was this, anyway?"

"On a Thursday night. October fifteenth."

"That doesn't help much. I don't keep track of all Sam's movements, any more than he does mine."

"All right. I'm only bringing this up because, although I've only met him once, the man really did look like Sam. This guy impressed me by his unusual speed when he ran away. I run regularly myself, and I know when someone is fast—and he was very fast, like a professional runner. Has Sam had experience in track?"

"Yes, in college," Anne said.

"Okay. What else has he told you about his athletic skills?"

Anne didn't reply, but remembered he had trained for the biathlon, and was an expert at skiing and shooting.

"Have you ever been to his house?" Paul asked.

"No."

Paul pulled his feet back against his chair and sat up, locking her eyes.

"How well do you know this man, Annie? You might want to ask him more questions about his time away from the office. Look, I don't want to harass you, and I'm not going to pursue this any further. It's up to you. But please be careful."

For the rest of the evening, Anne kept up polite but cool conversation with her friends. Relieved when it was over, she climbed into her car and drove home. She would never have tolerated the pointed questioning if Paul hadn't been such a strong supporter over the years. They had remained friends after they stopped dating in high school. Her head ached. It was too bad that so soon after she'd had her first serious argument with Sam, she now had another reason to distrust him. Paul had correctly assessed that she knew very little about the man. He never gave her a detailed accounting of his time away from the office, and his behavior the previous weekend had been odd, even if he had more or less explained it away. All the same, Paul had seen a man in the middle of the night who only resembled Sam. It could have been anyone, or if it had been Sam, there might be a good reason. She would ask him.

The phone rang early on Sunday morning.

"Morning, sweetheart. It's a lovely day. Want to go for a drive? We'll have a long, lazy lunch on the way," Sam said.

"Sounds great."

"Pick you up at ten o'clock."

His call was like a breath of cool, fall air. Anne got up, took a shower, and dressed in a pair of slacks, a white blouse, and a long necklace. It was indeed a lovely day, sunny, breezy, and comfortable; not hot, not humid. She peered through the window at the gently waving palm trees above and the green foliage lower down punctuated by red and white Cajun hibiscus flowers. They reminded her of Degas's picture of Estelle standing behind a vase of flowers in similar colors. Thinking back to Marguerite's journal, Anne wondered if Estelle had been pregnant when Degas completed that painting. Sam might know. She would ask him about that. As she saw his car pull up, she gathered a light jacket and ran out to meet him. She opened the passenger door and slipped onto the seat.

He gave her a brief kiss. "I decided we should go along the River Road and take a picnic," he said.

"Great idea. It'll be good to get out of town for a change."

As she saw him look approvingly at her, she noticed that his eyes matched his shirt and were a shade of pure blue, rather than their usual steel gray. A rush of attraction surged through her. They drove across the Huey P. Long Bridge and turned north along the River Road. She wound down the window and enjoyed the sensation of the wind blowing her hair. He rolled up his sleeves and touched her shoulder.

"Didn't see you this week. Where have you been hiding?"
he asked.

"Not hiding. I might ask the same of you," she said.

This would be the time to ask him more about his where-
abouts, she thought, but she was enjoying herself and him and
didn't want to spoil the day. The serious talk could wait.

They passed several plantation houses. Some had tall pillars
in front and long driveways bordered by oak trees leading to
the river, while others with more informal entrances stood
farther back from the water. A few of the houses appeared in
good repair, displaying fresh white paint and tended lawns;
others had fallen into ruin, reminders of times gone by, abandoned since the Civil War.

"Have you ever been on a plantation house tour?" Anne asked.

"No, I haven't. You?"

She shook her head. "Somehow it seems the wrong thing
to do, when you consider that those places only thrived because
of slavery."

"Not only the plantations, but the whole South, and New
Orleans in particular, owed their financial success to slavery," he
replied. "Once the war ended, the way of life in Southern cities
changed, and many families whose livelihood depended on the
cotton industry went bankrupt."

"I know. It must have been a terrible time. I know that during
Reconstruction laws were passed to grant rights to former slaves,
but these were not enforced. Though everyone struggled, from
what I'm learning through Marguerite's journal, the Creoles lived
a life of incredible luxury for a while after the war."

"Yes, but as you say, only for a while. Their way of life broke
down. Everything was in chaos, with carpetbaggers exploiting
everyone, blacks and whites alike, while Southerners adjusted to
the new way of life. The Creoles couldn't compete with the Americans who moved into the city around that time. They had a better
business sense, and they managed to survive more successfully."

"I guess so; their houses tell the story. The American-built ones on St. Charles Avenue are better preserved compared with the Creole places on Esplanade like mine."

"Exactly."

After they had driven farther along the river, Anne said, "Sam, tell me more about the painting of Estelle. We haven't had a chance to talk much about it."

"Okay. I told you the story of how the museum raised funds to buy it. Well, it had been in France until then. Degas took all the paintings he completed in New Orleans back to France. Critics think he valued the family portraits because they were all he had as reminders of his American relatives. Almost all of them remained in his studio until he died. Now only a few, including the one of Estelle, who was pregnant, by the way, are owned by museums in this country. He came from a wealthy family, but it looks as though after arriving in New Orleans, he came to consider his paintings as potential sources of income. Not famous in 1872, critics think he reached a turning point here. He gained confidence and believed that his reputation would improve when he returned to Paris."

"And obviously it did," Anne said.

"Yes, partly because of some family portraits he completed here, but mostly because of the masterpiece he called *A Cotton Office in New Orleans*. You know the one?"

"From art history courses, yes. Marguerite hasn't mentioned it so far in her journal, but because of her, I'm learning more about Degas's connection with my great-great-grandfather, Philippe Fontenot, who was himself an artist. Do you suppose he achieved any recognition?"

"Not that I'm aware of. The American Impressionists were never as highly regarded as the French ones. Did you know that Degas was the only French Impressionist painter to work in America?"

"No, I didn't. Makes his visit here even more significant. Thanks for the history lesson. Speaking of history, the termites in the house have gone," she said.

"Good, so what's next?"

"Woodwork. The doors, doorframes, floors, stairs, and windows need repairing along with the bathroom fixtures. Then I get to decide about the really interesting stuff, the finishes."

"In other words, everything. Sounds as if you're making progress, though."

"I think so."

"I'm getting hungry," Anne said. "Is there somewhere we can stop for that picnic?"

"Soon. I know a place on the levee with a good view of the river."

She glanced at him. Now would be the time to ask.

"Oh. Do you come here often?" she said.

"You're sounding like a cliché, Anne. You can do better than that," he said, teasingly.

"No, seriously. Do you fish?"

"No. Do you?"

"You know I don't. But how are you familiar with the river, and places to stop, if not for fishing?" she persisted.

He took a sideways glance at her.

"Do you really want to hear the answer? Remember I'm thirty-two, and you're not my first girlfriend," he replied.

"All right, enough said," she sighed.

He was not going to make it easy for her. She needed to ask him whether he had been there at night, but why bother? He would simply say no, or give some answer that she didn't want to hear, just as he'd implied.

He stopped the car, retrieved a blanket and basket from the trunk, and bounded up the levee. Anne followed at a slower pace. He laid out cheese, fruit, figs, crusty loaves of bread, and a bottle of red wine. He twisted the cork from the bottle and poured two glasses.

"To you and your Creole ancestors," he said.

"Thanks. We should invite them. What a nice way to spend a Sunday," she said with a smile.

From their blanket at the top of the levee, they watched the water swirling below. An occasional silvery fish jumped, making a faint splash as it dove back in. Rusty barges passed, creating waves and wakes in the muddy water, while white clouds raced across the sky. Anne lay back, a hand shielding her eyes from the sun. Sam sat forward, resting his hands on his raised knees. They finished the bottle of wine and most of the food.

"It'll be Thanksgiving soon. What are you doing?" he asked.

"Spending it with my father in Oxford. I go every year. Perhaps you'd like to come and meet him."

"I'd love to, if I'm free, but I may have to go away again. I'll know soon."

"No rush. I won't need to tell him until the week before. Where are you traveling to?"

"New York. We're negotiating the purchase of a new painting. It's not well known, but it would fill a hole in our collection."

"You do an awful lot of traveling," Anne said. "Don't you tire of it?"

"No. I hate routines, and this gives me a break."

He checked his watch.

"Time to get going," he said.

They gathered up the picnic items and headed back to the car. As they went, she realized that she had still not learned any answers to her questions; he had evaded them all. She took a deep breath and braced herself.

"Sam, what were you doing here on the levee after ten o'clock on October fifteenth?"

He took off fast, bounding down the levee, swinging the picnic basket like a weapon.

"What are you talking about? What goddamned nonsense is someone telling you? Must have been someone else, because it wasn't me," he shouted over his shoulder.

They drove back to New Orleans in silence. Once home, Anne suddenly felt tired, and her head buzzed. She needed to lie down for a while. She couldn't bear to think any more about the possibility that something was seriously wrong with Sam. Her mind ran over his virtues. She enjoyed his companionship. Her first serious boyfriend, she found him irresistible. He was good to her: he treated her to meals in good restaurants, encouraged her career at the museum, respected her, and made her feel special. Besides, it thrilled her to be dating such an attractive man who shared her passion for art. She wasn't sure he had behaved badly enough for her to give up on him, and the man on the levee that Paul had told her about might have been anyone. She had accused him without any evidence, and she couldn't blame him for saying that others had been talking nonsense. The purpose of dating was to get to know a person, and how would she do that if she broke up with him?

Chapter 14

November 1872

The morning after the recital Estelle dressed in her usual black clothes. She found Edgar sitting in the front room reading the newspaper.

"*Bonjour*, what a fine morning," he greeted her. "How are you today, *ma cousine*? It was a pleasure to listen to music again. I can't thank you enough for arranging everything and singing so beautifully."

"I'm glad you enjoyed it. New Orleans is not Paris, but we do love music here," she said stiffly, shutting the image of America's shocking performance out of her mind. "What are your plans for the day? Are you going to the office?"

"No. The music inspired me, and I will paint today. I still have almost all the family to paint, and I don't want to disappoint you."

"I'm pleased to hear this, Edgar," she said, her face softening. "Désirée might sit for you, or Mathilde."

"Yes, they would be good subjects. And you, what are you doing today?"

"Me? Nothing much. I plan to relax, now that the recital is over."

At that minute, Beulah bustled into the room carrying a large bouquet.

"Madame, these flowers arrived, a present to you from your husband, I believe," she said.

"What a surprise! I love flowers. Please put them here on the table and bring a vase. I'll arrange them right away."

Beulah nodded and went into the kitchen. She came back moments later carrying a container. Estelle reached for the red gladioli and white camellia stems. Edgar took up his notebook and a pencil. He sketched her quickly as she viewed the flowers, holding the flowers delicately as she placed them in the glass vessel one by one.

Estelle, glancing sideways, saw that Edgar was drawing her. "I hope you're focusing on the flowers in your picture," she said. "I'm not nearly as pleasing, or as colorful. Anyway, I can't pose for you now."

"I don't want you to pose. I like this scene as it is. It's about you, doing what you enjoy, an ordinary, everyday activity."

She continued arranging the flowers.

After a few minutes, Edgar said, "*Bon!* This will make a fine painting. I'll go upstairs and start it while the image is fresh in my mind."

Estelle put the last gladiolus into the arrangement. As she did so, the idea occurred to her that her husband had sent the flowers to compensate for his display of attention to America Olivier the night before and for his clumsy mistake about the handkerchief. Pain shot through her chest, and her eyes blurred with tears. Her task finished, she turned from the table. Not seeing a chair that stood nearby, she stumbled over it and fell with a thud to the floor.

"Madame, what happened? Are you hurt?" Beulah said, looking dismayed as she kneeled down beside Estelle, who was stifling her sobs and cursing herself for her carelessness.

"I don't know . . . the baby . . . call the doctor, please."

The maid dashed out to find a manservant. She instructed him to take the carriage and ask Doctor Lenoir in Rue Chartres to come immediately. When she returned, Estelle was sitting up, her back propped against a chair, rubbing her swollen stomach.

"Here's your fan. You're overheated, madame. Don't worry— the doctor should be here soon," Beulah said.

Estelle accepted the fan while the maid mopped her brow and wiped away the tears.

"Thank you, Beulah. Whatever would I do without you? Could you help me upstairs? I think I need to lie down for a while. I have some pains like contractions."

Beulah held her under the armpits and helped her to stand. They made their way up the stairs, and once in the bedroom, Beulah unbuttoned Estelle's dress and dropped a nightgown over her head.

Désirée arrived back at the house after her usual morning walk and met Doctor Lenoir on his way up the front steps.

"*Bonjour*, doctor, what brings you here?" she asked.

"Madame De Gas has had a fall."

"*Mon Dieu!*"

She rushed the doctor up the stairs to Estelle's room. The doctor entered first, shutting the door behind him. Désirée waited, pacing the hall. Soon Beulah emerged.

"How is she? Can I go in? What does the doctor say?" Désirée asked.

"The doctor says she's all right but must rest. He'll be able to tell you more."

The door opened again, and Doctor Lenoir came out. Désirée moved to grab his arm, then stepped back and met his gaze.

"She's resting now, and should sleep," he said.

"But the baby? Is everything fine?"

"The baby seems to be all right. Heartbeat is normal. Madame De Gas has had a shock. I've prescribed bed rest for the next week."

Désirée clasped her hands.

"Thank you, doctor. What a relief. Can you see yourself out?"

"I can. I'll be back tomorrow."

Désirée tiptoed in to find her sister lying in bed, her eyes closed. She took Estelle's hand and bending to her said, "Don't worry, dearest. You and the baby will be fine. Sleep now. I'll be close by."

Estelle opened her eyes briefly, with the ghost of a smile. Désirée pulled a chair closer to the bed and sat down beside her. "I'll stay near you, dear one," she said again in a whisper as she smoothed the bedcovers.

Estelle soon fell into a sound sleep. Désirée crept to the windows to close the shutters against the strong light invading the room.

Chapter 15

November 1970

*A*nne met Andrea at the house soon after the contractors had removed the termite tents. The air smelled fetid, but they saw no sign of the winged insects. Andrea stood at the entrance and gazed around.

"This place is amazing," she said. "Classic Greek Revival style. Corinthian columns, a marble fireplace, and great proportions."

She unfolded the floor plans that Anne had given her. "They're good. I wouldn't change a thing downstairs," she said. "If you want to preserve the character, I'd keep the moldings and medallions and paint the woodwork. I can advise you about colors."

"I thought I'd paint everything white. It's a clean, crisp look, and will create an airy, bright space."

"That's what I would suggest. The Creoles understood a lot about white. They used shades with dark undertones to add patina and to keep the homes from being blindingly bright in the strong sunlight."

"Really? How do you know this?" Anne asked.

"A designer who is an expert on color gave a lecture on the subject at school recently. I took notes. He recommends a certain combination of white shades that work well together and create what he calls 'a soulful ambience' for New Orleans interiors."

"Fascinating. Tell me more."

"It has to do with the undertones. Each white is mixed with a certain percentage of blue, yellow, or red. As an artist, you already understand how each tint produces warm or cool colors."

"Sure, but there are so many variations. Would I have to mix them myself?"

"No. It turns out there are colors commercially available that the designer claims are close to the ones the Creoles used." She opened a notebook and flipped through the pages. "The combination is Navajo White, Swiss Coffee, and White Dove. You can use them anyway you choose, on the walls, on the ceiling, or on the trim. The important thing is to have all three colors together in the same space. The different whites trick the eye so that they blend and balance the light in the room."

"This is fantastic information. Three shades of white! I'll try it. I can't thank you enough. This color scheme will make the house beautiful, perhaps even soulful."

"I'll be interested myself to see how it all turns out," Andrea said.

"And by the way, when's the wedding?" Anne asked.

"Next year. I'll be sure to invite you."

Another wedding, Anne mused. *Other women my age get married or have careers. I have a house. Am I living my life upside down?*

Next day Anne started her new project at the museum. She read the books Peter gave her and reviewed the list of the painters for the show on Western art. She needed to learn more about the various weapons that the cowboys and Indians used. Perhaps some of those could be part of the exhibit. She wasn't very familiar with the seminal battles of the frontier either; she would have to educate herself about those, too. As she worked, her thoughts kept returning to the wonderful color scheme Andrea had suggested, and she wished she had time to spend on things that interested her more. She determined to make time.

On Monday the following week she heard Sam's voice near her cubicle.

"What do you mean, you haven't yet talked to her? Well, get with it. She's an intern, and you're supposed to help," he said.

Anne peeked round the partition surrounding her desk. He was talking to a tall, thin, blond woman, with long, shapely legs, perfect makeup, and a disdainful expression on her chiseled features. She had piercing Prussian blue eyes and a form-fitting suit to match. Anne caught Sam's eye, and he beckoned to her.

"Anne, this is Mary Wharton," he said.

"Pleased to meet you," Anne said, rising and holding out her hand.

Mary took it. Her grasp was slippery, like a fish.

"We'll be working together, I understand," Mary said. "Pardon me for not coming by sooner. I've been out of the office. Let's talk now."

"Sure, if you have time."

"I'll call you later," Sam said, looking in Anne's direction.

Mary Wharton strode into Anne's cubicle and took a seat next to the desk.

"I take it you're researching the artists. What have you learned so far?"

"About Frederic Remington, Charles M. Russell, Charles Schreyvogel, and several others. I've also been studying the guns, bows, and arrows used by the frontiersmen and Indians."

"Guns and arrows? What on earth for? This is to be a painting exhibit, not a dog and pony show."

"I decided it might be useful to display some objects along with the paintings," Anne said.

"Waste of your time. I need a list of the artists and a theme for the show. When can you get those to me?"

"By the end of the week."

"Good. But why the interest in the guns? Has your friend Sam Mollineux perhaps piqued your curiosity about those?"

Anne blinked.

"Excuse me. What has Mr. Mollineux got to do with this?"

"Plenty, I would think. You must know that he's a sharp-shooter, in more ways than one."

"I didn't know, and no, he has nothing to do with my research or my ideas about the exhibit."

"Really? My advice to you is to keep professional and personal affairs separate. Have that information to me by Friday."

She got up to leave. Anne watched her go, noting her confident stride. She was a thoroughly objectionable woman. How dare she presume to give her advice about Sam, and how had she learned about their relationship? What was her relationship with him, anyway? Anne would make it her business to find out.

Sam called later that afternoon.

"Hi, sweetheart. How did the meeting go?"

"Mary told me what she expects by the end of the week. Didn't like her much. She said I shouldn't get my personal life mixed up with my professional one."

Sam roared with laughter. "She said that? The little hypocrite," he said.

"How well do you know her, anyway?"

"Better than I'd like. My advice is to steer clear of her as much as possible."

"Difficult to do, when she's now my boss," Anne said.

"Welcome to the world of work. It's good practice to get used to working for someone you don't find sympathetic. I expect she resents you because she thinks I had something to do with your getting the internship."

"I see. In other words, she doesn't think I'm qualified for the job," Anne said bitterly.

"Look, that's not the reason I called," Sam said. "Thanksgiving is this Thursday. Is it too late to accept your invitation to join you for dinner?"

"At my Dad's, you mean? No. He'd like to meet you."

"Good. I'd like to meet him, too. We can drive up together."

"Sam, what does Mary know about our relationship? What would cause her to give me that stern warning?"

"I've never told her anything about you. We no longer talk. But there may be gossip around—that's my guess, that she heard through the grapevine that we're dating."

"Is that bad?"

"It could be. She's the jealous type. We can talk more about that on Thursday, or should we drive up to Oxford on Wednesday night?"

"Wednesday night would be better. That way I'll be able help Dad with the meal, and we'll all have longer to visit. We can stay at his house."

"Sounds good. Talk to you later."

She put the phone down. Her father had wanted to meet her boyfriend for months now. She was a little surprised that Sam had accepted the invitation, but more than happy that he had. Suddenly she realized that she had a deadline to meet on Friday, and it would be a short week because of the holiday. That meant she had to get the information to her boss by Wednesday, two days from now. She wondered if Mary Wharton had expected that the short work week would give her less time to complete the assignment so she would fail . . . but she told herself not to be paranoid. She opened her books and applied herself to the task with renewed vigor.

After work she went home and, wanting to engage herself in something of greater interest, took out Marguerite's journal. She could plunge more happily into Marguerite's trials and tribulations in 1872 than her own a century later.

December 1, 1872

Maman went to visit Estelle today. She's had a fall and is bedridden. Her baby is due in a few weeks, and the doctor's concerned. Maman said Estelle asked her to read to her because she has poor eyesight. Apparently, her husband had suggested that Madame Olivier should keep Estelle company, but Estelle said she would prefer Maman. Maman wants to oblige because she is fond of Estelle and feels sorry for her. René is not always considerate, she says, and she does not like America Olivier. M. Degas, meanwhile, has been painting members of his family. Papa says the paintings are very good, but the faces are obscure. Why would he not portray faces clearly? I've been practicing portraits myself, and I always try to achieve a likeness. Papa says M. Degas has a unique style, unlike anything he's ever seen. I think he's a little envious. Now I have more questions for M. Degas, if I should ever have the chance of talking to him. My curiosity knows no bounds! I dream only of Paris.

Good observations, Anne mused. Who was America Olivier? Her great-great-grandfather Philippe and Degas were seeing each other. Marguerite had spent no time with the artist so far. She hoped Marguerite would chronicle their friendship, for it appeared there had been one. Marguerite must have been impatient, knowing that she didn't have the freedom to speak to the artist whenever she saw him. Well-bred young women had few options but to remain passive in those days. She, on the other hand, needed to take an active role in determining her future. She didn't need to follow rules as strictly, but deciding for herself wasn't so easy, either. It struck her that there were several Estelles: Estelle, Degas's cousin; Estelle, her half-sister, and Estelle, Etienne's sister and Stella's namesake. She resumed reading the journal.

December 7, 1872
So exciting! I had a good talk with M. Degas yesterday.
He showed Papa and me an oil painting of his niece
Carrie. It's lovely. The white dress (very white) is especially well done. I asked him about it, and he told me he
often paints ballerinas in Paris. He admires their costumes
called tutus. He explained that he has developed a technique of using a black monoprint as an undertone so that
the white brush strokes on top create a luminous effect
similar to the way the dancers' clothes appear under the
harsh glare of the spotlights on the stage.

Marguerite had spoken to the painter at last! Anne's excitement matched the girl's as she took in this new information. What
a coincidence! Just after she had learned from Andrea about the
best shades of white paint to use in her house, she'd now gained
valuable insight into Degas's special use of that color. And it *was* a
color. Now she would examine reproductions of Degas's ballerina
paintings, try to copy his style, and introduce some nuanced white
areas into her own paintings to create more striking luminosity,
as he had.

On Wednesday, Anne took her list of painters and theme for the
show to Mary Wharton's office. After a struggle she had come up
with a title: *War with Horses: Painters of the Wild West.* Mary wasn't
there, so she left her list on the desk attached to a cover note saying
she hoped it was acceptable and she would like to discuss it the
following week.

Sam had told her he would pick her up directly from work to
drive to Oxford. She met him on the curb at five o'clock.

"Hop in, and let's get on the road." he said.

She tossed her suitcase in the back seat of the car and climbed
in beside him.

"How wonderful to have a few days off," she said. "Now I understand why people look forward to weekends so much."

"What do you mean? Didn't you always look forward to them?"

"Not while I was in college. There were always tests to study for, papers to write, and there wasn't much difference from the rest of the week, except we didn't have classes."

"You surely don't mean you were dull, all work and no play, in those days. Didn't you go on dates?"

"Sure. To parties, and dances, too. Some debutante and Mardi Gras balls. Newcomb's a social school, you see."

"So I hear, not that I was there," he said.

"You wouldn't have fitted in at an all-women's school, but you dated Newcomb girls."

"How do you know that?" he asked. "More gossip?"

"No gossip. You told me yourself, when we first met."

"I don't remember that . . . what did I say?"

"No details, but you said when you asked me out that you expected I, like most Newcomb girls, wouldn't have a car, which implied that you knew others. Would you mind telling me who, by the way?"

"Better not," he said. "But I understood those girls didn't have cars because they expected their dates would drive them. Anyway, I never became involved with anyone as much as I am now, with you."

A smile played across her face as she savored his words and she settled down in her seat. There was no point in spoiling the moment and grilling him about his relationship with Mary Wharton. She was glad to be on a long trip with him, her first, and that he was interested in meeting her father. They had reached the outskirts of the city and would soon be on the road for Oxford. It was about a six-hour drive, and they should be there by eleven o'clock that evening.

"Tell me about your father," Sam said.

"Dad, François Gautier, is a professor of entomology at the University of Mississippi. He's had some success in research and is now studying mosquitoes with the worthy goal of reducing the number of the pests in places like New Orleans. Dad's an intellectual and strangely obsessed with insects, but lovable. He's been a good father."

"Your mother died during your freshman year, right? Has he remarried?"

"He was married for two years to a dreadful woman called Catherine. Luckily for him, she took off with a fellow graduate student. I believe she's gone from his life; hope so, anyway."

"Why do you suppose he married her?"

"I have my theories. She was young and attractive, and he was well established but lonely."

"Will he remarry?"

"No idea; actually, I'm not sure if he's divorced yet."

"How's he doing now?"

"Okay, I guess. I've no idea if he misses Catherine. As I said, she was awful. Lately he's been interested in helping me solve my termite problem."

"How so?"

Anne suppressed a smile. "He had the extraordinary idea that he could release some kind of predator ants to gobble up the termites."

"No kidding! Your dad sounds like a character."

"He's dead serious when it comes to insects. Don't tease him, please. That reminds me: my neighbor Homer got upset when I told him I was having the house tented. He became ferocious and told me my family has always killed things."

"Aha. Shades of dark deeds, don't you agree?"

"Nah. He accused my grandfather of killing Hen, his chicken."

"He had a chicken called Hen?" Sam laughed. "But the plot thickens: perhaps your family was involved in voodoo. The practitioners used to kill chickens, you know."

"Yeah, I know. Not likely. My family were respectable, well-to-do Creoles. They didn't dabble in black magic."

"Are you sure? I've always thought of you as an enchantress."

She smiled. "Flattery will get you everywhere with me," she said.

He blew her a kiss, and they drove on.

"Have you talked to Stella yet about the damage in the bathroom?"

"I have. I don't think she had anything to do with it."

"So you're still considering asking her to move in?"

"I am. I'm starting to like her. Actually, I sort of admire her."

"How so?"

"She's figured out what she wants to do in her life and has a career she loves. She's beautiful and accomplished."

"Well, it's your decision. Be careful, though," he said. "If someone lives with you, it's important to find out if you're compatible. How would you turn her out if things didn't work out?"

"I've considered that, and I do still need time to get to know her."

She had thought about the awkwardness that would result if Stella had friends she didn't like, or a boyfriend or husband who wanted to move in. For that matter, what would happen if Sam should want to marry her? She kept her musings to herself.

"Do you need a break?" he asked, some hours later. "Something to eat?"

"I'm more thirsty than hungry," she said. "Perhaps we could stop at a drive-in."

As they passed through the town of Winona, Sam saw a Dairy Queen sign.

"Not exciting, but perhaps good for a Coke, or something," he said.

"Fine with me. Mississippi's not New Orleans."

Sam pulled the car into the parking lot beside the fast-food joint. They both got out, and Anne went inside to find a bathroom. She joined Sam at the outside service window.

"Do you have anything to eat?" he asked.

The man inside, dressed in a T-shirt with a Dairy Queen logo and hat said,

"We-ell, we have some ice-cream, and cheese sandwiches. Kinda late for much else this time o' night."

"Okay. We'll have something to drink. Two Cokes, please," Sam said.

They watched the flies become dizzy as they hit the fan that swirled sluggishly in front of the Dairy Queen window. It was a sultry night, warm for November, and the flies were on their last legs.

"Dad would love them," Anne said, taking her drink. "He loves things out of sync, especially insects that are not welcome."

"Anne, the more you tell me about your father, the more I like him," Sam said.

She stared at him, but made no response. She hoped that he and her father would get along.

They reclaimed their seats in the car, and Sam drove out of the parking lot.

"I was wondering, while we're there, could I take a look at that painting your relative completed?" he asked.

"Sure, but why would you be interested? Philippe Fontenot is not a well-known artist."

"All the same, I'd like to see it."

"All right. Sure. I'd like to hear your opinion of it, anyway," she said.

They drove on through the night, chatting about nothing in particular, until they arrived at Anne's father's house on Magnolia Street in Oxford.

The porch light was on. After Sam turned off the ignition, Anne watched him observe what he could of the building. The clapboard walls, white columns, and porch of the traditional ante-bellum house gleamed eerily in the moonlight. Her childhood home, where she had grown up . . . she was trying not to regard it as *home* anymore. She needed to move on and establish her own place, the one she would restore and make hers, but as she viewed her father's house, a wave of nostalgia washed over her, and she imagined it would be a long time before she would experience a sense of homecoming there, as she did here.

Brushing her thoughts aside, she said, "Dad said he'd wait up for us, but I don't see any lights inside. Let's go in."

Sam lifted both suitcases, and Anne unlocked the imposing front door. She fumbled for the switch in the front hall, and lights soon lit up the foyer and curving staircase that led to the second floor.

"Lovely old Southern home," Sam said.

A man with dark hair graying at the temples, a smooth-shaven face, and horn-rimmed glasses appeared at the top of the stairs. He wore a checked shirt tucked into a pair of brown corduroy trousers.

"Hi, Dad," Anne called.

François Gautier came down to greet them, beaming. He gave his daughter a long hug, then extended his hand to Sam.

"So pleased to meet you at last," he said.

"How do you do, sir," Sam replied.

"Well, come in, make yourselves at home. Would you like anything to eat? How about a cocktail?"

"A cup of tea and something light to eat would be nice," Anne said. "What will you have, Sam?"

"Same for me," he said.

"Come on through to the kitchen. You can leave your bags in the hall," François said.

The kitchen at the end of the hallway was a wide room with a big wooden table in the middle. Anne put the kettle on and bustled around looking for sandwich materials.

"Looks like you've been shopping, Dad," she said, seeing a large turkey as she opened the fridge. "I wasn't sure what to expect, but it seems you have everything already."

"Yes, in middle age, I'm finally learning to take care of myself," he said, and turning to Sam added, "You see, I've always relied on my wives for domestic things, but I find I enjoy cooking, now that I understand more about it. It's all science, really."

"I'm proud of you," Anne said, "but I can help you with dinner tomorrow, if you'd like."

"Thank you. I'll welcome your help with the big meal, especially the pumpkin pie. All the science I've learned in my life won't teach me how to make the crust. Do you enjoy cooking, Sam?"

"Not really. I tend to eat on the fly or go out for good meals. My mother is a wonderful cook, and I appreciate good food."

"Where are you from?"

"I grew up in Charleston. My folks still live there."

Anne brought ham-and-cheese sandwiches and mugs of tea to the table where Sam and her father were sitting.

"Tea for you too, Dad?"

"Yes, thank you. How was your drive?" he asked.

"Dark, but straightforward. I'm not too familiar with Mississippi, and it's my first visit to this part of the state," Sam said.

"Well, we can't do much sightseeing tomorrow, it being Thanksgiving, but on Friday we can show you around. Oh, you are staying on for the weekend, aren't you?"

"If it's all right by you," Anne said.

"Glad to have you. I'm always glad to see you, my dear," he said, patting her hand.

At that moment Anne noticed a gray cat curled up in a basket in a corner. She crouched beside it and extended her hand. The cat raised its head and sniffed Anne's fingers. It had very green eyes.

"I didn't know you had a cat, Dad," she said.

"I've had her for about three weeks now. Her name's Luna. The color of her eyes reminds me of a Luna moth."

"Good name. Where did she come from?"

"She kind of adopted me. She had climbed up a tree, escaping from one of the vicious dogs next door. They're always causing problems in the neighborhood. I tried to coax her down, but she wouldn't come until later that evening, when I caught her meowing at the front door. I let her in, and she seems to have taken up residence."

"She looks like a nice cat," Anne said. Luna stepped delicately, one paw at a time, out of the basket and rubbed her head against Anne's hand, purring softly. "What breed of dogs are they?"

"Pit bulls. They're horrible. The woman who owns them, my neighbor, says she keeps them for protection. She lives alone, you see. But they're always getting loose and have chased people a couple of times, nipping at their heels. The police have warned her to keep them inside the fence."

Anne glanced at her father and concluded that he looked better than he had the last time she had seen him. She was glad he had a cat. That would comfort him. Perhaps he was also happier, now that Catherine was out of his life. She would talk to him later about that.

They finished their tea and sandwiches, and Anne took the plates and cups to the kitchen sink.

"It's late, and you all need your beauty sleep," François said.

"You, too," Anne said giving him a kiss. "Sleep well."

Anne opened the door to her old bedroom. It seemed strange having a man beside her in her childhood double bed, but she was happy Sam was there, and glad to be safe and at home. He reached to give her a kiss. Tomorrow was Thanksgiving Day. A day of thanks.

Chapter 16

December 1872

Estelle knew she had to follow the doctor's orders to stay in bed. She did not want to hurt the baby, and though it would mean taking a back seat to her sisters, Mathilde and Désirée, she decided to absent herself from family obligations for the next few weeks, until the baby was born. It was a difficult decision. Since their mother's death the previous year, she had taken over domestic matters for the household, now comprising seven adults and six children. Although the youngest of the three sisters, she was the one who had most willingly taken on responsibilities after their mother had died.

Mathilde came to her bedside the day after her fall.

"Estelle, I was so sorry to learn of your accident, but I hear all will be well if you take the doctor's advice to get some rest. What can I do to help?"

"Don't concern yourself, Tilda. You have more than enough to do with your three children. I'll be up in no time. Désirée has offered assistance, and she has more flexibility. Thank you for asking, dear one. Please talk to Edgar for me and make sure he has some way to fill his time productively."

After Mathilde left, Estelle again affirmed the necessity of taking care of the unborn baby and herself, though it was against her nature to ignore the others. But perhaps it was just as well: she suspected the more she knew about René and America, the more they would cause her anxiety. Why hadn't he come in to talk to her yet? He slept in an adjoining room, and it would be easy for him to stop by. Anyway, try as she might, she could not do a good job of running the house from her bed. She lay back helplessly and stared at the ceiling until she fell asleep.

Edgar talked to Mathilde at breakfast the next morning.

"What can I do for Estelle?" he asked. "I adore her, and I feel terrible. She's so kind to me, and I'd like to help."

"Estelle's very fond of you, Edgar, but expects nothing from any of us. She will gain strength, you'll see. In the meantime, if you would continue your paintings, that's what would please her the most."

"Certainly. I'll keep working. Please let her know that I look forward to being a godparent for the first time, too."

"She'll love hearing that. I'll be glad to tell her," Mathilde said.

Edgar rose, reached for his hat, and shut the front door firmly behind him as he left the house to go for his mail at the office.

Désirée came into the room and joined Mathilde at the breakfast table.

"It's my turn to sit with Estelle," she said. "How is she doing this morning?"

"She's resting but worries about Edgar. Has he asked you to pose for him yet?"

"Not yet."

"Estelle says he may be interested in marrying at last. He was courting you in France, wasn't he?"

"He was, but somehow I wasn't receptive to his advances then."

"And now?"

Desiree met her sister's eyes. "Estelle needs me. You saw the way René behaved with that woman at the recital."

"America. Yes. A disgraceful display."

"Estelle doesn't deserve that treatment. She has been a devoted wife and mother to his children. He should show her more love and respect."

"I agree, but what can we do?"

"I'll find a way to talk to him," Désirée replied. "America isn't half the woman that his wife is, and we should tell him that, if he can't figure it out for himself."

Her cheeks flushed pink, and she stood up, twisting her hands.

"Be careful," Mathilde said. "René can be cruel. You need to look out for yourself, dear. You have enough problems of your own."

"Don't worry about me. I blame René for Estelle's fall, and the very last thing our family needs is a scandal."

As the days progressed, the household fell into disarray without Estelle to manage things. Désirée did her best, but her heart wasn't in it. Missing Estelle's help in planning menus, Clarice served gumbo almost every night for dinner. Beulah spent most of her time ministering to her mistress as she lay in bed. The nurse watched the children, with Mathilde overseeing their care. René and Michel continued to go to work. Edgar took his daily walks to the cotton office until the end of the first week in December.

"May I call for the carriage?" Edgar asked one morning. "It's raining outside, such heavy rain as I've never seen before, and I fear I won't get through the streets to the office without soaking myself up to the knees."

"Of course you may," Désirée replied, "but Estelle suggested you might prefer to spend time at the Fontenot house. She says Philippe would welcome the opportunity to paint with you there."

"Good idea, thank you. He lives close by and I won't get very wet. I'll send a note to ask if it's convenient."

Edgar penned a quick message and asked a manservant to deliver it. Within the hour he received a response from Philippe, who would be most happy to have him. Edgar gathered his paints, pulled on some tall boots, and set out for the neighbor's house on foot.

For the next several weeks in December, the rain continued to fall. Without adequate drainage, water accumulated in the muddy streets and made walking all but impossible. The weather remained warm, and the steam, rising in dense clouds from the flooded roads, frayed everyone's nerves, straining patience to the breaking point and robbing the nights of any cooling relief.

"This is heat that we would welcome in Paris in June, but not now," Edgar said one evening to Désirée. They were sitting on the porch sipping cold drinks and fanning themselves. The chirping of late-season crickets kept them company.

"These mosquitoes are driving me crazy," he said, setting his glass aside and slapping his bare wrists.

"It's unusually hot, but the weather will change soon. It's often cold for Mardi Gras."

"For Mardi Gras? But that's two months from now. I'll never survive that long! I can stay until the baby is born and for the christening but I'll go home in January. What can I say? I love you all, but I'll leave you."

"Edgar, surely you tease. I . . . well, all of us, expected you to stay longer. Estelle will be so disappointed, and you haven't finished the family portraits."

"True, but it's difficult. The children won't sit still, and even pretty Mathilde, who wants to help, can only pose until the children beg her attention. Besides, I'm not painting anything worthwhile," he said, shifting away from her, his eyes downcast.

"Edgar, we're so happy you're here. You're part of the family; don't you value that?"

"Yes! Everyone has made me welcome, and I'm most grateful. But the light doesn't suit me, I worry about my eyes, and I miss Paris. I need to go home. Also, I see that I'm useless here. I'm of no help to the family—I've no interest in cotton—and from what I can tell, you're all doing just fine without me."

He stared at her with an earnest expression.

"But that's where you're wrong, *mon cousin*," she said, looking him in the eyes, frowning.

"*Comment?* How am I wrong? You live in luxurious surroundings, in this beautiful house. . . ."

"This house? Yes, it's beautiful, but it's not ours."

"Not yours? What do you mean?"

"Our father, your uncle Michel, took it when he sold the family's house on St. Charles Avenue."

"*Pardon*, perhaps I misunderstood. Are you saying that this house is rented, not owned?"

"Exactly."

Edgar took a deep breath. Then he ran his hand through his hair, letting it fall limp at his side.

"I had no idea. . . ." he said at last. "And the business?"

"Not doing well at all," Désirée said.

He sat for a long time saying nothing. Then he shook his head from side to side, stood up, and shuffled inside, shoulders hunched. Désirée watched him go. After a few minutes she went in to talk to Estelle.

"Are you awake, dearest?" she asked softly.

Estelle turned over in the bed and pulled herself upright. Désirée arranged the pillows behind her.

"I'm feeling better. Perhaps I'll go downstairs for a while tomorrow. How's Edgar?"

"That's what I wanted to talk to you about. He says he's leaving soon."

"So soon? But the baby's not born yet, and he wanted to be here for the christening."

"He does, and says he'll stay until then, but I believe he's tiring of our domestic routines. He complains about the children and thinks he's not useful here . . . I may have made a mistake. I told him we don't own this house and that the family business is in trouble."

Estelle gaped at her sister. "*Mon Dieu*, Désirée, why on earth would you tell him such private things? He does not need to know. René will be furious. You understand how proud he is, and about the effort he makes to keep up appearances."

Désirée pursed her lips. "Damn René," she said. "I disagree. It's more important that Edgar learns the truth. He's family, after all. Maybe now he'll try to help."

Estelle placed her hand on her forehead, settled back, and sighed. Désirée gave her a kiss.

"Now I've upset you. I'm sorry . . . only I wish Edgar would stay," she said in a whisper.

Estelle touched her arm. "I do, too, but only if he's happy here."

"I'll have Beulah bring you some tea," Désirée said as she left the room. Turning around she added, "I'll come back and read to you if you wish."

Estelle lay back down in the bed. Her heart ached for her sister, who perhaps still entertained hopes that Edgar would marry her. Estelle was aware that during the past few weeks Désirée had been an attentive companion at the bedside, ignoring her own needs. She burrowed her head in the pillow. What would René say if he found out that Désirée had told Edgar about the house and finances? And her father, too? She closed her eyes to soften her fears. What she didn't see couldn't hurt her.

René came home for lunch the next day. He sat down in his favorite stuffed chair in the front room and called to Clarice to bring him a drink. As he sipped it, Désirée came downstairs. She passed him on her way to the kitchen for a glass of water for Estelle without greeting him.

"How's the invalid?" René asked her.

"*Invalid?* Estelle's hardly an invalid. She's your pregnant wife, but perhaps you've forgotten."

René regarded her with surprise.

"What's the matter? What have I done to deserve a scolding?"

"You might go and see Estelle yourself, instead of asking me how she is. She lies in bed all day, and she could use some attention from you, her husband, I think."

"I'll go up when I've finished my drink. She needs some company, I agree. I've suggested that America Olivier might read to her, but Estelle hasn't asked for her yet. Perhaps I'll ask America myself."

Désirée's mouth dropped open. Glaring down at him she said in an icy tone, "I think America Olivier is the last person Estelle would wish to have around after her outrageous behavior at the recital."

He rose from his seat. Towering above her, he shouted, "What are you talking about? She was charming! Edgar thought her entertaining as well. She's a family friend, for heaven's sake, and a friend of Estelle's, too."

White-faced, Désirée stormed out of the room into the kitchen, slamming the door behind her.

The doorbell rang, and Clarice hurried to answer. Sophie stood outside, shaking an umbrella.

"I stopped by to visit Madame De Gas," she said. "Is she accepting visitors?"

"She's resting, but I'll ask. Please come in," Clarice replied.

Before Sophie could enter, another woman mounted the steps and pushed her way in.

"Terrible weather, isn't it? My feet are soaking. I came to read to Estelle." It was America. René set his drink down.

"How good of you to come. I was thinking of asking for you. How are you?" he said, ignoring Sophie and looking directly at America.

"I'm fine, couldn't be better, thank you," she said gaily.

Sophie mumbled to Clarice, "Perhaps I'm not needed. Two visitors at once are too many for Estelle. I'll come another day."

The maid nodded and ushered her out.

Addressing René, Clarice said, "If you'll excuse me, monsieur, I'll ask mademoiselle if madame wants a visitor."

"Of course, of course, talk to Désirée," he said impatiently. To America he said, "You're soaking wet. Let me help with your coat. Would you like something to drink?" He took her hand.

"Thank you, no. I came to see Estelle."

Clarice disappeared into the kitchen. Moments later, Désirée rushed into the room, her face contorted in anger.

"What do you mean, imposing yourself on our family without an invitation?" she said in a shrill voice. "Estelle is well cared for. Please leave."

America blushed and quickly removed her hand from René's grasp.

"Very well. Please send her my best wishes," she said as she moved toward the door.

"You should be ashamed of yourself, brother-in-law," Désirée said.

At that moment, Beulah clattered down the stairs. Upon seeing René she gasped, "Madame's time has come. Please send for the doctor at once."

René reached for his hat. "I'll take the carriage, and go myself," he growled.

Beulah and Désirée made for the kitchen. Carrying hot water and towels they rushed up to the bedroom. Estelle lay in the darkened room, her body twisting in pain.

Estelle was no stranger to childbirth, and this time would be no worse than the other three, she thought. The contractions were coming faster now. She was grateful to have Beulah and her sister to help. If things followed their usual course, she would be imprisoned in discomfort for the next several hours, even days. At least it was December and before Christmas, so the family's routine would not be upset. But the body-wrenching pain of labor was fierce, almost unbearable . . . the curse and privilege of being a woman, she told herself.

Chapter 17

November 1970

Thanksgiving Day dawned, warm and sunny. Anne woke before Sam, and seeing him peacefully asleep and not wanting to wake him, she slid out of bed, pulled on a bathrobe, and stole downstairs. Her father was sitting at the kitchen table nursing a cup of coffee.

"Good morning, Annie," he said. "Coffee?"

"Thanks," she said, fetching a cup.

"I love the aroma of a freshly brewed pot of this stuff in the morning," she said as she poured the coffee. "That's something I miss, living without a private kitchen."

"That will change once your house is ready. Speaking of that, how are things going?" François asked.

"Fine. The house is getting into shape."

"Annie, I worry about your safety. I worry that the vandals you told me about will return. Are you sure you should continue this project?"

"I'm not worried. We've installed a burglar alarm, and so far, there's been no more trouble. I'm determined to finish the work."

Her father nodded. "I understand how much the house means to you, and I respect your wishes," he said.

"They're working on the inside walls now," Anne said. "I've decided the paint colors. My neighbor Homer complained about the pest control. He was acquainted with my grandfather, it seems."

"Well, I guess he would be, since they were neighbors. Has he lived there long?"

"Apparently so. I believe he's the one who thought my grandfather had died in the house—told the police, I mean. He's a weird guy. He said my family always kills things."

"What? You mean, they were murderers?"

"Probably not. He mentioned a chicken that he claims my grandfather slaughtered. Sam said it sounds like voodoo."

François laughed. "I seriously doubt that, from what I knew about your mother's family, but perhaps he knows more than you give him credit for. He might know more than I do, for example. I never even met your grandfather. By the time your mother and I married, her relationship with her parents had broken down irreparably. Anyway, have you tried talking to that neighbor—Homer, is that his name—about your family?"

"No. As I said, he's weird. He has a parrot called Hurricane, and he thinks the house is haunted."

"Okay," her father said, smiling. "I wouldn't hold that against him."

"You're right. I should try to talk to him some more. The family history is still a mystery to me, though I'm learning a lot from Marguerite's journal. Oh, and Sam wants to look at the painting of my great-great-grandmother Sophie, the one you're keeping for me here. Where is it?"

"Still in the closet along with the chest that contained Degas's notebook and the old letters. Why does he want to see it? Does he think it will solve some of the family mysteries?"

"I'm not sure, but it was painted during Degas's time in the style of the Impressionists. It might be valuable, and he'll be able to appraise it, since that's his field."

François lowered his voice and said, "You've been seeing him for several months now. Do you think he's the one?"

"Maybe. Speaking of mysterious, there's a lot of mystery about him."

"That's a good thing, isn't it? Aren't mysterious people more likely to hold your interest?"

"That depends on what their secrets are. Anyway, I hope you can get to know him a little on this visit. Me too," she said with a smile.

She got up, refilled her cup, and sat back down next to her father.

"On the subject of becoming acquainted with people, I've met my half-sister, Stella, a few times."

"Estelle. Really? Are you still considering offering her a share in the house?"

"Not right away, not ownership, but I might allow her to move in. Seems she's being evicted."

"How so? For not paying rent? That doesn't speak well for her."

"Not for that reason. She's being forced out because of the city's urban renewal program."

"I see."

"Can you tell me more about Mama's family in New Orleans? You said you had no contact with them, but why was she so secretive, and why didn't she tell me earlier about Stella?"

François folded his arms across his chest and hesitated before answering. "It was always a sore spot between us. She married me without telling me she'd had a baby out of wedlock. When I found out, I felt betrayed, and that I'd made a bad decision in marrying her. The revelation almost broke us up, in fact. When you were on the way, we agreed to make a go of things." He paused. "I loved her, you see."

Anne touched his arm. "I understand that, Dad, and I'm so sorry we lost her. Thanks for telling me this, but let me ask again, why didn't she tell me earlier about the baby?"

"Mostly because we wanted to protect you. She finally decided before she died that you had a right to know the truth."

"All right, but she never mentioned that the father was a man of color."

"True. Attitudes are changing now, but it would not have helped your reputation then if people learned you had a sister of mixed race. You attended Newcomb, a school where such things mattered. You weren't a debutante, but you had friends who were, and you might have wanted to marry a Southern gentleman who cared about your family origins."

Anne scowled. "But that's ridiculous," she said. "I'm not a snob. I may have had a good education at a fine school, but the experience didn't make me ashamed that I have a sister of mixed race. That's so unfair! I can understand Stella's annoyance at being disinherited by our grandfather. He had no business disowning Mama. The whole situation is a disgrace."

Her face reddening, she stood up and paced around the room. Her father stared at her.

"Have some breakfast, Annie," he said.

She sighed and sat down.

He got up and put two pieces of bread in the toaster. "Want some eggs?" he asked.

"No, thanks. Toast is fine."

Anne stood up, spread butter and jam on the toast and carried the plate back to the table, along with another cup of coffee. She sat staring at the food before taking a bite.

"Feeling better?" he asked after a while. "You wanted the truth. That's always good."

"So I'm learning. It's not always easy," she said. "Speaking of Mama, I notice that her paintings are missing from the walls. She was a fine artist, and I liked her work. Besides, the paintings remind me of her. If you don't want them, I'd like to have a few for the new house."

"Catherine took them down. I like them, too, and I've been meaning to rehang them. You're welcome to choose some for yourself."

"Thanks. Well, how is Catherine?"

François shrugged. "I've no idea," he said. "She came back once to pick up her clothes, but hardly said a word."

"Do you miss her?"

"Not a bit. She was a mistake. You knew that."

Anne nodded. "Are you going to divorce her?"

"At some point. I'll wait for her to make the first move. I'm in no hurry to remarry. Actually, I find I rather like being on my own."

"You and me, both," Anne said, surprising herself. "Though I may want to marry at some point. My friend Isabelle is expecting a baby, and I sometimes envy her for transitioning from college to adult life so easily. I have things I want to do before I settle down."

"The important thing is to find the right person before you do," her father said. "Whatever you do, don't make a rash decision. To make a good decision about anything, you have to face the truth, and that takes time."

"You're right, of course," she said, meeting his eyes.

"You get my meaning. It's tempting to reach out to another person to fill a gap left by someone else dear to you."

She put her arms around his shoulders. "I know. Thank you, Dad," she said.

Sam appeared in the doorway wearing sweatpants and a loose T-shirt.

"Morning, all," he said.

"I hope you slept well. Help yourself to coffee," François said.

"We need to start preparing dinner. Do you want to help?" Anne asked, looking at Sam.

"Not really. I'd like to go for a run, if that's okay, get some exercise and work up an appetite for the big meal. I'll be glad to help clean up afterward."

"Fine. You can run through the campus a few blocks away," she said. "Turn left out of the driveway."

"Thanks. See you later," he said, turning to go out the front door.

The cat woke up from her nap in the corner and wandered, tail held high, to the kitchen door.

"You can let her out," François said. "She won't go far."

Anne opened the door to let the cat out and ran upstairs to take a shower and dress for the day. She wondered how Sam and her father would get along. She hadn't observed Sam's relationships with people other than those he worked with. How would she react if her father disapproved? Or worse, if he warned her about him, sensing something amiss, as Isabelle and Paul had done? She wished she didn't still feel so uncertain about him. So far, she had ignored the warnings and enjoyed the power of making her own decision about continuing to see Sam. Then she realized the tables weren't even: after this visit, he would have the advantage of knowing more about her, whereas she would probably learn nothing about his background. Perhaps he would invite her soon to Charleston to meet his family. It was still early, she reasoned: even though Isabelle and Paul had married within four months of their meeting, she would heed her father's warning and not make the mistake he had made in marrying the wrong person too fast, without knowing the truth.

When she came back downstairs, François was cutting up onions and celery for the stuffing. A recipe book lay open on the table.

"Dad, I didn't know you were learning to cook," she said.

"As I told you, it's all science. Anyway, it's a new way of looking at insects."

Anne recoiled. "Don't tell me you're using insects in your recipes."

"No, though it's a good idea. What I meant was that the practice of cooking is a good contrast to theoretical scientific studies. It has become a hobby of sorts. I find it relaxing, and I like eating good food."

"Glad to hear it. Do you want some help?"

"You can make the cranberry sauce and, as I said yesterday, the pie."

Anne and her father worked side by side preparing the meal. Soon the house filled with the fragrance of browning onions and sizzling butter.

"Could you open the front door?" François said. "If we open the back door as well, we'll have a cross-draft to keep the house cooler."

As she passed through the house to open the door she met Sam, dripping sweat, bounding up the steps.

"Stay away from me! I'm in desperate need of a shower," he said as he stepped into the foyer.

A loud wail sounded from the porch, and the cat bolted in, her leg bleeding badly. Close behind came a dog, foaming at the mouth, snarling, with bared teeth. It lurched forward poised to clamp down on the cat's narrow back, when two cracks rang out, so close together they merged almost as one, and the dog fell on its side, twitched for a few seconds, then was still.

Anne shrieked, and François came rushing out of the kitchen. They stood in stunned silence, the resonance of the shots ringing in their ears.

"It's dead," Sam said, holding a small gun in his hand. The acrid odor of gunpowder hung in the air.

"*My god*," Anne said, sitting down on the stairs, feeling sick. "You killed it."

"Quick work," said François. "You saved Luna's life. I can't thank you enough."

"I take it this is a pit bull from next door," Sam said.

"Yes," François replied. "No loss as far as I'm concerned, but Ms. Hiller will be upset. We can deal with that later. I need to get my cat to the vet."

Luna had slinked away to hide under a low chair in the living room. She was licking her hind leg and shivering. François took a towel, folded the cat into it, and picked her up. She purred softly.

"I'll drive you," Anne said. "Sam, could you please turn off the stove?" We'll be back as soon as we can."

"Let's take my car," François said. He handed Anne the keys, which she immediately dropped on the floor making a jarring, jangling sound. She stooped to retrieve them.

"Are you sure you're up to driving?" Sam asked.

"I think so."

She wasn't sure, but she needed to get away from Sam. Her father sat in the passenger seat holding the cat and, white-faced and still shaking, she backed the car out of the driveway and headed toward the animal hospital.

"Nice work, on Sam's part," her father said after a few minutes. "But how on earth did he learn to shoot like that, so fast, and with such precision?"

"He learned on the shooting team at Yale and trained there for the biathlon," Anne said.

"That may explain it, but why was he carrying a gun while running around the neighborhood here?" François asked.

"I have no idea, but I guess we're lucky he was," she said soberly.

François cradled the cat and gave her an occasional reassuring pat on the head.

"You had a close call, little one," he said. "That's the end of exploring outside for you for a while."

The minutes clicked by slowly at the animal hospital while they awaited their turn, but after they entered the examination room, the vet soon cleaned and stitched the cat's hurt leg.

"Here's an antibiotic salve to apply to the wound. She'll have to wear a cone for a week or two so she doesn't lick it and loosen the stitches, and she won't like that, but you can see it's necessary."

"I can. Thank you," François said, and paid the bill.

In the car he said, "Thank you for driving, my dear. It's already past noon. I think we'd best forget about Thanksgiving dinner for today. How about pasta? I can make a tomato-based sauce and a salad. We can have the turkey tomorrow."

"Pasta is fine with me," Anne said. "I've lost my appetite for a big meal today, and I'd like to go for a run when we get home. Guess you'll be dealing with the police and so on. We'll need to clean up the mess inside, too."

François nodded. They parked the car in the driveway and entered the house. There was no sign of the dog or any blood, and Sam, dressed in clean khaki pants and a short-sleeved shirt, sat in the living room, reading.

"What did you do with the dog? Did you call the police?" Anne asked.

"Don't worry about it. It's all taken care of," he replied.

"What did the police say? Does Ms. Hiller know about her dog?" François asked.

"I didn't call the police. There's no need to say anything. Much better to say nothing."

Anne and her father exchanged glances.

"I'm not sure about that . . . we ought to inform the authorities," François said.

"Believe me, we should leave them out of it. I've been in situations like this before. It'll be okay."

"You *are* a cool customer," Anne said. She looked at Sam and noticed that his eyes were steel gray.

"Actually, I can appreciate the sense in what you're saying," François said to him. "The house is large, surrounded by the garden on all sides, and even though the gunfire sounded loud to us here, our neighbors won't have heard it. If someone passing by on the street had overheard the noise, we'd have had a visit from the police by now."

"Exactly," Sam said.

"Anyway, I'd as soon not face Ms. Hiller."

He carried the cat to her bed in the corner, and she settled down, after shaking her head in an unsuccessful attempt to dislodge the plastic cone.

"I need to go for a run to clear my mind," Anne muttered. "Back in an hour."

François took a seat near Sam in the living room.

"Would you like a drink or something? We've decided against making the turkey today, but you're welcome to eat something to tide you over until dinner—a simpler dinner," François said.

"A beer would be great, if you have one."

"I'll join you," François said, as he left for the kitchen to fetch the drinks. He handed one to Sam.

"I suppose the appropriate toast is Happy Thanksgiving," Sam said.

"Yes. Cheers!"

They both took swigs of the cold amber liquid and sat still for a few minutes.

"I understand your field is entomology," Sam said.

"It is. I've always liked bugs of one kind or another. Do you know anything about insects?"

"Not much. I've seen beautiful butterflies in the rain forest and wish I'd studied more about those."

"Yes, they're spectacular, but they're not misunderstood. Most people like them. I find the outliers more interesting."

"Such as?"

"Rare cannibalistic ants. Gypsy moths. Dung beetles."

"Dung beetles?"

"Sometimes known as scarabs. Fascinating."

"Yeah, I guess there's more to learn about those and their nasty habits," Sam said, smiling.

"Speaking of habits, you seem to have developed some skill using a gun. That was quite a performance there this morning. How did you learn to shoot so well?"

"Anne may have told you I attended Yale. They had a shooting team, and I trained for the biathlon. I've had a lot of practice."

"Sure, but what you did had the mark of a true marksman, excuse the pun."

"Let's just say I've had advanced training since college."

"You mean, professionally?"

"Look, sir, I really can't talk about this. Can we leave it at that?"

"I see. I suppose that explains your decision to keep quiet about the dog."

Sam made no reply and took another swig of his beer. François stood up.

"Anne mentioned you wanted to look at a painting she owns. Perhaps you'd like to do that when she gets back. I'll have a bite to eat. Are you hungry?"

"No, thanks. I'll enjoy the beer, and perhaps another, if I may."

That evening François made pasta for dinner, as promised. They devoured it, drinking plenty of red wine to wash it down. They talked about insects; François did most of the talking.

"Tell me to stop when you've had enough," he said. "I can talk forever about this subject, and frequently do. It's a bad habit among people in my profession."

Sam and Anne, sitting upright, their heads propped on their hands, had both fallen asleep.

"Oh, I'm so sorry. My apologies," he said loudly.

Sam woke up, startled. "I'll turn in now. Thanks for dinner. See you tomorrow," he said, looking at François.

Anne woke up, also. "I'll do the dishes, Dad," she said.

"Thanks. Let's do them together. I want to talk to you."

They carried the plates to the kitchen and Anne put on a pair of rubber gloves. She filled the sink with soapy water and got to work. Her father dried each washed item with a dishtowel.

"Anne, I don't want to overstep boundaries here, but I have a few thoughts about Sam."

"I've many thoughts myself, especially after today. Go on," Anne said.

"All right. He has charm and he's polite. However, I'm fairly sure he has an agenda we don't know much about. He's well trained with weapons and didn't want to talk about it when I asked him. He may work for the FBI, using the museum job as a cover. Those people don't usually talk about their special skills. I only mention this because of the possibility that he won't ever make a long-term commitment to you."

Anne stopped scrubbing a pot. "Are you saying he'd never marry me, not that I necessarily want him to," she said.

"I don't know, but marriage rarely mixes well with that kind of work."

"All right, I hear you. Thanks," she said.

"Another thing. As you're aware, I try not to interfere in your life, but I have to say that the course you've chosen will make it more difficult for you. If you choose not to marry, it's essential that you find work that's meaningful."

"I know that, Dad."

They finished the dishes, and he gave her a hug before going upstairs to bed. Anne sat for a long time on the couch after he left, going through the events of the day in her mind until she fell asleep.

The next day Anne got up early. She hadn't slept well on the couch. She took a shower, leaving the bathroom damp and smelling of soap and the light cologne that she usually splashed on her neck, and threw on a T-shirt and a pair of jeans. When Sam came down an hour later, she was standing in the kitchen holding a cup of coffee and staring out of the window. A mockingbird trilled from the big magnolia tree outside, and late-season blooms shone white in the early morning sun. They evoked in her a sense of nostalgia, a longing for lost childhood.

"Hi, sweetheart," he said, drifting over and giving her a kiss on the back of her neck. "You smell like flowers. Want to come back to bed?"

"No. I didn't go to bed. I fell asleep on the couch. Guess you didn't notice. I'm up now and need to get on with the day. Today we're having Thanksgiving dinner, remember?"

"I do, and I look forward to it."

She moved away from him.

"Aren't you going for another run?" she asked. "Don't forget to take your gun."

"Not this morning. Hey, what's wrong?"

"I don't know, Sam. I don't understand you. Dad talked to me last night after you went to bed. He suspects you work for the FBI. Is that true?"

Sam put his arms round her waist. "Well, if it is, do you really expect me to tell you?"

"I guess not, but it makes me wonder if I should trust you," she said, twisting herself out of his grip.

"Why not? If anything, you should feel safe, since I can protect you."

"I'm not in need of protection. I don't involve myself in risky endeavors."

"No, but you can never tell who might turn out to be an evil person, out to harm you or anyone else, for no particular reason," he said.

"Guess I'll worry about that when I have to. I've realized that there's a lot I don't know about you, and that bothers me."

"Well, give us time. As you saw yesterday, it's useful to have someone around who knows how to shoot well."

"True. Dad is very grateful."

"To change the subject, how about showing me that painting?" he said.

"All right. I'll find it after breakfast. You do want breakfast, don't you?"

"Sure. I'll run up and take a shower and be right back."

He left the room, and Anne poured herself another cup of coffee. The strengthening sun streamed through the window spreading warmth through her body, and she again experienced the pleasure of being home, and of being secure. It was true that she had always felt safe around Sam, and despite her misgivings about his secrecy, she liked his calm confidence. It was all rather confusing and she remained alarmed about his apparent ease with a gun. Still, she didn't want the incident about the dog and the questions that had arisen to spoil the weekend. She would continue to enjoy the time with her father and put off the decision about whether she wanted to keep seeing Sam until later. As he'd reminded her, she had time. *What was it her father had said? To make a good decision, you have to face the truth. Yes, those were his words.*

Chapter 18

December 1872

The baby, named Jeanne, was born on December twentieth. Christmas was all but forgotten in the household amid all the excitement. René arranged for the christening to take place in early January, and Edgar announced his intention of leaving soon afterward. Estelle, relieved to be no longer pregnant, spent a few days in bed following the birth and soon involved herself in domestic routines again.

Friends stopped by to welcome the baby and congratulate the parents. Sophie Fontenot arrived, one of the first visitors.

"Estelle, it's so nice to meet Jeanne," she said one cold day. "She's a lovely baby. Too bad it's raining all the time. I'd love to take her out for a stroll. It has been a long time since I had my babies, and I'd like to help with this one."

Estelle patted her friend on the arm.

"I've been meaning to thank you for hosting Edgar so often recently," she said. "He was becoming tired of the intense domesticity of family life here, I think."

"We've been glad to have him. He and Philippe have spent many hours painting together. Edgar says the light in Philippe's studio is better for his eyes. He has done some sketches of Marguerite."

"Has he? Well, she's a very pretty girl, so I'm sure he enjoys that. He says he's leaving after the christening. I had hoped he would stay longer, but he has already booked his passage on the ship."

"Oh. Let's have a farewell party for him," Sophie said.

"That's a good idea. He might attend one or two Mardi Gras balls before he leaves, too. Those should amuse him."

"You're right. *Laissez les bons temps rouler;* let the good times roll. What does Jo think of her new sister? She's back from school for the holidays, isn't she?" Sophie asked.

"Yes. She's always been a helpful older sister, and she loves the baby. I'm treating her to a pedicure as a late Christmas present this week."

"What a luxury," Sophie said.

Estelle nodded. "It is a luxury, but she's a good girl and deserves a little pampering. That school she attends is not sympathetic to us Creoles."

"It's true. The Americans are different, stricter, and not fun-loving, like we are. No sense of style, either."

"That's what René says, too. But they're very good businessmen and take risks, which we tend not to do. He complains that they're fierce competitors."

"I wouldn't know about that, but they've definitely made their presence known in the city. Their mansions on St. Charles Avenue are overly grand," Sophie said, making a face.

"They are," Estelle agreed. "Are you acquainted with any American families?"

"Can't say I am, now that you mention it. We don't invite them to our Mardi Gras celebrations, and they don't attend the Catholic churches. Speaking of Mardi Gras, the first ball of the season is next week. Are you going?"

"I expect so. I'll talk to René. Is Philippe wearing a costume?"

"Yes. Well, a mask anyway. Marguerite is excited. It will be her first."

"I can imagine. I remember my first one well; don't you?"

"Yes. I wore a white dress, all floaty," Sophie said, smiling. "I felt so grown-up. The men were hard to recognize because they wore masks, and I danced with several people without ever knowing who they were."

Estelle laughed. "Me, too. Silly, isn't it? But fun."

"Yes. Well, I must go now. I'm glad to find you looking so well, my friend."

Sophie went out of the house, and Estelle sat for a minute, looking after her. Sophie was a good friend, a sensible woman with a fine family. Estelle wasn't familiar with her husband, Philippe, but Edgar had told her he was an accomplished painter, and they had developed a friendship. That he had found a companion pleased her, although she wished that he considered his brothers' company more satisfying. She also wished he had spent more time with Désirée. While grateful, she couldn't stop her remorse. Her sister had helped care for her, perhaps giving up all hope for a relationship with Edgar, as a result. She sighed. She knew she couldn't arrange the lives of all the people she loved.

René came in, back from work. He stooped and gave her a quick kiss.

"How was your day?" he asked. "I saw Sophie Fontenot on the way out."

"Yes, she came to see the baby, and we talked about the ball next week. She's going with Philippe and Marguerite. Is your costume ready yet?"

"Yes, and it's spectacular. I got many in Paris, and mine is of a cockroach. The mask is magnificent. It has antennae and jaws. Very realistic."

"Sounds creepy to me. Have you talked to Edgar about his costume?"

"He doesn't want to wear one, but I've convinced him to wear a mask, at least. He says he doesn't dance."

"Doesn't dance? Good heavens, where has he been all his life?"

"In Paris, I believe," René said, grinning.

"We must show him how to have a good time here. He loves the theater and tells me he has painted dancers often. How could he not enjoy our masked balls?"

"He will. Don't worry. Just wondering . . . has America come by to offer her congratulations?"

Estelle's pulse quickened and she drew a sharp breath.

"No. Why should she?"

"Well, she's a neighbor and a friend. She told me she would stop by."

"She did? When did she tell you that?" Estelle asked, frowning.

"Uh, not sure, but as you're aware, she's always pleased to have a new child in the neighborhood, someone else for her children to play with."

Estelle said nothing. Some of her and Mathilde's children were the same age as America's, and they played well together. But when had America told René she would come to offer congratulations? Had they seen each other in private? Her heart heavy, Estelle decided not to think about that. Not yet, anyway.

Chapter 19

November 1970

*A*nne took the painting out of the closet for Sam to examine. She unwrapped the brown paper and set the painting on the floor. The oil portrait depicted a young woman in a black gown resting her chin on one hand and holding a fan in the other. The faraway expression in her eyes suggested regret, as though she had returned from a ball and hadn't enjoyed it.

Sam studied it closely.

"Amazing resemblance! This attractive relative of yours looks exactly like you—no question now about where you inherited your looks," he said, looking back and forth between Anne and the picture. "She has your hair, your brown eyes. It's a fine painting, Impressionist. You said your great-great-grandfather Philippe painted it, and it's his wife, right? What was her name again?"

"Sophie. I gathered this because Marguerite mentioned the painting in her journal. It's not signed, but the name Sophie is written on the back."

She turned it round and showed him the scrawled name and date, 1872.

"Interesting that this painting is about the same size as the one the museum has of Estelle. If Philippe and Degas were friends, they may have shared canvases. The colors are muted too, like some of Degas's from that period. Perhaps they also borrowed paints, from each other, or painted together."

"They did paint together, and Philippe's painting makes Degas's connection with my family in New Orleans seem more real, doesn't it?"

"It does." He kneeled down to examine it again.

"I have an idea." he said excitedly. "Would you be willing to show the painting to the public? The Philadelphia Museum of Art is planning an exhibit of American Impressionist painters in the next few months, and this one would make a nice addition. It would help me professionally as well if I offered it to them, because I plan to ask the curators there to loan some of their paintings for the Impressionist exhibition we're planning to have at our museum."

"Sure. I'd be happy to loan it. You'll have to appraise it though, and it will need framing and insuring, won't it?"

"Right. I'll take care of those details and give you a receipt. This is a great find, a wonderful piece."

Anne wrapped it up again.

"I guess we can take it along when we go back to New Orleans tomorrow," she said.

"Let's do that. Well, this definitely makes the visit worthwhile."

Taken aback, Anne looked sharply at him.

"Uh, well, of course, the visit was fine in other ways, too," he said.

Staring past him so he couldn't read the hurt in her face, she said, "We'll have our Thanksgiving dinner today. Perhaps you can peel the potatoes."

She was happy to lend the painting for display, but Sam's obvious interest in it further diminished her pleasure in his visit.

François had placed the turkey to cook in the oven after breakfast, and the savory aroma of the stuffing filled the house.

He and Anne spent the next several hours preparing the meal while Sam watched football on television. They sat down at the table at two o'clock, raised glasses of red wine for toasts, and ate heartily.

"Great dinner. Thanks," Sam said as they finished the pumpkin pie. He helped with the dishes, and they put the kitchen back in order.

"How about taking a ride around town, Anne," Sam suggested. "You can tell me about your childhood memories here."

"Sure," she said without enthusiasm.

While they drove around the town of Oxford and she pointed out important places in the fading light, she sensed a rumbling deep inside that something wasn't right. They had a drink at a bar near the campus and returned home. Despite her failing spirits and exhaustion, she spent another restless night on the couch.

Next day Anne and Sam prepared to leave early. François was in the kitchen making coffee when they came downstairs lugging their bags. He pointed to two canvases propped against the wall.

"I wondered if you wanted to take these with you," he said.

She bent to look at them.

"My cemetery paintings, the ones I did during my senior year. I had almost forgotten them."

Sam squatted beside her and examined the pictures. "These are superb, Anne," he said. "Great atmosphere. Spooky, almost."

"Yeah, that's how the cemetery appeared. I stumbled on my Fontenot family gravesite—you know, one of those mausoleums they have in the St. Louis cemetery—and I did several paintings. In those days I believed in ghosts. While I was completing the paintings those spectral figures somehow appeared on the canvas next to the gravestones. Family members, I thought. Now I'm not so sure. I've seen no evidence of spirits at my house so far." She stood up. "I'm not sure that I'd be able to paint anything as successful now."

"Why ever not?"

"No inspiration. I need to find a subject that interests me first. I plan to, though." She glanced at her father. "No, I don't want to take them. Please keep them for me."

Luna came out of her basket in the corner and padded across the floor toward Anne.

"Poor cat. She seems to be doing better," Anne said, stroking her back.

"She'll be fine," François said. "I'll give her fish for a treat tonight. She doesn't like the cone and being confined to the house."

"Will you ever let her outside again?" Anne asked.

"Yes, I think so. She's learned a hard lesson, and will probably keep well clear of the house next door now."

"Dad, it's been a good visit. Perhaps you can come to New Orleans next time."

"Yes." He gave her a long hug, then held out his hand.

"Sam, I'm glad we met. Thanks again for saving Luna."

They shook hands.

"You're welcome. Thanks for your hospitality, sir."

Carrying the painting, François accompanied them to the car. They locked their things in the trunk and slid into their seats. Anne wound down the window.

"Bye, Dad, see you soon. Take good care of yourself," she said, waving.

The drive home was uneventful. Sam dropped Anne off at her place and drove on. They had agreed that he would take the painting of Sophie to his office and keep it there until he could appraise and prepare it for shipment to the museum in Philadelphia.

She inspected herself in the mirror. Two nights of sleeping on the couch had improved neither her appearance nor her state of mind. The visit had made her keenly aware of the contrast between her current accommodations and her father's comfortable house. But it had been good to be home again, despite the sad memories of her mother. Now back in New Orleans she'd work hard on the Esplanade house and find time to attend to the multitude of tasks that remained. Should she ask Sam for help? *Of course not* . . . that was the bad news. She wasn't sure she could trust him anymore.

It was still early, five o'clock, and a soft evening. Thinking she should check on progress at the house, Anne strolled the few blocks to the property. Her neighbor Homer was lounging on his porch.

"Hey there, missy," he called. "How's yer Thanksgivin'?"

"Pretty good, thank you. How about you?"

"All right, I guess. Had my sister over. She knew yer grandmother; they were friends, you know, but pr'haps you knew."

"No, I didn't know. What does she say about my grandmother?"

"Name was Charlotte. Nice lady. She used to help my sister with her children. She had eight, my sister. Eight! Don't know how she managed. Anyway, she loved them kids, all kinds, Charlotte did. She weren't like that husband o' hers, yer granddad. He could'a taken a walk in the river and drownded, any time. Parrot didn't like him neither. Always told him, 'Bad Boy.' Yes, siree."

The old man cackled, showing his yellow teeth. Anne recoiled, but remembered her father's advice that he could probably tell her more about her family history. She swallowed hard and attempted to keep the conversation going.

"Did you meet my grandmother Charlotte, yourself?" she asked.

"Like I said, nice lady. Gave me Hurricane, my parrot. Knew I'd lost my chicken and gave 'er to me in exchange. I got the better deal, I reckon. I'd take a parrot over a chicken any time. Lives longer, anyway."

"Can you remember the names of my grandmother Charlotte's parents?" she asked.

"Maurice, I think was his name. Forget the name of the wife."

"Do you know anything about him?"

"Not really. Might'a been a doctor or a vet. Oh . . . forgot to tell you. Saw ghosts at yer place last week. Blue lights. Heard some noises, too."

"Blue lights, and noises? What kind of noises?"

"Weepin' and wailin'."

"Did you go to see if anyone was there? Why didn't you call me?"

"Didn't have yer number. Don't like empty houses. Parrot kept squawkin'. Had to put a towel over 'er to get 'er to stop."

Anne cringed. Her mistake—she hadn't given Homer her number.

"Here's my phone number," she said, scribbling it on a piece of paper she had in her purse. "I'm glad you have your parrot, Mr. Jackson. Must be good company."

She didn't take Homer's sightings seriously, and as she had recently told Sam, she wasn't superstitious anymore. At least now she'd learned that her grandmother liked children and that her great-grandfather's name was Maurice. How was he related to Marguerite? She might learn more from his sister, but Homer himself was crazy. Delusional.

She saw that work had progressed and there had been no more attempts at unlawful entry to the house. The remains of the broken bathroom fixtures had been removed. Piles of sawdust covered the floor, and walls had been replaced and re-plastered. All seemed fine, and soon she would order the paint. Checking the house reminded her that Stella hadn't yet called to arrange a time to get together again. Anne would give her a ring.

But her father's words came back to haunt her: Homer might know more than she imagined.

Chapter 20

December 1872

The weather had turned cooler at last. Estelle grew stronger each day and watched her new baby with pleasure as she gurgled in her crib. She was glad to have a healthy child. The household, which had lost its rhythm during her confinement, returned to normal. She wondered how Edgar was faring and regretted again that she had spent so little time with him in recent weeks. He would leave after the christening, but there was still time for him to paint more family portraits.

He sat enjoying croissants for breakfast when she entered the dining room one bright winter day.

"*Bonjour, mon cher* Edgar," she said, touching him lightly on the shoulder.

"Good morning!" he said, loudly. "Listen, I speak English!"

"If you stay here longer, you'll soon be talking like a native. But really, it would be better if you spent your time painting. You still haven't painted Mathilde."

"You're right. She's a good subject, but antsy. Can't sit still. Perhaps she could sit for me this afternoon while her children are napping."

"I'll ask her," Estelle said, brightening. "I can't help wondering why you haven't painted any of the men, your brothers or your uncle. Aren't they good subjects?"

"Actually, I enjoy painting women. And then there's the problem of getting the men to take time off so I can sketch them. They work long hours at that office. Anyway, they're not pretty."

"But you don't care about that. You paint people as they are, often with their backs toward you. Even little Carrie had her back turned in the painting you did of her."

"True. You know, I consider these family portraits exercises, not great works of art. Someday I'd like to paint something of real significance, a work good enough to be worthy of preservation."

"You mean, preservation for the future, rather than preservation of the past," Estelle said.

"Exactly. But to do this, I need to find the right subject. I may have to return to France to do that."

Estelle regarded him sadly. "I'm sorry we're only family, and so ordinary."

"I beg your pardon, I spoke thoughtlessly. I didn't mean to offend you, dear. It's my shortcoming, not to observe well enough, to fail to see what's possible here. Other artists, friends of mine, would do much better in this exotic place. You see, only if I face the truth about something important will I be able to create a great painting. But I'm glad I've painted some family portraits—you, Carrie, Jo—to remember you by, and I'll paint Mathilde today, I hope."

"Thank you, Edgar. Where do you want her to sit?"

"On the balcony, I think."

"All right. I'll talk to her right away."

Later that day Mathilde took her place sitting on a chair on the second-floor balcony. She wore a light purple dress, orange ribbons laced around the bodice, and a black ribbon circling her neck.

"How do you want me to pose?" she asked.

"Just be yourself. I never want my models to assume unnatural expressions or attitudes," he said, as he adjusted his easel.

"Am I a model, then?"

"No, you are my cousin, and family. I wish to paint you as such. Please look at me as I work, and keep your hands as they are now, holding the fan and resting in your lap."

Mathilde raised her eyes and sat still as he had asked.

"Charming," Edgar said.

"If I may ask," she said a few minutes later, "how am I different from a model? Surely you could describe anyone who poses for you that way."

He smiled and paused before answering. "Tilda, I've no desire to offend your sensibilities, but sometimes my models are dressed less formally,"

She raised her eyebrows and said with a shy smile, "Oh, I see."

"Keep that expression; it's most appealing," he said.

He worked fast, sketching the outline and blocking the background, the balcony and the hint of the building beyond.

"Are you working on the drawing first? Will you start the painting soon?"

"I am outlining the shapes, but I won't paint. I'll use pastels, a good medium for a delicate woman like yourself. The pastels will highlight the softness of your beautiful dress."

He worked for an hour and she sat quietly, enjoying the moments of peace. Her three small children demanded much of her, and she had little time to relax. Suddenly Beulah's face appeared on the other side of the French doors. Mathilde jerked forwards.

"Beulah, is something the matter? Come in," she said, beckoning to the maid.

"*Mon Dieu*, you have moved!" Edgar shouted. "I told you to sit still! How can I finish my drawing when you are flapping around like a chicken?"

"*Excusez-moi, mais les enfants* . . . perhaps the children need my attention," Mathilde said, standing up and opening the glass doors.

"*Impossible!*" Edgar said. He gathered up his materials, took them to his room, and slammed the door.

❦

"How did it go with Mathilde?" Estelle asked him later, over the evening meal.

"She's a good subject, but as I said, she can't sit still. However, I have sketches and enough information to make a reasonable picture. All the same, it's only another family portrait: nice, but hardly a great work of art."

"Edgar, I hope you find something to inspire you soon. Can't you find even one subject to paint here that you think might be, as you say, worthy of preservation, something important enough?"

"No . . . but that's not to say I haven't met intriguing people."

Estelle wanted to ask more, to understand more of his thinking, but thought it imprudent. *Intriguing people?* Perhaps he had found what he was looking for but wouldn't tell her. He was secretive about his work until he considered it finished. She would wait, and hope.

Chapter 21

December 1970

Anne felt unsettled. She couldn't get the image of Sam firing the gun out of her head, and her father's suggestion that he might have a double life disturbed her. She was confused, and more than a little overwhelmed when she thought about the decisions she would need to make soon about Sam, her career, and her sister's request to move in. Her father's advice rang in her ears: to make a good decision about anything, she needed to face the truth.

As she left for work on Tuesday, she came across Officer Hammond outside.

"Good morning, Miss Gautier. I wanted to stop by and talk to you for a minute. Got a report last week about that house of yours down the street. Seems there was a racket in there. We went by to check but didn't hear or see anything. Gave you a call, but you didn't answer."

"I was away for Thanksgiving," she said. "What kind of racket?"

"The person calling said it sounded as though there was a fight. Screaming and hollering. Place looked empty."

"There's a burglar alarm now, so if there were intruders the person would have heard that."

"That wasn't in the report."

"Well, who was the caller?"

"Name of Smith, Darrell. Passerby."

"Don't know anyone with that name. Thanks for telling me. I visited the house on Sunday, and everything seemed fine."

"Okay. You might want to check again. Just wanted to give you the information."

Is the world going mad? she asked herself. First Sam kills a dog, now it appears the house is haunted, as Homer had warned her. *But who were the ghosts?* Her mother? Marguerite? The spirit of Homer's slaughtered chicken?

She ran to the building and disengaged the alarm.

Inspecting every corner, she crept through the house. The light beamed in, casting blue shadows from the trees. Only her footsteps echoed in the open space. She saw nothing amiss, no evidence of visitors of any kind, and no ghosts. Scratching her head, she drove to work. She refused to be frightened, but the recent events still disturbed her and rambled around in her mind.

She and Stella met for dinner later that week. Dressed in a demure brown dress and flat shoes, she entered Brennan's restaurant on Royal Street. It was one of her favorite places to eat, and she had invited Stella as her guest. Stella arrived before her and sat swilling a drink by a fountain in the courtyard.

"Thanks for coming," Anne said. "I'll join you in a cocktail."

She ordered her usual gin and tonic. Although she needed to ask Stella many questions, she wanted to become fond of her and, above all, to do the right thing and correct any injustice regarding the inheritance. She would ease her way into the more difficult topics of discussion. She smiled across the table at Stella.

"What are you doing for Christmas?" she asked.

"I have a few days off. I'll celebrate with my adoptive parents here in town."

"Where do they live?" Anne asked.

"In the Marigny area, in an apartment. They're getting older and want me to cook, which I'm glad to do."

"Will they decorate for the holiday?"

"A little. They're Catholics, and we always go to the cathedral for Mass on Christmas Eve."

The waiter announced that their table was ready, and they followed him inside. Anne admired Stella's outfit, a tailored black dress with delicate flared sleeves, and heels. Her dark hair, smooth and pinned, looked elegant, and her face glowed with health. She was an attractive young woman, five years older, and not for the first time, Anne felt flat and ordinary beside her. She wished she had worn her green dress.

The light was already fading, and candles on the tables glowed orange in the stately dining room. It resembled a room in a fine home rather than a restaurant. They took their seats and scanned the menu.

"How do the entrees compare with yours at Commander's Palace?" Anne asked.

"Very different, but this is a decent selection," Stella said. "I'll have lobster."

"Same for me."

They placed their orders and chose white wine.

"I've been learning more about our relatives by reading Marguerite's journal. You will enjoy it, too, I think."

"I know a little about Marguerite already. Her brother Maurice was our great-grandfather. His children were Etienne and Estelle. I understand that he named his daughter in honor of Estelle Musson, who was a family friend and the wife of René De Gas. I already told you that my name came from Estelle Fontenot, the one relative on our side who was good to me."

Anne stared at Stella. The slight was not lost on her: *the one relative who was good to her.* It was a direct challenge. Sweating under her long-sleeved dress, she told herself to cool down. She intended to do the right thing by her sister. She must not overreact. She cleared her throat.

"So, Marguerite wasn't our great-grandmother," Anne said. "Disappointing. I like her, from what I've read so far. Marguerite wrote about Estelle De Gas in her journal, but I wish we had writings from some other family members. I turned up another discovery recently. This building was Edgar Degas's mother's home before she moved to Paris."

"You mean, this restaurant?"

Anne nodded and smiled. "Isn't that something? You can easily imagine these rooms as living spaces for the family. Our relatives may even have visited here."

Stella scanned the room and Anne watched her face. Stella's eyes narrowed.

"Did it occur to you that the apartments in back, the ones in the courtyard, were the slave quarters? That's where I would have lived," she said in a low voice. Then she leaned forward and added, "*I would never have visited this house alongside the rest of the family in those days.*"

Anne flushed, and she almost knocked her wine glass off the table. Stella stabbed the lobster on her plate with a fork and it spun around, staining the tablecloth with a shower of butter.

Anne blinked and gripped the arms of her chair.

"I didn't mean to be so insensitive. I never thought . . ."

"It's okay," Stella said, looking down at the broken shellfish.

They ate in silence and Anne ordered a second glass of wine. The waiter brought the dessert menu and asked if they would like the special of the day, baked Alaska.

Anne said, "Not for me, but go ahead, Stella, if you'd like something."

Stella's expression brightened.

"You know, I've always wanted to try cherries jubilee. It's famous, and it's the first time I've come here. We don't serve that at my restaurant."

"All right. I'll share it with you. I like flamed desserts."

"My friend Mary has them all the time. In fact, I think she comes here only for them, sometimes. She loves drama of any kind."

The waiter wheeled a tray next to their table. A chafing dish held a silver pot containing cherries in a thick red sauce. The glow of the flame underneath lit up the space in the darkened room. The man stirred the cherries until they bubbled.

"I can't wait to tell Mary about this," Stella said. "She'll be surprised, because she said the only person she knew that came here was Sam, who brought her often."

Anne's heart jumped. Was this *her* Sam? And *her* boss?

"You don't mean Mary Wharton, do you?" she asked, her voice rising.

"Yes, do you know her? Oh, that's right . . . she works at the museum."

"Damn you for bringing this up, and for spoiling the evening," Anne said tersely, bursting into tears. "She's my boss, and Sam's my boyfriend!"

At that moment, the waiter splashed brandy into the boiling cherries and, with a quick motion, lit the mixture. It burst into flames. Stella, shocked by Anne's outburst, stood up. The cuff of her flared sleeve touched the flaming dessert and caught fire. Someone nearby screamed. Anne held her hands to her mouth and stood up as well, pushing her chair back. It fell, crashing to the floor. The waiter emptied a pitcher of water over Stella's burning sleeve, dousing the flames. The smell of scorched silk and skin infused the air.

Stella, her sleeve smoking and dripping, sat down, trembling. The waiter moved the tray aside and picked up Anne's fallen chair. An older woman sitting at a nearby table came and put her arm round Stella's shoulders.

"I'm a nurse. Stay calm and let me take a look at your hand." The nurse examined Stella's hand and wrist. "The skin's a little singed, but you're not badly hurt," she said. "You might want to put some salve on the burn. Sit quietly for a while. You've had a shock. Have a glass of water."

White-faced, Anne sat down, too stunned to speak. Her outburst had caused this dreadful accident. She didn't bother to wipe the tears from her cheeks, now stained with mascara.

"How terrifying," someone said.

"Is she hurt?" someone else asked.

The diners sitting close by stared at the two young women. The maître d' swept through the room.

"Please continue to enjoy your meals, everyone," he said in a loud voice. "We apologize for the unfortunate accident, but the young lady is fine."

Chatter and clatter resounded as people resumed eating their food. Anne perused the room, suddenly aware that all the diners were white. Stella was the only person of color in the place other than the waiters. Bringing her here had been a mistake.

Bending to their table, the maître d' said to Anne and Stella, "I'm so sorry this happened. May I help in any way? Call a cab? An ambulance? Naturally, your dinners are on the house."

Stella said nothing but stared blankly at the man. Anne answered uncertainly, "Thank you for your concern. I can drive my sister home or to the hospital, whatever she wishes."

"May I offer you some tea or coffee?"

"No, thank you," she said. Stella shook her head.

The maître d' turned to Anne.

"Perhaps you'd like to go to the ladies' room. There's a couch and comfortable chairs there if you both need to rest awhile before leaving."

Stella raised her head.

"I think I would like to go to the hospital, after all. Please call an ambulance," she said.

"I'll come with you," Anne blurted.

"No, there's no need. I'll have a friend meet me there," Stella said, avoiding eye contact and holding up her burned hand in the space between them.

"If that's what you want. I'm so sorry."

Anne's stomach knotted. Stella continued to sit across from her at the table as the busboy cleared the dishes. Soon uniformed medical aides arrived and escorted Stella out of the restaurant to the ambulance. She moved past Anne without speaking, her face expressionless. Anne stood up and slipped to the ladies' room where she would be less conspicuous and could rest until she was calm enough to drive. In the restroom, overwhelmed by her emotions and the wine, she became drowsy. Glancing at her tear-streaked face in the mirror, she knew she appeared a wreck. She wanted to sleep and wake up to find that the scene at the restaurant had been nothing more than a bad dream. After a while, dazed, but no longer shaking, she left the restaurant and drove slowly home.

Chapter 22

January 1873

The christening was set for January third at the St. Rose of Lima Catholic Church, where the family regularly attended services conducted in French. The day before the event, Estelle noticed that the baby felt hot.

"I'm afraid she has a fever," she said to René. "We'd better send for the doctor right away."

The doctor arrived a few hours later.

"Keep her as cool as you can," Dr. Lenoir said, after examining the child. "I don't think she has yellow fever because the signs are not all there and because it's winter, but you never know. Has she been exposed to any mosquitoes?"

"No. She hasn't been outside, and we've kept the bedroom window closed."

"Good. I'll come again tomorrow."

Estelle burst into tears. Yellow fever had been rampant the previous summer, and many had died. René touched her arm.

"Let's hope for the best," he said. "We had better postpone the christening, though."

"You're right. Please tell the family. And talk to the nurse. She mustn't let the children anywhere near the baby's bedroom. We don't want them to be at risk."

"No. Yellow fever is all we need," he said. "Damn it all."

He thumped down the stairs. In the parlor, Edgar sat at the piano.

"What are you doing, trying to be a musician now, as well as an artist?" he said. "Maybe you'll have better success playing the piano and actually earn a living."

"*Imbécile!* You . . . turkey buzzard! I'm leaving soon, you know. You won't have to put up with me or the smell of my paints for much longer," Edgar said, his face creased in anger.

"Well, we've canceled the christening. The baby's sick. Guess you won't be able to stand as godfather after all."

"We'll see about that," Edgar said. He stood up from the piano bench and stomped up to his room. A few minutes later, he clattered downstairs and out the door, banging it behind him as he left.

"What's going on?" Mathilde asked, coming out of the kitchen.

"Nothing. Edgar's pouting, that's all," René said.

"He's ready to go home. We should try to give him a good send off, don't you agree?"

"That's up to you. Achille has already promised to accompany him to the train station. I'll be working."

"I'm sure Désirée and Estelle would want to make a fuss of him before he leaves. I'll talk to them."

"As you wish," René said, jamming on his hat. "I'm off to work."

After the doctor and her husband had left, Estelle sat rocking the baby's cradle, tears streaming down her face. She gazed with eyes full of love at the child's small, flushed face and tiny body and dabbed her skin with a damp towel. Prayers would be the only savior now, she thought.

Mathilde opened the door and peeked in.

"I'm so sorry, dear," she said to Estelle.

"Thank you. We must wait to see what will happen; that's the worst part."

"It is. Would you like a cup of tea or something?"

"That would be nice," Estelle said.

Mathilde crept back downstairs to find Clarice.

Estelle wiped her tears with the towel. These were difficult times. René was distracted by his failing business; that might explain his recent behavior as well as his interest in America Olivier. Perhaps she should be more understanding . . . but his flirtation at the recital had hurt her, and she needed his support now more than ever. Edgar would leave soon, having painted nothing worthwhile in New Orleans, or so he said. Now he might lose his role as godfather; such a disappointment. All the same, she didn't want to fall into the trap of self-pity. There were plenty of things to look forward to, she told herself, sniffing, including Mardi Gras. She had always enjoyed the festivities and the break from sadness that the carnival season provided, and this year they all needed cheering more than usual.

Clarice arrived bearing a cup of hot tea. She put it on the table near Estelle and viewed the baby. She shook her head.

"*Pauvre petite. Voici le thé, madame*," she said.

Estelle thanked her and took the cup. The warm liquid calmed her, and she peeked out of the tall window at the garden. If she focused, she could make out a dim view of palm tree fronds waving in the breeze and bright spots of red camellias glowing among the deep green foliage. It was still too early for the roses, her favorite flowers. She could almost see the roof of the Oliviers' house on Tonti Street, a few yards behind the garden fence. *That awful woman,* she fumed. She stifled her anger and turned her thoughts to spring and new growth. She hoped with all her heart that the child lived long enough to see it.

Baby Jeanne's illness did not worsen during the following days. The doctor examined her daily. One day he announced, "The fever has gone. She's out of danger."

"Thank God!" Estelle said, beaming, clasping her hands together.

The melancholy atmosphere that had pervaded the household for the past few days lifted. Strains of songs came from the piano again, and the children were no longer admonished to whisper when they crept upstairs. Estelle donned a green gown and started spending her days downstairs.

During the second week of January she asked Edgar when he expected to leave.

"I postponed my departure until we had news about the baby, but I can't wait much longer. There are exhibits to prepare for in Paris."

"Well, then, we must plan your farewell. You will come to the ball this weekend, won't you?"

"I don't enjoy such events as a rule, but if it would please you, I'll make an exception this time. What should I wear?"

"René has a costume in mind, I think. Why don't you talk to him?"

"I'll do that, but I have no desire to look foolish."

"Don't worry. You'll wear a mask. No one will know who you are."

He shrugged. "So what? No one knows who I am, anyway," he said.

Chapter 23

December 1970

The morning after her dinner with Stella, Anne woke up groggy, as though she had passed out the night before from too much drinking. As she lay in bed recalling the events, she groaned and turned her face to the wall. She'd made a fool of herself by overreacting and had caused such a ghastly scene. It was all very embarrassing. Stella was furious with her and would not now want to move in, but even if she and Stella made amends, the complicated relationships remained: Mary Wharton was a friend of Stella's, and Sam was Mary's former boyfriend. Anne didn't belong in that trio and didn't want to. She cringed at the idea. Despite her good intentions, nothing seemed to go well these days.

Realizing it was getting late and a workday, she called in sick. She needed time to sort out her thoughts. This would be a good time to visit the blighted neighborhoods, Section C, among others. She wanted to understand the situation better, and she could take her camera to record what she saw. She already knew the history of the Tremé area now undergoing development mere blocks away from where she lived. It had been the location of Congo Square, where slaves were allowed to meet on Sundays to get food and clothing. Jazz had been born there, and Louis Armstrong had grown up in those streets. All remnants of history had disappeared, and in the 1930s the Municipal Auditorium had displaced the square. More recently, much of the area had been cleared to make way for the expressway and future Superdome. The concrete elevated I-10 expressway soared above the ground, its giant legs cutting through former residences around it.

Anne drove to North Rampart Street, the beginning of the Tremé district. It was not a safe part of town for walking. She cruised under the enormous overpass. Barriers placed along the middle of the streets kept onlookers away from the work. Backhoes clawed at piles of bricks, raising dust. A sign dangled from a fence: HOUSING IS A HUMAN RIGHT. Losing her way because of the construction, she circled through the maze of narrow roads.

Sitting on the steps in front of a dilapidated wooden shotgun house she saw a black woman and a small child. She stopped and wound down the window.

"Excuse me," Anne called, "may I have a word with you?"

The woman's dark eyes met hers.

"What 'bout?"

"I'd just like to talk to you. Is this your house?"

"Is ma home, sure, not ma house. Lived here fer years. Not anymore. They's gonna tear it down, rip its heart out."

"I'm sorry. Don't you want to leave?"

"'Course I don't. No one do. We all get along 'round here."

"Are they going to find you a new place to live?"

"Na. Homeless, guess we'll be."

"That's terrible. I'm so sorry. . . ." Anne couldn't think of anything to say to comfort the woman. She saw that the house and others beside it had character. If they had been on a better street, perhaps they would have been deemed historic and worthy of preservation.

She got out of the car and approached the woman. "I'm an artist, and I'd like to capture some images of the neighborhood," she said. "Would you mind if I took your picture?"

"A'right with me."

Anne took several shots, nodded her thanks, returned to her car, and drove on. Entire blocks of housing had been razed and turned into rubble.

City Hall stood on the corner of Perdido and Loyola Street. A crowd of people of different races holding signs gathered on the steps. Anne parked the car and approached a man whose placard said KEEP THE RIVERFRONT A FRONT FOR THE RIVER.

"Excuse me, but may I ask what this means?" she said, pointing to the sign.

"We're protesting the riverfront expressway. They want to build a highway in the French Quarter right in front of the river, through Jackson Square. Preposterous!"

"I agree. Are you a member of a group, or here for yourself?"

"Don't you listen to the news? We're a preservation community."

"Glad to hear this. Are you interested in protecting other areas of the city from demolition as well? In the Tremé, for example?"

"Sure, but they're hopeless causes. The residents there are too poor to have much influence, and there's only so much we can do to take on the city. Those bastards don't care about preservation. We have to fight for the strongest causes, and the riverfront expressway is one. Look, if you want to know more about Tremé, go over there and talk to James Hayes. He's the one with the red hair."

She walked to him and held out her hand.

"I'm Anne. I have a sister who's about to be evicted because of redevelopment. Can you tell me more about what you're doing to stop this madness?"

"I could write a book about it," he said. "I'm a member of the Tremé Community Improvement Association. We're one of several groups fighting for neighborhood rights. I live in the district.

Most people there are racially mixed, and the city has labeled it as a blight, full of crime, prostitution, drugs, and derelict buildings. There are some old houses that have no plumbing or hot water, and those need to be dealt with. But they could be renovated rather than demolished. A lot of the residents like living in the area and don't want to move."

"So I've learned," Anne said. "The HANO guys are supposed to rehouse them. What's the truth about that?"

James shook his head. "Public housing. Right. Even when they build it, it's horrible. Here's a pamphlet to read that will help you understand what's going on. If you're really interested in helping, you should come to one of our meetings."

"Thanks. I think I will," Anne said.

A dog barked incessantly, and she twisted her head to look. A pit bull strained at its leash while a woman dressed in a tie-dyed T-shirt and untidy wiry hair struggled to hold it. In the scuffle she dropped a sign saying Save Tremé. Anne froze and gasped. It was Stella. Not wanting to be seen, Anne slunk back into the crowd. Her legs shook. She watched as Stella, laughing with a group of friends, pulled the dog toward her and gave it a slap. Someone yelled at the animal to stop barking. The dog continued snarling, saliva dripping from its mouth.

Still reeling from the shock, Anne stumbled to her car. She sat there for a long time, hands resting on the steering wheel. Well, that made everything clearer. Even if she wasn't responsible for the vandalism, Stella had told her nothing about her real beliefs about urban renewal. She was an activist! And Anne would never want a pit bull in her home. While sympathetic to her sister's situation, she realized that she no longer wanted Stella there.

But she had discovered new subject matter for her art: she could use the photograph of the woman and child in front of the old building as the basis for a new painting. If done well, it might be useful as a way of bringing more attention to the plight of poverty-stricken displaced residents. She resolved to start right away. The subject inspired her and might be worthy of her best efforts. And the subject had importance.

Placing the painting she had abandoned earlier on the easel, Anne laid down a thin glaze of white paint over the surface. She allowed the mass of dark horses underneath to emerge faintly as an undertone, following the technique she admired in Degas's paintings of dancers. She would allow time for the white paint to dry before adding more pigment. Satisfied with the results so far, she cleaned her brushes.

Next day she continued working. Using her memory of the photograph she had taken of the woman and child sitting barefoot in front of their soon-to-be-demolished home, she took a brush and sketched the details of the house and figures in burnt sienna. The woman's apron and the child's dress were white. As she painted the background in monochromatic brown tones, she carefully avoided covering the darker images of the horses. Then she layered paint on top of the horses using bold strokes of blue-tinted white to portray the clothes. The result astonished her: the colors jumped off the canvas, illuminating the clothing and reflecting soft lights in the figures' faces. The woman's and child's postures suggested quiet resignation; only their eyes mirrored their distress. After she finished, Anne stepped back to appraise her work and pose the all-important question: *Does it tell the truth?*

Chapter 24

January 1873

Sophie came across Marguerite writing in her journal one morning.

"What do you have to say that keeps you working with such concentration, *chérie*?" she asked.

"The thought of Mardi Gras around the corner. I'm so excited to be going to the balls this year, and I love my new dress. Thank you for that, *Maman*."

"It's time you had a becoming gown. Don't forget our party at home tomorrow evening. You can wear it then."

"No, I want to keep it for the first ball. I'll wear my pink dress tomorrow. It still fits, even if it's a little childish. Who's coming to the party?"

"Maurice will be back from school. Several of our friends. I invited the De Gas family, but the ladies can't come. Edgar has accepted, though."

"Edgar's coming? Well, that's lovely."

"I'll send Nicole to help you with your hair. You should try wearing it up now that you're sixteen."

"Thank you. I'd like that."

Marguerite pranced around the room. Edgar would be there! She hoped she could dance with him. Recently he'd sat beside her as she completed some drawings and given some advice. He'd done so kindly, without condescending, and she liked him for that. When he guided her hand, she felt a quiver up her back.

Next day she dressed with care. Nicole drew her hair off her neck and tied it with ribbons on top of her head. She needed a necklace and earrings to complete the outfit; perhaps her mother would lend some. When she heard strains of music drifting from the rooms below, she took up her fan and made her way down.

The guests were arriving in twos and threes. Everyone seemed so elegant. Her eyes wandered around the candlelit room. In the subdued light she could barely make out the figure of Edgar talking to her father. She passed a waiter carrying a tray of drinks and took a glass of wine.

Her brother Maurice approached her.

"Drinking wine are you, little sister?" he said. "Be careful."

"I'm old enough. *Maman* told me so herself."

"Well then, you can dance with me. You're the belle of the ball tonight."

"*Merci*," she said, putting down her glass. He led her to the dance floor, put his arm around her and swung her across the room.

"Not so fast, you're making me dizzy," she said.

"That's how you're supposed to dance: dizzily."

"Stop. I've had enough, big brother," she said.

"You're quite a good dancer. I'll ask you again later," he said.

He left her standing a few feet away from Edgar.

"*Bonsoir, mademoiselle*," he said. "I see you dance divinely."

"Not with my brother, I'm afraid," she said. "He sweeps me off my feet, and I almost fall over."

"Brothers are like that. Affectionate, but lacking in understanding. I know it well."

"Monsieur Degas . . ."

"Edgar, please . . ."

"Edgar. I've done a new drawing. May I show it to you?"

"Now? Here?" he asked, looking at her, a puzzled expression on his face.

"No. It's upstairs."

"Uh, well . . . *très bien*, if we take just a minute."

They pushed their way through the crowd and mounted the stairs.

"In here," Marguerite said, opening the door. They went inside, leaving the door open. It was a feminine bedroom with a big four-poster bed covered in a flowery quilt. Big fluffy pillows lined the headboard. Marguerite fetched her sketchbook and sat on the chair by her dressing table. She opened it and showed him a drawing of her mother.

"That's very good," he said, taking the book from her and looking at it closely. "You have improved. The face bears a good resemblance and the hands are nicely done. You might want to turn this into a painting."

Marguerite beamed.

"You have taught me well, Edgar. I so admire your work." She stood up.

"Perhaps we should go back downstairs before they miss us," Edgar said.

At that moment a particularly melodious passage resonated from below.

"Let me dance with you," Edgar said, drawing her close to him and folding his arms around her waist.

They danced slowly, gently, swaying to the sounds.

Am I dreaming? Marguerite wondered. When the music stopped Edgar took her hand, kissed it, and bowed.

"How enchanting you are," he said.

She blushed and moved away from him. Her heart beat so fast she feared she would faint.

Philippe interrupted them.

"*What's going on?*" he shouted. "Edgar, what in heaven's name are you doing in my daughter's room? You have no right to be there. *Get out!*"

"It's all right, Papa," Marguerite said, trembling. Her father's anger scared her. "He was only helping me with my drawing."

"Well, this is neither the time nor the place. Go back downstairs, both of you."

As Edgar slid quickly past her father he said firmly, "My apologies. I meant no harm."

Philippe scowled. "You are a welcome guest in our house, but there are limits. My daughter's bedchamber is out of bounds for you. Don't ever go there again."

They rejoined the party and Edgar soon took his leave. Marguerite had no more appetite for dancing and refused her brother's offers. She positioned herself behind a potted plant out of sight. Her heart throbbed with the memory of Edgar's arms encircling her. She wanted to see him again. And soon.

Chapter 25

December 1970

*A*nne needed to talk to Isabelle. She wanted advice, and now she was willing to listen. Fraught with anxiety and too impatient to call ahead, she drove straight to her friend's house.

"Sorry to barge in uninvited. Are you busy?" Anne asked.

"Come on in and have a drink," Isabelle said. "I see you could use one. What'll it be?"

"Gin and tonic, please. On second thoughts, a glass of water. I don't need liquor." She collapsed on the couch.

"What's wrong, Anne?" Isabelle asked.

"I'll tell you in a minute. Let me collect my thoughts. First tell me how you are, Izzy."

"Fine. No problems so far with the pregnancy. See, I'm showing now."

She patted her swelling stomach and grinned. "I'm getting things for the baby's room, though Mama says I should wait until later. She's superstitious. Paul will be here soon; if you're not too hungry, we'll wait for him and have dinner together."

"Thanks. What are you making?"

"It's Monday. Red beans and rice day."

"Good New Orleans tradition."

"Let me fetch the water. Back in a sec."

Isabelle handed Anne a glass and sat next to her on the couch.

"Okay, talk. What's going on?"

"You know me well, my friend." Anne sighed. "And these days, I'm not sure I even know myself. I seem to make one mistake after another, but mostly I want to talk to you about Sam."

"Thought so. Well, tell me everything."

"There have been red flags all along, but I've ignored them. You and Paul tried to warn me, and I've had reason to worry about him on my own, too. Perhaps it *was* Sam on the levee that night, as Paul suspected."

"All right, but we don't know what he was doing, do we? It may have been something innocent, like fishing."

"He doesn't fish. He also runs very fast, just as Paul observed."

"All right," Isabelle said again. "What else bothers you about the man?"

"He's away a lot, supposedly on business, but he never tells me what he's doing, or that he's going. One morning after staying the night with me he left without saying good-bye. No word of thanks, nothing about how much he enjoyed the evening. I felt used."

"Strange. Have you talked to him about these things? Perhaps he has good explanations," Isabelle said.

"He evades the questions and doesn't give any explanations."

"I agree, something sounds suspicious. Paul told me you've never been to Sam's house. Is it possible he's married?"

"I don't think so. We're dating, and he seems to have a lot of recent girlfriends," Anne said, trying to forget the image of Mary Wharton. "He doesn't wear a wedding ring."

Isabelle rolled her eyes.

"I'd ask him the question, at least," she said.

"Actually, assuming he's not married, the things I've mentioned aren't the reasons I'm most concerned." Anne paused. "We went to my dad's for Thanksgiving, and Sam shot the neighbor's dog . . . no, don't worry, it wasn't crazy behavior on his part; the dog attacked Dad's cat. What bothered me—and Dad—was how efficiently he used his gun, and how calmly he reacted. He had been out for a run, and had a gun with him. Why? Dad thinks he works for the FBI. When I asked Sam later point blank, he said even if it were true, he couldn't tell me. So that shuts down further questions."

"Well, from what you've told me, it all fits, doesn't it?" Isabelle said. "He's secretive, he travels but doesn't tell you where to or why; he's comfortable, and no doubt skilled using guns; he goes out for mysterious rendezvous at night in remote areas along the river. My guess is he does work for the FBI, or for some equivalent undercover organization. He'd need a gun permit to carry one around, and FBI agents have those as a matter of course. Does that bother you enough to end the relationship?"

"I don't know. I would need to understand why he engages in this line of work, and if he sees it as something useful and honorable that he can do well. If he simply doesn't mind living a double life, or needs the drama, that wouldn't be acceptable. Dad also mentioned another problem: he may not want a permanent relationship, ever. Such people usually don't, he says. That makes sense to me. Domestic life—marriage—might be too humdrum."

Isabelle smiled. "Come on now, marriage isn't always humdrum. What kind of word is that, anyway? But seriously, these are troubling questions, for sure, Anne. My advice would be to wait and see what happens. You're only dating the guy. You have no permanent commitment to him, any more than he has to you. I thought you weren't interested in marriage, anyway."

"I wasn't, but I've been rethinking that."

Isabelle raised her eyebrows.

"Well, great balls of fire, as Scarlett would say. Whatever happened to Miss No-Responsibility?"

"Guess I'm growing up, like you," Anne smiled. "Or maybe I want a partner."

"Okay. Let me put it another way. If you want marriage, why stick around with this guy, who doesn't look like a likely candidate?"

"Good question, though marriage isn't the deal breaker here."

"Well, do you love him?"

"I thought I did, but now I'm not so sure. Dad gave me some good advice. He said to make a good decision, you must first face the truth. In this case, the truth might be the deal breaker."

"Annie, I wish you the best, you know that. It's hard to advise you about someone I've never met. Why don't you invite him over sometime?"

"I did already, and he couldn't come, or perhaps . . ." her words trailed off.

". . . he didn't want to meet your friends?" Isabelle said, finishing the thought.

"Although he did accept the invitation to meet my father," Anne said. "But, damn it all, he wanted to see my painting, the one in the attic. I'm starting to feel like the biggest fool."

"Don't be too hard on yourself. This is your first serious relationship, and you want it to work out. You'll figure this out in time."

"Oh my God! That reminds me, I gave the painting to Sam to appraise, and I never even wrote my name on it. It's not signed, so no one would know who painted it, or who it belongs to. I'll have to talk to him. Sam wanted to send it to the Philadelphia Museum of Art for an exhibit. Glad I thought of this."

"So now you have another reason to talk to him, and soon," Isabelle said.

The front door opened, and Paul came into the room.

"Hi, sweetheart," he said, giving Isabelle a kiss. "Hello, Anne. Great to see you!"

She stood up, and he gave her a hug.

"How's it going?" he asked.

"You missed the big discussion. Isabelle can fill you in on the details. Let's talk about you and law school."

"Nothing much to tell, I'm afraid. It's fine. Dull, but fine. How are the house renovations coming along? Did you ever figure out who destroyed the bathroom?"

"Not exactly, though I now believe someone who knows Stella was trying to send me a message that I should let her move in."

"And are you going to?"

"No."

"Really? Why not?"

Anne fidgeted in her seat. She didn't want an interrogation about that uncomfortable subject. But Isabelle and Paul were her friends . . . possibly they would offer a different point of view.

"She and I are not compatible. I ran into her recently in the Tremé, and she seemed very different from when I've seen her before. I saw a new side of her, one that made me suspect she hasn't been honest. She was with friends. Worse yet, she had a pit bull."

"How does that make her incompatible? As you would be the first to admit, appearances aren't everything. And what's wrong with a dog?" Isabelle asked.

Anne's heart beat faster. Her voice shrill, she said, "Don't you know anything about those dogs? *They're vicious!* The dog that Sam killed because it attacked Dad's cat was a *pit bull!*"

Isabelle and Paul exchanged glances.

"Don't think the worse of me if I can't have her live with me. I couldn't share the house with a dog like that."

"Well, maybe she won't bring it. People often use those dogs for protection. If she lives in a dangerous neighborhood, she might need it."

"I hadn't considered that," Anne said, her voice calmer. "Perhaps I overreacted. I have a habit of doing that. I don't know. All this business with Sam and the dog and my job has made me very edgy, and I have so many decisions to make right now."

"We know you do. Let me ask, do you like Stella?" Isabelle said.

"I was starting to, but we had a bad experience at Brennan's recently, probably my fault."

"What happened?"

"We were having dinner, and I learned she and my boss Mary are friends, good friends, and that she knows about Sam through Mary, who used to be Sam's girlfriend. I got upset and she had an accident."

"What kind of accident?"

"Her sleeve caught fire on a flaming dessert. She's okay."

"Well, bless your heart. Annie, I must say your life these days doesn't lack drama," Isabelle said, smiling. "That's an awkward situation, but are you sure you're thinking clearly here? You told us you had sympathy for your sister and wanted to make amends for the way your family treated her. What's changed?"

"Nothing. I'm cautious for reasons I've mentioned: she and I may not have a compatible lifestyle. But now that I think she hasn't been straightforward, and that bothers me."

"You may be right, but this is a big decision for both of you. I know you. If you don't do what's right, you'll have that on your conscience. Couldn't you talk to her about the dog?"

"I guess so, but after our dinner at Brennan's, I'm not sure she wants to live with me, anyway."

"So that's different, if she chooses not to. Good luck, Annie," Isabelle said. "We're aware that this isn't easy."

"I'll say," Paul said. "But I'd like to hear more about Sam. He had another girlfriend, you say? Is he a two-timer?"

Anne burst into tears. "I hope not," she said, sniffing.

Isabelle gave her a hug. "Paul, don't make things worse for her."

"Sorry," he said quietly.

"Are you okay, Annie?" Isabelle asked.

"Yes. Just stressed out. I need to go home now," Anne said, blowing her nose.

"Wait. What about dinner?"

"Lost my appetite."

"All right, if you're sure," Isabelle said. "I'll call you tomorrow."

⟡⟡⟡

Next day, Anne stopped by Sam's office to find her painting. His secretary told her he wasn't in and that she didn't know when to expect him. Anne had an appointment with Mary Wharton, whose office was on the same floor.

"Come in," Mary said, not looking up. "Sit down. We'll go down the names on your list, one by one. Jedediah Paris. I've never heard of him or Ledbetter Pickens. Why did you include them?"

"They were experts with rifles. Jedediah had a reputation for killing rattlesnakes, and Ledbetter painted him in the act of firing at them. Ledbetter could follow trails as cleverly as Indians. Jedediah did sketches of him identifying footprints."

"Interesting historically, and story worthy, but the art isn't any good. We can't include them. My goodness, you have guns on the brain, don't you? As I've said to you already, this isn't a dog and pony show."

Anne bit her lip and refrained from commenting sarcastically that there were no dogs or ponies on her list. She almost hated the woman.

The phone rang, and Mary reached across her desk to answer it.

"Oh, hi there, Jerry," she said. "No, I can't talk now. Call you later."

Her voice had taken on a sultry tone, whispery and deep.

"Your other suggestions are okay," she said, matter-of-factly, "though I wonder how you discovered the more obscure painters. Are you sure you didn't get any help? Perhaps from your boyfriend?"

Anne drew a sharp breath. She wrapped her arms tightly in front of her and replied, "My personal life has nothing to do with this project, and I'd prefer to keep things professional here."

Mary tossed a lock of her blond hair out of her eyes. She looked with disdain at Anne in her bellbottoms and loose shirt.

"Well, if you want things to be more professional, you might start by dressing the part. I have no desire to work with Sam on this assignment, anyway. He's so unreliable."

Feeling stung, Anne burst out, "Whatever do you mean, unreliable? He's a good curator and works damn hard at his job."

"Let's say he's unpredictable, then. Especially with women. You'll see. He uses them, and when he doesn't need them anymore, he drops them cold. You know he has other things on his mind besides the museum."

Anne felt nauseous. She stood up.

"Well, if that's all you want from me for now, I'll catch you later."

"Hold on a minute. Not so fast. I haven't given you your next assignment. Find the names, addresses, and phone numbers for the owners of paintings from this list and draft letters for my signature asking for the loans. They will have to authorize loans for the exhibition, you understand."

"I understand."

"Fine. See you next week."

Weak-kneed, Anne stopped by Sam's office. She knocked at the door but got no answer. She remembered that Peter Knight had offered assistance if she ran into problems and decided to find out if he was available. He was sitting at his desk.

"Nice to see you, Anne. What brings you here?"

"I wonder if you can help me," she said.

"What's the problem?"

"I need to get into Sam Mollineux's office. Would you have a key to let me in?"

"I do, but what for?"

"He has a painting of mine in there. It's an American Impressionist painting by a relative of mine, and he's having it appraised. When I gave it to him, I forgot to write my name on it. The artist didn't sign it, and I want to be sure it doesn't get lost or attributed to someone else."

"Well, we wouldn't want that. Sam left for New York last night on an assignment. and won't be back until the day after tomorrow."

They reached Sam's office, and Peter unlocked and opened the door.

"Do you see the painting?" he asked.

"That looks like it, over there," she said, as she saw a flat object wrapped in brown paper propped against the wall.

A curator appeared in the doorway. "Peter, could you talk to that donor again? She's on the phone, and I don't have answers to her millions of questions."

"Okay," he said, groaning. "Anne, gotta take this call. Please close the door when you're done."

"Many thanks," she said.

She crossed the room to the painting. Strange, she hadn't remembered using that kind of tape to fasten it, she thought. Perhaps Sam had re-wrapped it. She tore open the paper and the canvas came into view. She gasped. Degas's portrait of Estelle De Gas, the one that had hung on the museum wall at the top of the stairwell, stood before her. She examined it closely. The textured paint identified it as an unframed original. Puzzled, she wondered why the painting would have been taken down for reframing so soon after being rehung. Then a stab of fear gripped her. *What if this was a forgery?* It was the same size as her painting; she remembered that Sam had commented that both paintings had the same dimensions. So where was her painting? Starting to panic, she searched the room. She discovered another brown-packaged object beside Sam's desk. The tape enclosing that one seemed more familiar. She tore it open. She had found her painting. With relief, she sat down in Sam's leather desk chair, her heart pounding. Taking a black pen from the desk she jotted the name of her relative Philippe Fontenot, artist, on the back, then printed her own name underneath: Anne Gautier, owner. She wasn't sure of the convention for identifying paintings, but at least she had recorded the information. She re-wrapped both canvases and deliberated for a long time. What should she do next? Obviously the first step would be to learn if the painting of Estelle had disappeared from its place on the wall.

Anne left the office, making sure the door locked behind her. She headed for the stairwell where the portrait hung. It was there.

She scrutinized it. The same woman, Estelle, gazed down at her. It, too, was an original, with strong brush strokes. But which was the true original? With a sinking heart, she began to suspect that one of them was a forgery. It could be an authorized copy, of course; she knew many artists who learned to paint by replicating works of other artists. She would find out, and she knew without hesitation that the very last person she could ask was Sam.

Chapter 26

January 1873

*E*stelle and Désirée anticipated the ball with excitement as the family made preparations. It would be one of the first parties of the two-month carnival season that would end on February twenty-fifth, Mardi Gras, the day before Ash Wednesday and the beginning of Lent.

"Perhaps I can persuade Edgar to dance with me," Désirée said to Estelle one morning as they helped each other to put on their necklaces.

Estelle smiled. Perhaps if he whirled Désirée around in his arms, he would renew his romantic overtures. She knew from experience the spell that dancing and good music could cast over even the most reluctant suitors.

The women chose their finest dresses, and the men tried on their costumes. The Comus Krewe's carnival theme for the year was Darwin's *Origin of Species,* and insect masks were popular.

"Achille, what will you wear?" Edgar asked his brother.

"I'll be a grasshopper. It's fitting for me, and I like green. What about you?"

"René won't tell me. He's giving me a mask. I don't want a complete outfit. This is all pretty silly really, you know."

"We do know. We love it," Achille said.

On the evening of the event, the family members assembled in front of the house and waited for the carriages that would transport them to the auditorium where the ball would take place. Everyone talked at the same time. The women laughed at the men's outrageous costumes. They were brightly colored, and some had feathers for added panache.

"You're the best-looking cockroach I ever saw," Désirée said to René, laughing.

Edgar peered at her through his gold butterfly mask.

"You look delicious yourself tonight, Didi. Your dress ruffles resemble whipped cream," he said.

She beamed and flicked her fan.

William was dressed as a parrot, and Michel wore the bright red costume of a ladybug.

Estelle, wearing a blue dress, surveyed the family with satisfaction. Mathilde, always beautiful, was dressed in black lace and held her husband's arm. They would have fun at the ball. The carriages soon arrived, and the three sisters and the men stepped inside.

The auditorium boasted a large dance floor. An orchestra stood at one end, and musicians in black jackets and white shirts busily tuned their instruments, resulting in a cacophony of sounds.

The costumed guests made their way in, the women's long silk skirts rustling. Perfume pervaded the air. Chairs and tables draped with white cloths lined the edges of the room, and ribbons of green, purple, and gold hung from the chandeliers. René chose a table near the orchestra, and the men held chairs for the women as they took their seats.

A brown spider crawled toward them.

"*Bonsoir, mes amis,*" he said. "I don't know who these insects are, but I recognize you lovely ladies. I'm Philippe."

"Please join us," René said. The men raised their masks, and everyone laughed. They moved another table close, and minutes later the Fontenot women, Sophie and Marguerite, arrived.

Estelle gazed at Marguerite in astonishment. *She looks exquisite, and so grown-up.* The last time she had seen her, she had been pretty, but still a girl. Now she had become a beautiful young woman. Straining to see, she noticed that Edgar had taken his mask off and was staring at her in frank admiration. Her dark hair, arranged on top of her head, sparkled with diamonds. She wore a silvery gown with a full skirt that fitted her slim figure perfectly. When she moved, the layers floated around her. With a start, Estelle understood Edgar's reaction: Marguerite looked like a dancer, exactly like sketches she had seen in his notebook.

Philippe's voice broke into her thoughts.

"What would you ladies like to drink?" he asked. They answered in turn.

"Wait a minute, I can't remember it all," he said. "White wine for Désirée and Estelle, red for Mathilde. Sophie, what did you say?"

"I'll help," Edgar said. Looking at Marguerite, he asked, "What will you have?"

She smiled. "Champagne, please."

"For me, too," her mother said.

Sitting beside Désirée, Estelle appreciated the swish of air from her sister's fan cooling her burning face. She had forgotten to bring one in all the excitement as they left home. She watched as Désirée's gaze settled on Marguerite, who waited quietly for her champagne. Edgar returned to the table and handed Sophie a glass, then offered one to Marguerite, who extended a graceful hand to accept it, smiling up at him. Edgar returned her smile and sat down beside her. The lump in Estelle's throat swelled as she saw the longing in Désirée's eyes. She gulped. Her sister could hardly compete with a younger woman who resembled a ballerina, a favorite subject in Edgar's art.

Philippe returned to the table with a tray of drinks and passed them round. Estelle took a mouthful of wine. The orchestra struck a chord, the violins soared, and soon the familiar music of waltzes filled the space. Colorfully attired guests who chatted together and admired each other's clothes now occupied all the tables, and peals of laughter rang across the room.

A large tiger-costumed figure mounted the stage. Motioning for the music to stop, he lifted his mask to address the crowd.

"*Mesdames et Messieurs*, welcome to our celebration. After the parade of the men in their attire, the dancing will begin. Thank you for attending, and we wish you all a festive evening. *Laissez les bons temps rouler!*"

Everyone clapped, and the orchestra resumed playing. Estelle continued to sip her wine. Edgar, sitting across the table, turned to look in her direction. She caught his eye.

"What are you drinking, Edgar?" she asked.

"Absinthe. We have it in France, but I've never tasted it before. René recommended it. He says he wants to be sure I have a good time."

Overhearing this remark, René said, "Absolutely. We can't send him back to Paris saying he had no fun in la Nouvelle-Orléans."

"Take care with that drink," Estelle said. "It's dangerous, especially if you're not accustomed to it."

"Let him be, it's fine. We drink it all the time, don't we, Achille?" René replied.

Achille nodded. His grasshopper mouth didn't allow him much room for talking.

The waiters were slow in bringing food, and René stood up to order another round of drinks. Finally, a plate of crawfish, condiments, and asparagus appeared in front of each guest at their table. René proposed a toast to Edgar, thanking him for coming and wishing him a safe journey home. Edgar stood up, raising his voice so that all could hear.

"*Merci beaucoup*," he said. "It has been a pleasure to share all your lives and to get acquainted with my new relatives. I leave tomorrow. I'll take back happy memories, and I will miss you all."

"Will you leave behind any of your paintings of the family?" Désirée asked him after he had sat down.

"No. I want to keep them. They're all I have to remind me of you. I've already arranged for them to be sent on."

"Too bad. They're lovely. I especially like the one of Jo having a pedicure," Désirée said. "But perhaps you'll come back and paint us again."

He met her stare, but made no answer.

More food arrived, including cheese, bread, and fruit arranged on a platter: figs, bananas, oranges, and pears. Everyone ate heartily, and the crowd's conversation and clatter of silverware increased in volume as the meal reached its conclusion. The band struck a few notes, and the tiger-costumed man remounted the stage.

"Now that everyone has eaten, let's see what creative ideas have been inspired by this year's theme, Darwin's *Origin of Species*," he said. "Will the men who have costumes please make a circle in the middle of the dance floor."

Hundreds stood up and moved into the circle. Edgar remained in his seat. The orchestra struck up a lively tune, and the costumed men paraded around making sounds appropriate to their creature. A turkey strutted, a chicken flapped its wings, a lion roared, a parrot squawked, and René the cockroach zig-zagged across the floor. The audience clapped, and the actors, their vision obscured by their masks, bumped into each other, collapsing in heaps on the ground.

After a while, the men returned to their seats, many laughing uncontrollably. After slapping each other on the back, René, Achille, and Philippe sat back down at the table.

"That was fun, but next year I'll choose a costume that allows me to make more noise," René said. "I don't know what sound cockroaches make, unless you count the cracking sound they make when you step on them."

Estelle eyed her husband with disapproval. He was behaving like a schoolboy. Still, it was Mardi Gras, a time for frivolity. She glanced at Edgar, who was staring again at Marguerite, seemingly unaware of the activity going on around him. Désirée hid her face behind her fan. Estelle kept her face neutral, but couldn't ignore the sadness about her sister's lost opportunity.

The music began, the cue for dancing. Philippe stood up, taking his wife's hand. René touched Estelle on the shoulder and escorted her to the floor. Achille invited Désirée to dance, and Mathilde and William joined them. As she twirled about the floor in her husband's arms, Estelle caught sight of Edgar leading Marguerite to dance. He had taken off his butterfly mask. She reluctantly admitted the couple made a handsome pair as they waltzed around the room, Marguerite's skirts flying as they spun.

Two dances later, the couples returned to the table, out of breath, with flushed cheeks.

"It's so good to dance again," Estelle said.

"Yes, it makes me ten years younger," Désirée agreed. To Estelle she whispered, "I thought Edgar said he doesn't dance."

"Yes, he did say that," Estelle replied.

They exchanged glances, and Estelle's heart flew to her sister's. Marguerite appeared entranced, and her eyes shone almost as brightly as the diamonds in her hair. Edgar stood behind her, his hands resting on her chair. Désirée took a long, slow, drink as she observed the couple from across the table.

"Have another drink, Edgar. You won't have another occasion like this for a while," René said, smiling like a devil.

"I've had enough, but why not? This is a special night," Edgar said.

"It'll fortify you for the ship, and the terrible food," René said.

He crossed to the bar to bring more drinks, and the orchestra began playing music with a slower rhythm.

"Please dance with me again," Edgar said, bending down to Marguerite.

"With pleasure," she said, getting up.

They held each other perhaps a little too closely, Estelle thought. They also seemed to have an intimacy that could not have developed on the dance floor. Perhaps they had become better acquainted at the Fontenots'—perhaps *she* was the reason Edgar had been spending so much time there recently. She should have guessed! Marguerite seemed to be as taken with Edgar as he was with her. Maybe this was a romance in the making. But he planned to leave the next day . . . she averted her eyes. She wanted to enjoy herself tonight.

"I wish I had more dance partners. I do so love to dance," Désirée said wistfully. "Achille, let's dance again."

"All right, but these grasshopper antennae get in my way, bobbing up and down. Do you mind if I take off the mask?"

"Not at all. I'd be happy to dance with a headless grasshopper," she said.

They moved onto the floor, and made a strange couple, but no stranger than others, Estelle thought. It was all ridiculous, but Edgar didn't seem to care. In fact, he gave the impression that he liked it all, or at least that he liked dancing with Marguerite very much indeed. Estelle continued to sit at the table viewing the dancers with blurred vision as they careened around the room. Her eyes burned. At least America Olivier didn't appear to be present. The last thing she wanted to witness was her husband dancing with *that woman*.

Finally, after midnight, the evening came to an end, and the exhausted dancers took their leave. The family members waited for carriages to take them home. Edgar stood close to Marguerite and said something to her in a whisper before they stepped into separate vehicles.

Estelle faced him as he sat across from her in the carriage.

"Well, *mon cousin*, what did you think of our Mardi Gras event?" she asked.

"I hardly know what to say, it was so magnificent. I'm dizzy from all the excitement."

"From all the absinthe, you mean, *mon frère*," René said, laughing.

"I drank a bit too much, but at this moment I am happy," Edgar replied.

"Are you ready, all packed, for tomorrow?" Estelle asked.

"Yes. Everything is prepared," he said.

Their carriages brought them to their house on Esplanade. Edgar dismounted rather shakily, and René helped him up the steps to the front porch. Achille, who lived in the French Quarter and would travel farther, called to Edgar, "I'll bring the carriage round for you at eight."

The family members filed inside and straight to their rooms. It had been a successful evening, Estelle thought, and a fitting end to her cousin's visit. But poor Désirée . . . what had happened between Edgar and Marguerite? She'd find out. She had her ways.

Chapter 27

December 1970

Anne left work early after her discovery of the second painting of Estelle in Sam's office. She needed time to digest the new information. It had been a shock. She wished she trusted Sam, and that he would have a logical explanation. Sadly, she suspected that he would lie or attempt to distract her from learning the truth. He was turning out to be a great disappointment. She knew she should report the finding to someone who would know about the legality of the matter, and she needed advice again. She dialed Isabelle and Paul's number.

Paul answered the phone.

"Hi, it's me, Anne," she said. "I hate to impose on you again so soon, but I've got a problem. Is Isabelle there?"

"No, she's at her mother's for dinner. Shall I give her a message?"

"Something's come up, and I need to talk to someone. Would you be available? It's important, and discretion is crucial."

"You have me intrigued. I'm home. If you'd like to come by, I can put together something for us to eat and you can talk your heart out."

"It's not about my love life. I need some advice; it may even end up as a legal matter, so you're the perfect person for the job."

"Job?" he asked.

"Not really, but I'm glad you'll talk to me. I'll be right over."

Anne *was* glad Paul would talk to her. She had always turned to him for advice before he'd met Isabelle, and she trusted him implicitly. She drove to the Cherokee Street house and rang the bell.

"How about a glass of wine?" Paul greeted her. "Sounds like you could use some strong liquid refreshment."

"No thanks," she said, as she sat down on the couch. "I need a clear head. Water, please."

"This sounds serious," he said as he scooted into the kitchen. He returned with a glass of water for her and wine for himself.

"Cheers," he said.

They clinked glasses.

"I know you're already suspicious about Sam," Anne began. "I agree that his behavior implies that he has a life apart from the one at the museum. So far, though, I've had no proof, only the sense that there's more going on than I know about. I've had no reason to suspect he's involved in any kind of illegal activity, until now."

Paul raised his eyebrows.

"Annie, I don't want to make you a worry wart, or see things that aren't there."

"Hear me out. You haven't done anything to turn me against him. The problem is. . . ." She caught her breath. "He may have a forgery of an important painting by Degas."

"What on earth makes you suspect that?"

"I was in his office looking for the painting of my great-great-grandmother Sophie and I accidentally came upon it."

"Hold on a minute, Anne. Please explain why Sam has a painting of your relative in his office."

"Sorry. I'm getting ahead of myself," she said, trying to calm her racing mind. After a minute she continued. "You've seen the one of Sophie left in the Esplanade house attic."

"Yes, I remember it. Sophie's the one who resembles you, isn't she?"

"She's the one. Well, Sam asked to see the picture when we were at my dad's for Thanksgiving, and it impressed him. He asked if he could borrow it for an exhibition at the Philadelphia Museum of Art, and I agreed, and gave it to him. Later I remembered I'd forgotten to put any kind of identification on it, and today I went into his office to find it. That's when I discovered the portrait of Estelle De Gas by Degas. Another identical painting is hanging on the museum's walls."

"My god. This is serious, if one is a fake, and no one has authorized a copy."

"Exactly. I don't know if it's legitimate. Who should I talk to? I've decided that even though this will surely end my relationship with Sam, I must do the right thing and report this finding."

"I agree. In fact, if you don't and someone finds out, they could find you guilty as an accomplice. He eyed her sharply. "I'd say you should talk to your boss at the museum for starters."

"Probably so. However, my boss now is a woman I don't like, who used to be romantically involved with Sam."

"Hm. Can you go over her head?"

"Yes, but if this matter turns out to be legitimate—if an art student or someone had permission to copy the painting—reporting it would put my career in jeopardy, don't you think?"

"Maybe. You need to do the right thing, Anne, whatever that is, and keep your hands clean. That's my advice."

"I agree," she said, nodding. "Thank you, Paul. You've always helped me out of the messes I get myself into."

"Yeah, I remember. Sometimes you overindulge with the booze." He grinned and winked at her, and she relaxed and smiled.

"Let's find something to eat," he said. "How about leftover chicken marsala?"

"Sounds good."

They went into the kitchen and Paul heated the food.

"How are you doing at finding out about your family, anyway?" he asked.

"I've sort of let this go. Life has gotten in the way."

"Relationships can do that, while you're trying to work things out," he said.

"That's what I'm finding, but I'll get back to my family story, if only because if I don't, it might get lost. Even Degas's family members would have been lost, if he hadn't painted them."

"Good point. Dinner's ready. Would you like a glass of wine now?"

"Yes, please. If I stay long enough, I may even get to see Isabelle. I have to say, I'm still getting used to the thought of you all as parents."

"Me, too, but I'm looking forward to it."

They chatted as they ate, and after a while Anne realized it was getting late. She thanked Paul and drove home. On the way she reaffirmed what a good friend he'd been to her throughout the years and wondered if she had made a mistake in discouraging him as a potential romantic partner in the past. Isabelle had seen his good qualities right away and had fallen in love with him. They were well suited, though, and neither was cursed with the desire to renovate a recalcitrant old house . . . not that she had done much toward achieving that goal. In fact, she had lately been engaged only in trying to figure out Sam. Perhaps things needed to change.

Chapter 28

January 1873

The household woke early on the morning of Edgar's departure. Michel and René had said good-bye the night before and had already left for work when the other family members gathered downstairs. Estelle and Mathilde rushed around getting the children into the front room. Clarice packed a hamper of food for the journey and served coffee to the adults. Everyone kept so busy that no one noticed the hour until Achille arrived with the carriage.

"Where's Edgar?" he said. "We don't have much time to get to the station. Are these his trunks? Robert, please put them in the carriage."

"Yessir," the manservant said.

"Edgar hasn't come downstairs yet," Estelle said. "I'll tell him you're here."

She went upstairs and knocked on his door. No answer.

"Edgar, are you ready?" she called.

Still no answer. She opened the door and saw that Edgar was still in bed, sleeping soundly.

"Wake up! Achille is here."

Edgar opened his eyes.

"I feel terrible," he said, rubbing his eyes. "What a headache! Did I oversleep?"

"Yes. You need to get dressed right away. The train won't wait." She left him to join the others.

"He's still in bed, with a headache. Must be the absinthe; I knew he shouldn't have had so much to drink last night."

"I'll help him," Achille said, going up to Edgar's room.

The children chased each other around the room noisily, and Estelle sat down on the couch holding baby Jeanne.

"Be quiet and stop scampering. Behave yourselves!" the wet nurse said, coming into the room.

Carrie flopped onto the floor.

"I've got a flower to give to *Oncle* Edgar," she said, "but he's not here. Did he leave already?"

"No, *chérie*, he's coming down soon to say good-bye."

Edgar finally appeared, his eyes slits as he strained to keep out the light.

"*Au revoir, Oncle* Edgar," the children said. Carrie held out the flower.

"*Au revoir, mes enfants, et merci*," Edgar said, bending down to embrace each child.

"I wish I had more time to thank all of you for your hospitality," Edgar said, kissing each family member on both cheeks. "I'm sorry to miss the baby's christening, too."

He held a hand to his forehead as he stood up, wincing as if in pain.

"Come, Edgar, we must go, or you'll miss your train," Achille said.

They got into the carriage. All the family crowded on the porch and waved as they drove off. The nurse ushered the children back to the parlor and took the baby from Estelle's arms.

"Do you think he liked his visit?" Désirée asked Estelle.

"In his own way, I believe he did, but he's not used to family life and the mundane domestic routines. He was ready to go home."

"He seemed to enjoy himself at the ball yesterday, dancing with Marguerite," Désirée said.

Estelle searched her sister's face for signs of sadness or hurt, but her expression remained calm.

"I know. I'm glad you're not too disappointed, dear."

"Only a little."

Estelle gave her sister a hug.

"I wouldn't have wanted you to go away and live in Paris, and you would, if you married him," Estelle said.

"True. I belong here, and I'm afraid I never would have fitted in with his artist's life and friends."

"Edgar truly is an artist. He's different from his brothers, and he became tired of hearing their endless talk about cotton."

"Yes. He thought cotton pervaded everything. He told me that dirty cotton even hangs on the trees here!"

Estelle laughed.

"He meant Spanish moss, I presume."

"That's what I told him. I'm not sure he believed me."

"Well, he's gone. I wonder if we will ever see him again. I *am* sorry that he didn't paint New Orleans. He only painted portraits of us."

"Oh, well. I'm going for my walk now. Would you like to come along?" Désirée asked.

"I would. It's a fine day."

The sisters donned their shawls and bonnets and set off toward the river. Estelle was grateful that Désirée was still at home, even though she wished her sister would marry. At thirty-four, she was almost too old to hope for a husband. She remembered how enamored of Marguerite Edgar seemed to be, and how often they had danced together the night before. Had Sophie observed their attachment? She would ask.

Désirée and Estelle wandered for an hour before stopping at the French Market for coffee and pastry. They arrived home at noon and found Edgar sitting in the front room in his shirt sleeves looking at the newspaper.

"Edgar! What are you doing here? Did you change your mind about leaving?" Estelle asked.

"I missed the train," he said, looking up.

"*Missed the train?*" Désirée said. "For goodness' sake! Well, now what will you do?"

He shrugged. "I'll book another passage on the ship. Anyway, I'll stay on for a while, if you'll have me."

"Of course you can stay," Estelle said. "What a surprise."

"I'm still tired, and my head aches. I'll rest for a while and come down for dinner."

"As you wish," Estelle said. "Unfortunate that the train left without you."

"Trains don't wait. It was my fault. Maybe now I can be a true godfather and stand at the christening."

"That will be lovely. It's on February fifth."

Edgar went upstairs, and the sisters exchanged glances, trying to keep from smiling.

"Did you notice his red eyes?" Désirée whispered.

"Yes. They're like beacons. We love him dearly, but he can't hold his liquor," Estelle replied.

As soon as he had gone, they collapsed on the couch, bursting with laughter.

The following day, Edgar came down for coffee as usual. Estelle opened windows to let the fresh air in.

"Good morning, Edgar," she said. "I hope you're better now. You will find cooler weather here at last. That should make things more pleasant. Did you unpack?"

"Not completely. My painting materials are still in boxes, but I have my notebook here, and pencils. I'll go to the office. I might do portraits of my brothers. After all, I've not painted them, only the women in the family, and I doubt the men would want to take the time to pose for me at home, as you all did."

"Good idea. Will you go on foot, or ride to Carondelet Street?"

"As you say, the weather's fine today, and it's not raining. I'll walk."

"Will you come home for lunch?"

"Not today. I'll take René and Achille out. I owe them, and they're going to have to put up with me for a while longer."

"We're glad you're staying on," Estelle said.

"I'll stop by the Fontenot house on the way home. I need to tell Philippe that I'm still here."

"All right. We'll expect you for dinner."

Estelle watched as he ambled out, pausing for a while on the porch and blinking in the sunshine before going down the steps and through the garden to the street. She wondered if his purpose in going to the Fontenots was to see Marguerite as well as Philippe. She would ask Sophie to come over to find out what she knew about the connection between her daughter and Edgar. Estelle scribbled a note to her friend and gave it to a manservant to deliver.

Later that day, she waited in the front room for Sophie. The pale winter sun streamed through the window, and the crystal chandelier flung rainbow prisms against the wall, highlighting the flowers on the table. Estelle took note of it all. She wanted to trap such things in her memory.

Sophie arrived and sat down next to her friend, and shortly afterward Clarice came in with the tea.

"What did you think of the ball?" Estelle asked.

"Wonderful, don't you agree? The costumes were so amusing, the orchestra played well, and I enjoyed dancing. Marguerite was thrilled with it all, too."

"She looked beautiful in that silvery dress. Wherever did you find it?"

"We ordered it from Paris. I decided she should wear something special for her first ball."

"Edgar was very impressed."

"Was he? Well, she likes him. Lately she and he have been talking about Paris, she says. He sketched her, and I believe he has finished a couple of paintings."

"Really? Have you seen them?"

"Only briefly, and he said they weren't finished. I think he likes her as a model. He takes great pains with the drawings, and she sits for him for hours."

"Does Philippe paint her too, when she's posing?"

"No. He's never painted her."

"I understood that they painted together, Edgar and Philippe."

"Occasionally, but not often. They talk about painting all the time. Philippe admires your cousin's work and says he will be recognized as a great artist someday."

"Why does he say that?" Estelle asked.

"Because of how original Edgar's work is. Philippe says his compositions are unusual as he usually places the subject on one side of the painting instead of in the middle, which is the conventional way. His bold use of color, especially white. I don't understand all the reasons."

"We all like his work, but we're not artists and don't know how to judge it. Are you saying that Edgar spends a lot of his time with Marguerite?"

"A fair amount, yes. They talk in the parlor, mostly. She has always loved drawing, and he has been helping her."

"I see. Do you suppose she's interested in him?"

"I don't know . . . she's young, and he's more than twice her age," Sophie said, knitting her brows.

"They danced together at the ball; didn't you notice?"

"No. I danced with Philippe most of the time. She's said nothing to me about him except that she likes him, but then perhaps she wouldn't."

"Why not?"

"Because I've told her she's too young for him, and besides, he's French."

"So what? She could do worse, and if she wants to see Paris, she would have an opportunity."

"Only if they marry, and I'm against that idea."

"Well, if I were you, I'd watch to be sure she doesn't compromise her reputation," Estelle said gravely.

"You're right. I'll have a talk with her," Sophie said, "though I don't suppose that matters, since he's gone back to France."

"But he hasn't gone. He missed his train, and plans to stay for a while."

"Oh . . . well, Philippe will be pleased. So will Marguerite. So am I, for that matter. We all like him."

At dinner time Sophie rose to go home.

Estelle mused about the conversation for a while. She realized that Sophie didn't know much about her daughter's relationship with Edgar. However, the fact that they had spent time together— possibly a lot of time—explained the closeness she had observed at the ball. She perceived a romance in the making; however, it would probably not develop if Sophie opposed the match. Edgar could certainly take care of himself, and she would not mention the matter to him. She wondered how Edgar would amuse himself for the next few weeks. Would he paint the family as he had said, or would he prefer to spend his time with Marguerite?

Chapter 29

December 1970

Dressed in a skirt and blouse, her hair tied into a loose braid, Anne strode to Peter Knight's office and knocked at the door.

"Come in," he said.

"Good morning, Peter. Do you have a minute? I need to talk to you about something important."

"Have a seat. What's up? Couldn't you talk to Mary about this?"

"I'd rather not," Anne said. "Remember I told you yesterday that Sam Mollineux had a painting in his office that belonged to me? Well, while I was trying to find it, I saw another painting, one identical to the one of Estelle that the museum owns. Do you know if anyone had permission to copy it?"

"I don't, but the director would. Before I ask, perhaps we should take a look at it."

"Is Sam in his office? If so, we can't do that."

"I'll see."

Peter knocked. Sam called out, "Hold on a minute," then came to the door.

"Ah, Sam. I wanted to see if you were back. How was New York?" Peter said.

"Great. Good trip. You'll hear more about it at the meeting later today."

"Okay. See you then," Peter said.

He returned to his office.

"Sam's there. Anne, are you sure the painting was identical to the one that we have here?" he asked.

"Absolutely," she said. "Now what should we do?"

"I'll find out if the painting is an approved copy," he replied. "If it is, we'll do nothing more. I have no reason to suspect Sam of wrongdoing, you know. He's been a respected member of the staff here for years. I'll get back to you."

Anne returned to her desk crestfallen. She had put herself on the line, and if they found no proof to back up her statement, they would question her credibility. She didn't know what to do next and chastised herself for not bringing her discovery to someone's attention sooner, before Sam's return. Picking up the papers on her desk, she tried to work on her assignment. She waited by the phone on tenterhooks, wishing every second that Peter would call with information. Finally, at four o'clock, the phone rang.

"Peter Knight here. No one has been given permission to copy the painting of Estelle, but we checked Sam's office and didn't find the painting you mentioned. I'm not accusing you of bringing false accusations against anyone, but we have no reason to investigate this matter any further. In the future, you must address any concerns to your supervisor, Mary Wharton."

"I understand. Thank you for letting me know," Anne said.

Putting the phone down, she rested her head in her hands and closed her eyes. She had made a mess of things and began to wonder if she'd had a hallucination and only imagined that she'd seen the painting. She'd been prepared to think the worst of Sam. What would she do now? Perhaps she should resign from the museum. She didn't know what to say to Sam and felt more confused than ever about his character. But she really had seen a painting that resembled the one in the museum and now knew it wasn't an approved copy. She wanted to know the truth.

Chapter 30

January 1873

René arrived early at work the day after Edgar's planned departure.

"I'd like to go over the numbers again," he said to John Livaudais, the accountant. "I know that profits are down, and I want to discuss ways to increase revenues."

John turned to the most recent pages in the ledger. "The numbers don't lie. Not encouraging," he said. "You've missed payments on those loans. When can we expect repayment?"

"Soon. I expect great returns from the cotton futures and from my import–export wine business."

"Look here, René, you've been saying this for years. That's not good enough. I've had several letters from creditors about your new wine business. You drew far too much money from the accounts during your last business trips abroad."

René scowled. "You must trust me," he said. "This is the family's business, after all. Why would I want to ruin it?"

"Why, indeed," John replied, shaking his head.

Achille arrived, lit a cigar, and sat down.

"So we're to have the pleasure of our brother's company for a while longer," he said. "It was a sight to behold, Edgar running after the train, and shouting for it to stop."

"We should put him to work to earn his keep," René replied. "Here he comes, now."

"*Bonjour*," Edgar said. "Is there any mail for me? I need to write to them at home to tell them I have delayed my departure."

"No mail today," René said.

Michel came in and nodded to his nephews without smiling.

"Here," René said, offering a wad of cotton to Edgar, "perhaps you'd like to examine it."

"No, thanks. I have other plans. Today I will do portraits of the men in the family: you, Achille, Michel, and William. What do you think about that?"

"We don't have time to pose, if that's what you want," René said.

"No need for that. I can sketch you all here, at work."

"All right. If you don't distract us, I see no problem," Michel interjected.

René scowled at him, the crease between his brows deepening.

"Excuse me, Uncle, but since when have you supported Edgar's art? If he's here in the office, he should be doing business, not amusing himself making drawings."

Michel glared at René, cleared his throat, and grabbed a handful of cotton.

Edgar positioned himself on a chair by the door and took out his sketchbook. Michel sat down facing him. Wearing his glasses and top hat, he pulled strands of cotton between his fingers. Achille, also wearing a top hat, leaned against the window on the left side of the room. William, half-seated on the table, showed cotton to a customer, and René sat stretched out reading the newspaper, allowing his cigar to hang out of his mouth.

Any visitor glancing around at the family members would discern that they, perhaps unconsciously, had taken typical poses. Anyone looking at them would wonder about the industriousness of the owners, since they all seemed to be relaxing. Edgar would paint the truth about his family's business.

After a few minutes, René put his paper aside and stood up.

"Please sit down; I'm still drawing you with the newspaper," Edgar called.

René sat back down. "I thought you understood we would not pose for you," he said.

"Only if you're working, which you don't appear to be doing," Edgar replied.

After a few minutes René stood up again.

"I can't sit still any longer. I assume you're finished with me," he said.

Edgar nodded and continued working on his drawing. The morning wore on, and soon it was time for lunch.

"I'll take you out; my treat," Edgar offered.

"I accept," René said.

"You go, too, Achille. William and I can stay and mind the business," Michel said.

"I'll take all of you out tomorrow," said Edgar. "I'd like to thank you for your continuing hospitality."

"Much appreciated," said Achille. "Let's go."

They went downstairs into the street and turned toward Antoine's. René allowed Edgar to take the lead. He spoke to Achille beside him.

"I suppose he's at least doing something worthwhile by painting the office. The cotton business is an important part of the family's history, and it'll be good to have it all documented."

"And he's treating us to lunch. I could use a glass or two of good bourbon at his expense," Achille replied, smiling.

Estelle planned a tasty meal in honor of Edgar's extended visit. She sent Clarice with a long shopping list to the French Market: smoked sausage, shrimp, oysters, and any ingredients she could find that would make a delicious jambalaya dish. She knew Edgar liked it. They would have bread pudding for dessert, another favorite. She wondered what meals at the Fontenot residence were like, and if the food there had enticed him to stay for dinner sometimes. There were few cooks to rival Clarice.

Edgar arrived at home. He took off his hat and greeted her as he came in.

"How did your day go, Edgar? What did you do, if I may ask?"

"I started some family portraits at the office," he said. "I find I like the subject, and I'll be able to do a decent painting."

"Only one painting? Aren't you going to do individual portraits of each person?" she asked.

"No. I'll paint the scene just as it is: a cotton office in New Orleans."

"Good. Then it will be a larger work, yes? A masterpiece, perhaps?" she smiled. "Dinner will be ready at six."

"I'll be ready. I've worked up quite an appetite," he said as he disappeared upstairs.

Estelle noted that he seemed in good spirits, and happier than he had been most days after only coming back from the office with his mail. Perhaps at last he had noticed something to paint in New Orleans that he considered worth his time.

For the rest of the month of January, Edgar worked feverishly in his studio. He took breaks and sometimes stayed away for most of the afternoon, but he always returned in time for dinner. His eyes took on a glassy, almost wild appearance.

"Are you still working on the cotton office painting?" Estelle asked one day.

"Yes. It's a more ambitious work than the others I've done recently, but it's giving me more pleasure, and it's coming along well."

"When will it be finished?"

"I don't know. I never think my paintings are finished. There are always improvements to make. It doesn't matter. I often finish paintings later, once I've worked out the basic composition and figures. I'm happy with the figures in this one, so far, and there's a good likeness between them and the subjects."

"When can we see it?"

"Not for a while yet. This is the best painting I've done since I came to New Orleans. I'd like to sell it to a textile manufacturer in England, and I may even do another on the same theme. Now I must go to the office to pick up my mail. I've been neglecting my correspondence."

It thrilled Estelle to see him so positive about his art. She wanted to ask if he had been seeing Marguerite, and if she had anything to do with his changed disposition, but she didn't want to intrude. Meanwhile, February approached, and the christening.

Chapter 34

December 1970

Anne left the museum distraught. She had destroyed her prospective career along with her relationship with Sam. While she now knew she would break up with him, she wished she had used better discretion in the matter of the forged painting. She should have respected the chain of command and told Mary Wharton, and she should have heeded the early warnings about Sam and ended the relationship months before. She had mixed her private and professional lives together as Sam and others had advised her not to do. Too embarrassed to talk to anyone about it all and apprehensive about what would happen during the next few days, she got into her car and drove out of the museum parking lot.

The squeal of brakes pierced through her. She had driven straight through a stop sign, causing the car in the intersection to nearly collide with her. The driver wound down his window and yelled obscenities at her. She drove on, vowing to be more careful, and parked the car. As she approached the house she stopped, changed her mind, and turned toward the Black Cat bar. She needed a drink.

The waiter passed by her table.

"What'll it be, young lady?" he said.

"A Sazerac, please."

She wondered why she ordered that drink, her celebratory cocktail. This was anything but a celebration, but perhaps she had been given a signpost to pursue a different course. She didn't enjoy the museum work, and Sam was part of that world. She could give up both and start again, making better choices next time. The more she considered it, the more appealing the idea became. After two drinks, her confidence rose. She knew her stubborn nature caused her to resist following advice, but she might have to swallow her pride and do what others expected of her, at least until she found her feet. Why had she defied Sam for so long and refused to dress up for her internship, a privileged position? Clothes mattered; she could make that correction relatively easily. Acquiring better judgment, particularly where men were concerned, would be more challenging. However, now she had more experience and would heed warning signs in the future. She had always been a dreamer and avoided facing the truth. It was time to renovate herself, along with her outdated house.

A man's voice called her name, catching her attention. Homer smiled at her.

"Hello there, missy. What brings you here, drinkin' by yerself? Mind if I join you?"

"I'm leaving in a minute, but you're welcome to have my table," she said.

He sat down, called the waiter, and ordered a bourbon and Coke.

"'Twas yer grandfather's favorite drink," he said. "In the old days we had 'em often, before he went sour, that is. Sat on the porch, summer evenings."

"I didn't know you were so friendly," she said.

"Yep, for a while. He changed after the girl had her baby. That was yer mother, I reckon. Didn't approve. I heard the shoutin' and wailin' though the walls. Sent her packin', he did. Now his sister, she were a fine lady. She were heartbroken when your mom left home."

"I'm familiar with most of this story, but thank you for telling me," Anne said.

"Runs in the family," he said.

"What runs in the family?"

"Bad behavior. Marguerite had trouble, too."

Anne sat forward.

"Marguerite? I know a little about her. Did my grandfather talk to you about her?"

"She were his aunt, very beautiful, I understand. Dunno if she ever got married. Always wanted to go to Paris, but the parents wouldn't allow it."

"What happened to her?"

"Dunno. Died, I guess."

"That's a good guess. Do you know anything more about her?"

"I do, a bit. Etienne said she were like yer mother. Loose, like."

Anne remembered her mother, pregnant with Stella at age fifteen, the result of a liaison with an artist, a man of a different race. But surely Marguerite hadn't misbehaved.

"What did Marguerite do to make my grandfather disapprove, if you don't mind my asking," Anne said cautiously.

"She were friends with that French painter, the one that lived here fer a while. Etienne said she sat for him, buck nekkid."

"How would he know that?" Anne asked.

"Think her dad found a drawin'. Destroyed it, a course."

He grinned and winked. Anne scraped her chair back and stood up. Then she sat back down.

"I want to thank you, Mr. Jackson. You've told me a lot about my family, and I appreciate that," she said. "Please allow me to pay for your drink."

He smiled. "Much obliged," he said then moved closer and spoke again, lowering his gravelly voice.

"There's more. Didn't wanna tell you before, but I saw someone near yer house. Someone bad."

"Really? When was this?"

"It were the night before the police came. Before you put that alarm in. Man had a sledge hammer."

Anne's pulse beat faster. "Oh my God. The vandal," she said. "Can you describe him, what he looked like?"

"Big with a dark face. Think he had a scar on his cheek. Scary. Acted drunk. Couldn't walk straight."

"I wish you had called the police," Anne said. "Perhaps they could have caught him."

Homer shook his head. "Them types, they mean. Take it out on old folks, if you know what I'm sayin'."

"So you were scared. Well, that makes sense."

"I think you need to move into that house o' yers. Never liked it empty."

"Do you really think it's haunted?" she asked.

"Nah. Only needs to be lived in. Old place is lonely."

"I agree. The work will be done soon, and I'll move in. I'll be glad to have you as a neighbor."

"That's all right then, missy," he said, with a small grin. "I'll keep an eye on things till then."

"Thank you," she said, leaving money on the table for the drinks as she left.

Now she had a clue about the vandal's identity, but not enough to report him to the police. At least, whoever it was had done no more damage to the house. If Homer's story about Marguerite was true, that would explain Degas's sudden departure without saying good-bye to her or her family. *What a scandal.* She felt acutely sorry for the girl. She hurried home, newly motivated to finish reading Marguerite's journal, which she had put aside during the previous busy weeks. When she got there, she found Sam sitting on the front steps.

"Where have you been? I've been calling for hours. I got worried."

"Hello, Sam," she said.

"Let's have dinner."

"I'm not hungry. We can talk here."

Weak-kneed, she was glad she had fortified herself with two drinks. This would be difficult.

"Well, I'm starving. Let's go to Camellia Grill."

"Really, I'd rather not go out anywhere. I need to talk to you."

"Hey, what's going on? You look like you've been hit by a thunderbolt," he said, reaching for her hand. She pulled away from him.

"Perhaps I have," she said gravely.

"Out with it. I'm all ears," he said.

She took a slow breath and met his eyes.

"Sam, I uncovered an original painting of Estelle in your office, a duplicate of the one in the museum. I didn't mean to pry. I only wanted to locate the painting of Sophie to mark it with my name. The Estelle painting seems to have vanished, so I have no proof that it was there, but I have to tell you that I reported it."

He blinked. "Oh, that painting. It's an authorized copy. Did you think it's a forgery?"

"I did, and I believe it is. The museum director said they had not given anyone permission to copy it."

Sam inhaled deeply.

"I just got back to town. No one has said anything to me about this. Are you sure it's not all in your imagination? You're out of touch, you know, sometimes."

"You'll probably hear about this tomorrow. By the time I reported it, the painting had disappeared from your office."

"Ah, so now I understand. You're in trouble because you blew the whistle when nothing was wrong. Bad move, Anne."

She shook her head.

"I'd like to know the truth. What did you have to do with the forgery?"

"There's nothing to tell. I don't know anything about a forgery."

"Well, I'm sorry you have so many secrets. I don't know you, and will never trust you, so I'm afraid I can't see you anymore."

Sam sat silent for a minute, and a muscle twitched in his cheek. "Very well," he said, and walked down the steps.

"Nice knowing you," he called. "Have a good life."

She watched him go, reeling as though it had all been a bad dream in slow motion. Then she raced up to her room and threw herself down on her bed, weeping uncontrollably.

Chapter 32

January–February 1873

Chaos reigned at the office. Papers lay on the floor, and the pile of cotton on the table spilled untidily over the edge.

"You've made terrible investments, everyone knows that," René shouted at Michel. *"These Confederate bonds are worthless."*

"Who are you to talk, with all those loans against the business?" Michel retorted. "John said you promised to repay them, but so far we've seen not one nickel from you. You're reckless and irresponsible!"

René grabbed his uncle by the shoulders to shake him, but quickly let go when he saw Edgar staring at him.

"Business is difficult, sometimes," he said. "I'm going for a stroll."

Michel shrugged and glanced at Edgar.

"He's a hothead, that brother of yours," he said. Edgar made no reply, picked up some letters, and turned to leave.

On the last day of January, Michel gathered the family together at the Musson household, saying he had an announcement. Everyone assembled in the parlor after dinner. He looked grim.

"Some of you know already, but I want to tell you myself that a notice will appear in tomorrow's newspaper that the firm of Musson, Prestidge, and Company will be dissolved as of February first, 1873. We're bankrupt."

Estelle and Désirée burst into tears. They had known of the increasing problems with the business, but it was hard to hear the words. William and Achille looked at their feet, and René gazed through the window. Edgar regarded them open-mouthed.

"*Comment?*" he said. "This cannot be true; I had no idea. *Terrible! Impossible!*"

"It has been coming for some time," Michel said. "I am so very sorry, but as you know, business has been declining since the war, and not only for us. Everything is changing. Cotton prices have fallen, cotton exports are reduced, and the expansion of the railroad and telegraph systems has undermined our factorage system of selling our wares. Small family businesses have suffered because cotton can be exchanged and purchased more efficiently by telegraph. I don't want to bore you with details and reasons, ladies, but rest assured that I'll do my best to find another business to invest in. We won't starve."

No one spoke, and each family member stood up slowly, embraced Michel, and left. Edgar sat white-faced until he was the only one in the room besides his uncle.

"What about Désirée, Estelle, and the children? How will they eat?"

"As I said, we won't starve. I still have resources, and we can always move to a smaller house. As you may be aware, we don't own this one," he said.

"I heard," Edgar said. "This disturbs me more than I can say. I'll go home; I don't want to impose any further on your hospitality."

"There's no rush," Michel said.

"I'm so sorry," Edgar said.

Head bowed, he ambled out of the room and up to his studio.

The christening took place on February fifth. Edgar stood up as godfather, and all the relatives gathered at the church. The Fontenot family attended. After the short ceremony, everyone returned to the house for coffee and pastry. Michel had instructed the men to say nothing about the family's financial misfortune, and no one else at the small gathering could have guessed about the dismal state of affairs.

"Are you coming to the ball next week?" Sophie asked Estelle.

"No. We've done enough celebrating for Mardi Gras already," she said.

"No one's ever done celebrating Mardi Gras," her friend answered. "Please come. We can all go together. It will cheer everyone up. I've noticed that René and Michel look sad, even though the christening is a happy occasion. They need cheering up. Edgar liked the last ball, too."

"You're right. Perhaps everyone does need entertainment. I've always considered Mardi Gras to be an antidote for sadness. I'll talk to them. They can be cockroaches and grasshoppers again."

"Let me know."

Marguerite stood nearby and seemed to be following the conversation. She said nothing, but Estelle saw her brighten when they talked about the ball. She would want to dance with Edgar again, of course.

Later that evening Estelle approached René.

"Sophie asked if we're planning to attend the ball next week. We should go. What do you say?"

"I say no. We don't need to spend more money just now."

"The Fontenots invited us to go with them. I think we will be their guests."

"*No,* I said. I don't want to rely on others' charity," René growled.

"What about Edgar? He's not responsible for the business problems, and he might enjoy going again."

"Well, let him go. He can be their guest."

"I'll suggest it," Estelle said.

Her heart sank. She knew her husband was distraught about the failed business, and she didn't want to injure his pride further by bringing the matter up, but she knew there would be hard times ahead.

Edgar continued to work on his painting of the cotton office and accepted the Fontenots' invitation to attend the ball.

Two weeks later Estelle met Sophie for tea at the Fontenots' house.

"How did you like the ball, Sophie?" Estelle asked.

"Very well, but not as much as the first one. Only the three of us were there, you know, and Edgar."

"Did Philippe wear his spider costume? Did the men parade around the room again?"

"Yes, Philippe dressed up, but there was no parade. Some actors presented a tableau, and we enjoyed dancing. We missed you."

"I assume Edgar danced with Marguerite."

"He did. They seem to get along well. I had a talk with her, and she says she likes him better than any of the men her age she has met. She's invited to a lot of parties, you know, now that she's out in society. She's very popular."

"No surprise there."

"I tell her she needs to meet a lot of young men, but she's resistant. She says she'd rather learn about drawing from Edgar. He brought her a bouquet of calla lilies last time he visited. They're her favorite flowers."

"*Mon Dieu.* Are you concerned about this friendship? Do you think he's courting her?"

Sophie looked uncomfortable. "I don't know."

"He'll be leaving for Paris soon, I believe," Estelle said.

"Will he? Perhaps that's for the best."

"If it's any consolation, I don't think he'll let anything interfere with his art. I'm now convinced this is the reason he hasn't married."

"You may be right, but he said something strange the other day. He said marriage might be a good idea because it would free him from the need to be gallant. What do you suppose he meant by that?"

Estelle thought for a few minutes before she answered.

"That etiquette is more important for people in society who are single. René told me he has quite a reputation for rudeness in Paris. He comes from a family of good standing, and is well versed in society's ways, but he may chafe at the requirements. He's an artist, after all, a freethinker."

"That's part of what bothers me," Sophie said. "Between you and me, he's not the best prospect for my daughter."

"I understand," Estelle said, "but if he's interested in marriage, he'll have to ask her father for her hand first, anyway."

"True, and Philippe may not agree. He and Edgar had a falling out recently."

"How so? I wasn't aware of that."

"I don't imagine it's something Edgar would want to talk to you about, and I believe they have patched things up now, anyway."

Estelle walked the short distance home after thanking her friend for the visit. So, Edgar did appear to be courting Marguerite. He had said nothing to anyone about this, as far as she knew, and he had mentioned no disagreement with Philippe. She wondered how much longer he would stay in New Orleans, and if he would propose marriage before he left. But how could he, when the family's fortunes were lost?

Chapter 33

January 1971

*A*nne's stomach felt queasy. She had no doubts about her decision to end the relationship with Sam, but how could she face him and everyone else at the museum when she had disgraced herself by reporting the forgery? She called Mary Wharton to tell her she wouldn't be coming into the office that day.

"Why not? You can't keep taking days off. You have work to do," Mary said.

"I understand, but after recent events, I may not be able to continue my job, and I'm not feeling well."

"That's up to you, but there's no reason for you to quit."

Anne hung up the phone. Obviously, Mary hadn't heard the news, or if she had, she wasn't letting on. Strange.

She stayed in bed until noon, when a shower revived her enough for a walk in Audubon Park, a haven she often sought when trying to work out problems. She sat for a while and gazed at the green lawns, lakes, and live oaks smothered with moss. Mist hovered above the ground, softening the contours and creating an atmosphere of tranquility, just as the three shades of white paint inside the house were supposed to do. *Soulful ambience,* Andrea had called it. Anne wanted to experience it and tame her chronic anxiety. Strolling through the park, she reached the river. It flowed like molasses, its surface shining silver in the diffused sunlight. An egret flapped by, head pulled in tight against his shoulder.

She knew she had made many mistakes and would live with the effects for a long time. Her mind ran through an inventory of recent problems. At least Stella had resolved one for her: she had sent Anne a note that day saying she'd changed her plans, had a new place to live, and no longer wished to move into the Esplanade house. Sam was out of her life. Both actions had left her with a sense of remorse. Despite her desire to make amends for the blatant racism that had cut Stella out of her grandfather's will, she had failed to make a good connection with her. Did she bear the responsibility for that, or was Stella too resentful to forgive and to accept overtures of friendship?

She had waited too long to read the signs that Sam was not trustworthy. If she had broken up with him earlier, she might not have discovered the forgery and would not now be losing her job. As for her career, she couldn't see any positive outcome at the museum. Even if she didn't want to continue in that line of work, a false accusation was an embarrassment that would damage her reputation. No one would take her word over Sam's about the forgery, and she had broken a cardinal rule by going above her boss's head.

She gazed up at the Spanish moss dripping from oaks above her. It was an epiphytic, she remembered from a botany class, living on the surface of trees. None of the oaks objected to its presence. Why? Maybe because the gray moss added an element of mystery but did no damage and had nothing nefarious to hide. Perhaps that explained in part her attraction to Sam: his outward appearance pleased her, as did the mystery surrounding him, but not in bad ways until she learned about the forgery. She had uncovered the truth at last, and now she needed to consider her job, and the repercussions. As she retraced her steps home, she could come up with no better solution than going to work the following day with a letter of resignation.

She read Marguerite's journal to pass the time.

February 17, 1873

Edgar is so romantic! He brought me a bouquet of white calla lilies yesterday. He told me they're not as beautiful as I am, that he should have brought roses instead. I like lilies better, myself. Their lines are cleaner, and they're easier to draw. I couldn't help throwing my arms around his neck when he gave me the flowers. Perhaps I shouldn't have—Maman tells me always to let a man take the lead in showing physical affection—but I don't think he minded. He kissed me on my forehead. Sometimes I worry that he sees me as a child, young and inexperienced. But he tells me that's what appeals to him: I have the freshness of a spring morning in Paris. Paris! How I wish he would take me there. He has told me about the wide boulevards, boating parties, and the wonderful opera and ballet performances. We usually sit in the parlor when he visits in the afternoons. Sometimes Maman is out, and we can sit close together on the sofa. My heart pounds so loudly I'm afraid he will hear it.

Last week he told me he will be coming less often, not because he doesn't want to see me, but because he has started work on an important painting of his family's cotton business. His beautiful eyes glow when he tells me about his progress, the colors he uses, the layers of paint that he applies. I've never seen him so excited about a painting. He wants to sell it in England. I asked him why this one is special, and he said it tells a story, and until now he has mostly painted smaller individual family portraits, not larger scenes. Estelle has encouraged him, he says. He admires her so much and has painted her several times. She doesn't have much time to pose for him, and once he sketched her while she arranged flowers in a vase. I wish I could see these paintings, but he tells me they're not finished.

The hours fly by when we're together—he must think so too, as he often jumps up and looks at his pocket watch when he leaves, asking where the light went.

Anne took a deep breath. So, a romantic relationship had developed between Marguerite and the painter, and now she had learned more about Degas's work, including the portrait of Estelle arranging flowers, the wonderful painting that would cost Anne her job. She closed her eyes for a minute, then continued reading.

February 19, 1873
Maman talked to me today about Edgar. Estelle has noticed our close friendship and expressed concern about my reputation. Maman warned me to protect myself from gossip and said if my reputation is lost, it might hurt my chances for a good marriage. She respects and admires Estelle, who graciously accepts her increasing blindness and family misfortunes without complaining. I suppose I should heed her warning. But how can I resist dear Edgar's attention?

March 3, 1873
I hardly know what to write. I'm afraid Maman will never forgive me if she reads these words so I'm hiding this book in the attic.

Papa found one of Edgar's drawings yesterday, a woman with no clothes on. Papa thought it was me. It wasn't, but he wouldn't believe Edgar, or me. He held the picture up and yelled at poor Edgar. He tried to explain that it was a sketch of someone he had known in Paris, but Papa wouldn't listen and said he would meet Edgar at dawn in the park and for him to bring his weapon. Edgar said, "Take a hold of yourself, this is ridiculous nonsense. You're an artist, you know better." I may have fainted because the next thing I remember is sitting in the bathtub with Nicole scrubbing my back. Maman doesn't know, or if she does, she hasn't said anything. This is terrible. Everything is ruined.

Anne put the journal down. In 1873 if Marguerite had posed naked and anyone knew, this would have destroyed her reputation and chances for marriage. Had Philippe fought a duel to defend his daughter's honor? She guessed not, since both had lived on. Either that, or both were terrible shots. She felt enormous sympathy for the girl. Had she married? Homer didn't know, and there were no more entries in her journal after that spring. Anne sincerely hoped that Marguerite had recovered from her youthful love affair and married a worthy husband, though she suspected that Edgar would remain in her heart forever.

But what impressed her most was Estelle's abiding concern for the welfare of those she loved despite her many challenges. Anne felt ashamed. She had been selfishly preoccupied with her recent problems, many of which she had brought on herself. She needed to take a leaf from Estelle's book and find her own source of strength.

Chapter 34

March 1873

*M*ardi Gras was over. The big celebration dubbed Fat Tuesday took place without the De Gas and Musson families' participation in either the grand parade or final ball on February twenty-fifth. The failure of the business had taken its toll, and no one felt festive. Also, the news about the bankruptcy had spread, and the family wished to stay out of the limelight.

Estelle understood that her husband cared deeply about the tragedy and that, even if he didn't talk about it, was acutely aware of his part in bringing financial ruin on the family. Her father shared the blame with his bad investments in Confederate bonds. Estelle feared for her children's future.

She expected that Edgar would leave soon. He had been spending hours in his studio painting the cotton office. There was still something feverish about him. One morning, she saw him sitting in the parlor looking dispirited.

"Edgar, what's wrong?" she asked.

He raised his eyes. "I've booked my passage back to France. I leave tomorrow."

"So soon?"

"It's time, for several reasons." He lowered his gaze. "I don't wish to impose myself on you all any longer, and I don't wish to bring shame on you all. I've finished as much of the cotton office paintings as I can. Perhaps I can sell the bigger painting and be of some help to the family."

"Dearest Edgar, how kind you are," she said gently. "How could you bring shame on us? Have you told the others you're leaving?"

"No. You're the first to know. I don't want any fuss, only a ride to the train, which I won't miss this time."

"I'm so sorry about the way things have turned out," Estelle said.

"Me too. Sorry for you, my dear cousin . . . and about your eyes."

"Don't worry about me. I have become accustomed to my failing eyesight. I do quite well, as you've seen, and I'll always be able to see in my mind's eye the things of beauty in this world—the palm trees with their green fronds, the roses, the golden evening light, the faces of my children, even your wonderful paintings. No, especially your wonderful paintings. I know you paint things as they are, Edgar, and I expect that you will soon be recognized as a great artist."

His face softened, and a tear ran down his cheek.

"Thank you for your belief in me, and for the generous words," he said, looking up at her. "I'm so pleased to have spent this time with you. No one else has cared about me with such—with almost motherly concern. Rest assured that I'll look out for you in the future and ensure that your welfare is protected."

"You are dear to me, too, *mon cousin*," she said, moving to embrace him.

They stood with their arms around each other for a while. Estelle hoped he would talk more to her about the reason he wanted to leave so abruptly and wondered if it involved the fallout with Philippe. She didn't want to pry, but did want to understand.

She said in a small voice, "Edgar, have you said good-bye to Marguerite?"

He started, and a flush spread across his cheeks.

"No. Philippe has forbidden me to talk to her. Let me just say that we had a misunderstanding."

Estelle observed his embarrassment and wanted to learn more, but held her tongue.

"Will you write to her?" she asked.

"I plan to. She's a lovely young woman, and I admit I was captivated by her, almost mesmerized, in fact . . . but the life of an artist is not one easily shared with another. I need time for my art, and I'm on the brink of doing some good work. I'd like to sell some of it and help ease your financial burdens. I can work better in Paris, and it's time to go home."

"I understand," Estelle whispered.

"Good-bye, my dear," he said at last.

"Will Achille take you to the train again?" she asked.

"I haven't asked him yet, but I will. He's less distracted these days than René seems to be."

"Yes. René has taken the news very hard. How are you planning to announce your departure to everyone?"

"I'll tell them at dinner tonight. Don't go to any special trouble with the meal. I've already packed my things and arranged for the paintings to be sent on."

"Very well."

Edgar spent the rest of the day in his room, only reappearing for dinner. He left the next morning with Achille. No one expressed regret to see him go, and his uncle and brothers sighed with relief.

Estelle called on her friend Sophie the following day. They sat in the Fontenots' front room.

"This is a pleasant surprise; what brings you here, my friend?" Sophie said, offering tea.

"Edgar has gone home. He left yesterday."

"What? He left without saying good-bye? Why? *Mon Dieu*! Now I understand what's wrong with Marguerite. She's been crying for days. I wonder if she knew he planned to go. I'll have to talk to her."

"So, he didn't propose, then," said Estelle.

"Well, if he did, she didn't accept."

"You must be relieved," Estelle said. "I'll go now. I only wanted to bring you the news. You'll be wanting to spend time with Marguerite."

"Yes. Thank you for coming," Sophie said, and escorted her friend to the door.

On the way home, Estelle thought they might never know what had happened between Edgar and Marguerite. She believed he cared about Marguerite, but accepted his explanation that he was first and foremost an artist. He needed to return to Paris to continue to paint with a plan of earning his living and contributing to the family's expenses. She liked him the better for it and felt satisfied that he had left having accomplished at least one work while in New Orleans that he considered worthwhile. She remembered his words: *Only if I can face the truth about something important will I be able to create a great painting.* He had learned the truth about the family's lost fortunes at last. She remained convinced that because of this understanding, he had created an important work of art.

Estelle opened the front door to her home. How much longer would they live there? And René, so proud, how would he hold his head up now that the business had failed? How would he support her and the children? Despite his flirtation with America, she, Estelle, was his wife. She would do her best to reawaken his interest in her. It would be easier, now that she was no longer pregnant. She resolved to remake some of her finer dresses. That would be less expensive than buying new ones, in addition to making her more stylish. And she would sing again, alone this time, with him accompanying her on the piano.

Chapter 35

January 1974

*D*ressed in a suit, Anne arrived at work with her letter of resignation. She wanted to leave her desk in good order before
she left, so she was sorting out the papers cluttering the top when
her phone rang.

"Anne, Tom McDermott here. Could you stop by my office,
please?"

"Yes, sir," she said, surprised. Why did the museum director
want to see her? She hoped she would not get a dressing down.
Clasping the letter in shaking hands, she told herself not to drop
it. She hoped to leave her job with as much dignity as possible. She
stood tall but advanced with sinking spirits to the director's office.

"Come in," he said, after the secretary announced her arrival.
"Take a seat, here on the couch."

She sat down, and he eased himself into a stuffed chair at
her side.

"I want to thank you for reporting the forged painting of
Estelle De Gas," he said.

Anne gasped. "Oh, I thought I'd made . . . um, you'd made . . .
or rather, you thought I'd made a mistake," she stammered.

"It appeared that way at first, but Mary Wharton discovered the painting. It was most definitely a forgery, and a good one, that seems to have been executed at the request of Sam Mollineux."

Her mouth dropped open, and she stared at him wide-eyed. "How did Mary find the painting, and how did she know about the forgery?"

"Turns out Mary had suspected Sam of wrongdoing for a long time. You may be aware that she and he were an item a few years back. They broke up, rather publicly and with some bitterness, I understand. I'm not privy to all the details, but it seems that while she and Sam were together, she noticed a stranger spending a lot of time looking at the museum's painting of Estelle. Sometime later, at Sam's house, the same person turned up. Sam tried to shoo him away. She recognized that same man when he came into the museum two days ago carrying what looked like a painting. Her suspicions aroused, and realizing that Sam was away, Mary got a key to his office, located the forgery, and removed it. Like you, she recognized it right away as a replica of the museum's painting."

"Amazing! A forgery, just as I thought. What has happened to Sam?"

"He's disappeared. We don't know where he is, but we've alerted the police and the FBI."

"Sir, I may be wrong, but there may be a conflict of interest by the FBI," she said.

"How so?"

"I believe he works for them."

"Is that so? Interesting. Well, that's their affair. Anyway, he's no longer working for the museum."

"How authentic is the forgery?" she asked.

"Impressively authentic. The forger used French oil paints that would almost pass for those used by Degas. Mary said they must have been smuggled into the country, because otherwise customs would have confiscated them."

Anne inhaled deeply and raised her hands to her mouth.

"I may have the answer to that question," she said. "A friend of mine saw a man who resembled Sam on the riverbank late at night last October. He received a package thrown to him from a boat. Perhaps the paints. . . ."

"Good heavens!" he interrupted her. "Cloak and dagger stuff. Very puzzling—shocking—the whole thing."

"But why on earth would Sam order a forged painting?" she asked.

"Mary says he made a deal with the donors, the ones who gave the money that enabled the museum to purchase the painting of Estelle. Sam got credit for arranging the last-minute donation, and the museum hired him. Apparently, he agreed to give the donors the original painting in exchange for their generous gift. He planned to replace it with the forged painting. He was running out of time, and the donors were becoming impatient. Sam may have feared for his life."

Anne nodded. Perhaps that explained why he carried a gun.

"Thank you for telling me all of this," she said.

"I'm sorry if you thought we distrusted you when you reported the forgery, but you can understand why we didn't believe you. Mary must have taken the picture between the time that you saw it and Peter went to look for it."

"Yes. That would explain the timing. I waited until the next day to report it, and I shouldn't have," she said.

"Don't worry about it. We're glad we saved our original. Forgeries, if they're good, sometimes take a long time to be recognized, sometimes never. If Sam had replaced the original with the forgery, we might not have noticed until it was too late. It's happened before, even at the best museums."

"Goodness, I had no idea," she said.

"Thanks again for your help," he said. "Keep up the good work."

As she stood up to leave, she saw a painting on the wall. It depicted her own street, Esplanade Avenue.

"What a lovely painting," Anne said, turning to face the Director. "Who's the artist?"

"I am," he said, smiling.

"Excuse me, but if you're a painter, why are you working at the museum?" she asked.

"Ah, that's easy. How many artists are like Degas, and how many make a living painting? Even he struggled at first. Most artists these days have a day job."

"You're right, of course."

She smiled her thanks and left the office. Now what should she do? Sam had gone, but should she resign? Not yet, anyway. She needed the income. She tore the letter of resignation in two, tossed it into a nearby wastebasket, and glided back to her desk.

At home that evening, she could hardly make out how her fortunes had changed for the better. One question remained, however: what to do about Stella. They needed to talk. Stella accepted her invitation to meet for lunch.

They sat together at the Black Cat on a rainy Saturday morning. Many people around them were wearing costumes before heading out to watch the Mardi Gras parade later that day. Stella had dressed as she had most of the other times Anne had met her: in stylish, conservative clothes that suited her. Her hair, however, seemed fuller, Afro style. Anne wore her usual blue jeans. She fiddled with her napkin and cleared her throat as she faced her sister.

"Thank you for coming," she said. "I wanted to see you again and apologize for the awful scene at the restaurant last time we met. I hope your hand and arm have recovered."

Stella gave her a feeble smile.

"They have," Stella said. "Thanks for asking. I'll admit your reaction to my telling you I'm a friend of Mary Wharton's surprised me, but I shouldn't have been so insensitive myself. You graciously invited me to dinner at a fine restaurant, and you had good intentions. I'll admit I've been the target of prejudice over the years, and I bear some resentment at the way I've been treated, but I'm not vengeful.

Anne listened carefully. Stella seemed to be telling the truth matter-of-factly, without hostility.

"I'm sympathetic, as I hope you know," Anne said. "People should get along, regardless of race, but perhaps that's a naive view."

"I agree. People should get along and treat each other with consideration, but not everyone shares that opinion. Look at the urban renewal projects, for example. Are you aware of what's going on there?" Stella asked.

"I am now, though I didn't used to be. I admit I've been naive. In college, I focused on school and ignored what was happening in the world outside. I didn't even get involved, as many students did, in protests about the war in Vietnam. I painted a lot. It's easy to lose yourself in art—in fact, that's one of the best things about it. But now I've started a series of paintings of buildings and inhabitants in the Tremé because I want to illustrate and record the destruction of homes there."

"Really?" Stella's eyes lit up. "Well, that's cool. We didn't talk about this before, but I'm involved in a preservation group. We're trying to save areas like that from destruction. It's where I used to live. There are some historic buildings there, many as important culturally speaking as the ones on Esplanade Avenue."

"There are, and I'd like to help with that preservation effort."

Stella smiled. "So we agree. I imagined you had no clue about what's been going on. Mary and I work all the time, trying to raise awareness."

"I didn't know that. I guess she and Sam have ended their friendship, such as it was."

"Yes, and I heard about Sam and the forgery. Bummer. Must've been difficult for you," Stella said.

"It was, but I learned something from the experience. I broke up with him. I believe I dodged a bullet."

"We all dodge bullets sometimes. I've made my own mistakes and have had threats from people I should've known to avoid. Mary told me Sam works for the FBI and would never marry because of his work."

"I suspected as much. What threats?"

"I had a boyfriend once who dealt drugs. Scary. Had to get a dog for protection. He'd show up in the middle of the night, banging on the door. Crazed out of his mind."

"I agree. Very scary. Just curious, did he know about your plans to move into my house?"

"Let me think. Yes, I was seeing him when we talked about that. . . ." She hesitated. "Oh, I guess I know where you're going with this: perhaps he was responsible for the vandalism. Well, it's possible. He sometimes got violent when he used drugs."

Anne inhaled deeply. "I'd love to know who the culprit is. What did your boyfriend look like?"

"Darker skin than mine, and muscular."

"Did he have a scar on his face?"

"Yes. From an old fight. On his cheek. Why do you ask?"

"My neighbor saw a man on the night of the vandalism at the house who fits that description. Is he around?"

"No. He died of an overdose two months ago."

"Oh. Were you still seeing him?"

"No. We had broken up."

Stella's shoulders slumped. She stared down at the table.

"I'm sorry," Anne said.

The waiter came to take their order.

"We need more time, please," Anne said. "Actually, I'm not hungry."

"Me neither," Stella said. "We've both had our problems, I guess."

"People need to talk honestly if they're going to be true friends," Anne said.

"You're right. I'll admit I didn't tell you much about myself before, but I wanted you to like me, to feel we were sisters."

"Same with me. And I do like you. We need to get to know one another better, that's all."

Stella met Anne's eyes. "I hope that we will be friends and love each other as sisters, but I've decided I can't move into the house."

Anne met her gaze. "I've come to the same conclusion. Our lives are too different. Maybe someday . . . but it doesn't mean we can't be friends, as you've said."

"Right. I'd like to be your friend, sister Anne."

"And you will be. This is a good beginning."

They grasped hands across the table and smiled at one another.

Chapter 36

June 1971

*W*earing her suit, Anne walked up to the podium at the
Isaac Delgado Museum of Art in New Orleans. She
had been invited to talk to the curators about her painting, her
great-great-grandfather Philippe's portrait of her great-great-
grandmother Sophie Fontenot. The museum planned to exhibit
it, and the curators wanted to know the story behind it. Anne had
invited her father to the presentation. The director introduced her
as an intern who had completed a year's work at the museum and
who had restored and now lived in her Creole ancestors' house on
Esplanade Avenue. Anne held up Marguerite's diary.

"First, I'd like to say that if I hadn't discovered this journal
in my attic, stories about Philippe and Sophie Fontenot would
have disappeared into thin air, along with information about my
family's connection with Edgar Degas. He stayed a few houses
away when he visited in 1872 and '73, and the two families established a friendship. As most of you know, Degas had a special
fondness for his sister-in-law Estelle, whose portrait hangs in the
museum. She influenced his career, and if Degas hadn't painted

her and other family members while in New Orleans, they would have been lost to us as well, and he might never have achieved the fame that *A Cotton Office* afforded him."

She went on to summarize other information she had learned from the journal. Enthusiastic applause followed her presentation, and she answered the audience's questions. A man asked about her plans for the future.

"I'll stay on for another year at the museum, but with reduced hours. I'll be working with Peter Knight on the upcoming Degas exhibit. The new schedule will allow me time to complete paintings of buildings that are being demolished and of inhabitants who are being displaced because of the urban renewal projects in the city. I've received a few commissions for this work and hope for more."

Mary Wharton spoke up.

"Excuse me, but isn't that a bit hypocritical, to create paintings to raise consciousness about the lack of public housing when you're obviously living in luxurious accommodations, yourself?"

Anne took a sip of water, cleared her throat and composed herself. She spoke out in a clear voice. "I hoped someone would ask me that question. I've decided that destroying beautiful houses with historic value doesn't improve anything. It's like, uh, throwing the baby out with the bathwater, to use a trite expression." She paused. "Please excuse that one—my best friend has just had a baby. Let me rephrase. I think both are important: preserving great buildings of artistic value and keeping less affluent historical neighborhoods intact as well. Community and culture are shaped by many levels of prosperity."

She caught Mary's eye and observed a flicker of a smile.

After she had answered a few more questions, the audience applauded, and she stepped down from the podium. Her father rushed to meet her.

"A fine presentation. I'm proud of you," he said, giving her a hug.

"Thanks, Dad. I think it went well."

"Let me treat you to a meal to celebrate. I'd guess you might miss those good dinners these days. At least, I hope you miss the food more than . . . uh, that young man of yours."

"Sam, you mean. Don't worry. I'm glad he's gone. Disappeared, probably undercover. I'm not sitting home much these days, and I have occasional invitations for meals."

"I must say, I'm relieved to hear this," François said. "Now, where shall we go?"

They decided on Antoine's, one of François's favorite restaurants.

After dinner, they returned to Anne's house. They mounted the freshly painted steps of her front porch and entered the house. Several of her mother's paintings hung in the hallway beside two of her own cemetery paintings.

"It's really wonderful, everything that you've done here," François said approvingly, as he glanced around. "You've managed to create a beautiful home out of that mangled old dwelling. I love the inviting warmth. Must be the color of the walls."

She smiled with satisfaction. "I'm glad you like it. Come and stay whenever you want. I'll show you to your room."

They climbed the stairs to the second floor. The bathroom door stood open, the new fixtures gleaming white. Anne smiled to herself with a deep sense of pleasure that the work had recreated such a lovely home, one worthy of her ancestors' early investment.

"I'll turn in now, if you don't mind. It's been a long day," François said.

She kissed him lightly on the cheek. "See you in the morning," she said.

Grateful for a few minutes to herself, she poured a glass of iced tea. Relaxing in the living room in a comfortable armchair, she opened Marguerite's journal and re-read the last entry, written a few days before Degas had left New Orleans for good.

> March 10, 1873
>
> I took up Edgar's notebook again today. There are sketches of me, the De Gas family, ballerinas, and horses, and notes about us all. Estelle appears in several places in different poses. I like her so much. She's kind and embraces life, despite her blindness. Edgar said she has encouraged him to paint more than anyone. I know he'll be famous one day.
>
> He told me nothing is more important to him than his art, not even me. I couldn't help crying when he said that; I hoped he might propose marriage. When he saw how upset I was, he gave me the notebook, and said I can keep it in memory of him. I prefer his company to all the young men I've met, even though Maman says he's too old for me. Why did he say I should keep his notebook "in memory of him"? Is he planning to leave soon? Oh, I hope not.

Anne heaved a sigh as she closed the journal. Poor Marguerite. Had she continued to paint, only to become another artist lost in the thrust of time? Well, at least she, Anne, would keep her memory alive. Marguerite had been resolute, never wavering in her interest in Degas.

Perhaps Homer had been right about the forlornness of empty houses. No ghosts had appeared since Anne had moved in, and probably wouldn't, now that she understood the truths about some of her more troubled ancestors.

Remembering the portrait of Estelle, she bowed her head. Estelle had left a poignant memory, and she could almost hear her strong voice echoing from the walls urging courage, kindness, and hope.

She stood up, ambled to the window and lifted the sash. Cool breezes fanned her face, and the honey aroma of magnolia filled her with the familiar longing for understanding. Beyond the garden she could see twisted live oak branches covered with Spanish moss swaying in the wind, ghostly gray objects, blending with green and blue shadows. Too bad Degas had never painted those.

Or had he?

Epilogue

This is a work of historical fiction. The Degas and Musson characters existed in real life, but Anne Gautier and her friends, associates, and relatives, including the Fontenots, and Marguerite's journal, are entirely fictitious. Summarized below are some of the facts about the Degas–Musson family members, as well as some true events included in the story and after Edgar Degas's return to Paris in March 1873.

Degas's masterpiece *A Cotton Office in New Orleans* was shown at the second Impressionist Exhibition in Paris in 1876. Highly praised, it was sold to the Musée des Beaux-Arts in Pau, France in 1878. Gail Feigenbaum, Curator of European Painting and coauthor of the book, *Degas and New Orleans: A French Impressionist in America*, that was prepared to accompany the exhibit of Degas paintings at the New Orleans Museum of Art in 1999, stated, "He had not painted New Orleans. With *A Cotton Office*, he had redeemed his experience: He had painted America."[1]

Degas kept notebooks of sketches and his comments throughout his life, many of which still exist in collections. No notebook has ever been found containing sketches of New Orleans or of the approximately two dozen paintings started or completed there.

Edgar Degas was the only French Impressionist painter to work in America. Many scholars believe that the five months in New Orleans represented a turning point in his life and art. Upon his return to Paris he eased the family's financial burdens by selling some paintings. He had planned to stay in New Orleans for only two months, but he missed his train, for unknown reasons, and stayed on. It is possible that, had he left earlier, there would have been no *Cotton Office* painting.[2] Later in 1873, Degas's father died, his estate greatly in debt. Degas never married, and kept most of the paintings of his New Orleans family in his studio for the rest of his life. He died in Paris in 1917 at age eighty-three, almost blind.

The family's cotton business, the firm of Musson, Prestidge, and Company, declared bankruptcy on February 1, 1873.

Degas's painting of Estelle, *Portrait of Mme. René De Gas, née Estelle Musson*, 1872–3, was purchased in 1964 by the New Orleans Museum of Art by means of the "Bringing Estelle Home" fundraising campaign. On the day before the museum's option to buy it was due to expire, a last-minute donation was made, and the museum acquired the painting. It remains in the museum's collection today.

Estelle De Gas, née Musson, married René De Gas, her second husband, in 1869. They had five children together (two were born after Degas left New Orleans). René abandoned her and the children in 1878. The Musson family moved from the house on Esplanade Avenue that year, and lived temporarily in a house in the French Quarter. Meanwhile, Estelle's cousin James Freret built a house for her at 125 Esplanade Avenue, and she and Désirée lived there until Désirée's death. Estelle lost vision in her left eye in 1868 and her right eye in 1875. She was known for her spirit, kindness and fortitude, and died in 1909 at age sixty-six.

René De Gas left Estelle and their children in 1878, five years after Edgar's visit to New Orleans, and eloped with America Durrive Olivier. They married bigamously in Cleveland, Ohio, soon afterward. After obtaining a divorce and marrying legally in 1879, René moved with his wife to Paris. They had three children together. René was unreliable in his childcare payments to Estelle, and never repaid the debts he owed to the bankrupt cotton business. The abandonment caused a rift in the family, particularly between René and the Musson family and between René and Edgar. Many years later, the brothers reconciled, and Edgar left René half his estate. René died in 1921 at age seventy-six.

Achille De Gas caused a scandal when he returned to Paris and wounded the husband of his former mistress. He spent a month in prison. Five years later he married a woman from New Orleans. He died in 1893 at age fifty-five.

Matilde Bell, née Musson, and six-year-old Jeanne De Gas, Estelle and René's third child and Degas's godchild, died of yellow fever in 1878.

Jo Balfour, Estelle's daughter from her first marriage, died in 1881 at age eighteen of scarlet fever. Pierre De Gas, Estelle and René's oldest son, died the same year at age eleven, also of scarlet fever.

Désirée Musson never married, and died in 1902 at age sixty-four. She was devoted to her family and assisted her father when he became deranged at the end of his life.

Michel Musson made poor investments in Confederate bonds, which hastened the demise of his cotton business in 1873. He was furious with René for leaving Estelle and their five children, whom he legally adopted, changing their names to Musson. He became mentally unstable at the end of his life, and died in 1885 at age seventy-one.

A word about New Orleans

During the 1970s, the city was engaged in a number of urban renewal projects. Large areas of the Tremé district and other low-income neighborhoods had been or were in the process of being demolished. Esplanade Avenue had deteriorated; crime-ridden and dangerous, it was no longer considered a safe area, and most of the fine Creole houses built in the 1850s had fallen into disrepair. A number of preservation groups fought to save historic buildings in several areas of the city, and some were successful. Now, in 2020, many houses have been renovated, despite the destruction of Hurricane Katrina in 2005. Anne's house is a composite of several of these restored houses and does not exist; however, 2306 Esplanade, the former Musson residence, still stands. Smaller than the original estate, part of the old mansion has been preserved, and it is now a bed and breakfast.

Afterword

Although this is a work of historical fiction, I have attempted to portray Degas's character as accurately as possible during that period of his life. He acquired a reputation for being surly, difficult, and a misogynist, though witty and capable of generosity. But while in New Orleans, he wrote to friends in Paris of his interest in marriage and children. Gail Feigenbaum in her essay "Edgar Degas, Almost a Son of Louisiana," states, "Edgar was immediately at ease with his Louisiana relatives. They brought out a gentler side of his personality in contrast to the sharpness remarked on by many of his familiars."[3]

The Notes section provides references for many actual quotes that are scattered throughout the story. I hope the novel captures something of the spirit of the era and that I have done justice to the painter and his family at a remarkable time, both in his life and in the city of New Orleans in 1872–73. I believe it's a story worth telling.

A list at the end of the book provides details about the paintings referred to in the story that Degas started or completed during his time in New Orleans. He is thought to have painted about two dozen there. I tried to weave references to the paintings into the tale and to write scenes describing several of them. I regret that we are unable to publish all the images here, but they may be found online or in art books. All of them appear in the New Orleans Museum of Art's publication *Degas and New Orleans: A French Impressionist in America.*[4]

Notes

Throughout the notes section, where translations from the French are used, the exact words may differ from the source. Translations reprinted from Degas's letters reprinted by Marcel Guerin are by Marguerite Kay.

Frontispiece
Genealogical Chart: De Gas–Musson Family in New Orleans/ Fontenot Family.

Modified version of chart. In Feigenbaum, Gail, and Jean Sutherland Boggs, 1999. *Degas in New Orleans: A French Impressionist in America* by James B. Byrnes and Victoria Cooke, Appendix I, p. 277. The New Orleans Museum of Art.

Chapter 2
"great *artiste.*" The actual words used mockingly by René appear in a letter he wrote to Estelle on July 17, 1872: "Prepare a fitting reception for the Grrrande Artiste." Quoted by Feigenbaum, *Degas in New Orleans: A French Impressionist in America,* p. 12.

Creoles are sometimes defined as descendants of colonial New Orleanians.

Chapter 4

"what a good thing family is." From a letter written by Degas to Désiré Dihau on November 11, 1872. In Guerin, Marcel, ed. 1947. *Degas Letters*.

"turkey buzzard." René wrote to Estelle on July 12, 1872, "Edgar . . . is crazy to learn to pronounce English words . . . he has been repeating *turkey buzzard* for a whole week." Quoted by Benfey, Chris, in Feigenbaum, *Degas in New Orleans: A French Impressionist in America*, p. 25.

"a good woman, a few children of my own, is that excessive?" From a letter written by Degas to Henri Rouart on December 5, 1872. In Guerin, *Degas Letters*.

Chapter 8

"I prefer to paint what is familiar." Degas wrote, "one loves and gives art only to which one is accustomed." From a letter written to Henri Rouart on December 5, 1872. In Guerin, *Degas Letters*.

Chapter 10

"everything here attracts me," Degas wrote to Lorenz Froehlich. He also described his pleasure at seeing white children in black arms. From a letter dated November 27, 1872. In Guerin, *Degas Letters*.

"I promised Estelle I would paint the family, and I will content myself with that." Degas wrote to Rouart on December 5th, "A few family portraits will be the sum total of my efforts, I was unable to avoid that and assuredly would not wish to complain if it were less difficult and if the models less restless. Oh well, it will be a journey I have done and very little else." In Guerin, *Degas Letters*.

"I've no interest in cotton." Degas wrote to Rouart, "One does nothing here, it lies in the climate, nothing but cotton, one lives for cotton and from cotton." December 5, 1872. In Guerin, *Degas Letters*.

Chapter 30

"This is the best painting I've done since I came to New Orleans." On February 18,1873, Degas wrote to his friend James Tissot, "After having wasted time in the family trying to do portraits in the worst conditions of day that I have ever found or imagined, I have attached myself to a fairly vigorous picture." He was referring to *A Cotton Office in New Orleans.* In Guerin, *Degas Letters.*

Chapter 32

"marriage . . . free him from the need to be gallant." His words in a letter to Tissot were, "A good family: it is really a good thing to be married, to have good children, to be free of the need of being gallant. Ye gods, it is really time one thought about it." November 19, 1872. In Guerin, *Degas Letters.*

Epilogue

1. Feigenbaum, Gail, and Jean Sutherland Boggs, *Degas and New Orleans: A French Impressionist in America.* "Edgar Degas, almost a son of Louisiana," p. 16. New Orleans Museum of Art, 1999.

2. Feigenbaum, p. 17.

Afterward

3. Feigenbaum, p. 9.

4. Ibid., Jean Sutherland Boggs, Catalogue, p. 105 onward.

Paintings by Degas in New Orleans referred to in the story

Painting	Chapter(s) in story
*Young Girl in a White Dress (*Carrie Bell*)* 1872 Oil on canvas 10 ½ x 8 ⅝ inches Private Collection, The Bahamas	10
Children on a Doorstep 1872 Oil on canvas 23 ⅝ x 29 ½ inches Ordrupgaard, Copenhagen, Denmark	10, 12
Portrait of Mme René de Gas, *née Estelle Musson* 1872-73 Oil on canvas 39 ⅜ x 54 inches New Orleans Museum of Art: Museum Purchase through Public Subscription	11, 14, 25, 29, 31, 35

Painting	Chapter(s) in story
The Song Rehearsal 1872-73 Oil on canvas 31 ⅞ x 25 ⅝ inches Dumbarton Oaks Research Library and Collection, Washington, D.C.	12
Woman Seated on a Balcony *(*Mathilde Musson Bell*)* 1872 Pastel 24 ⅜ x 29 ⅞ inches Ordrupgaard, Copenhagen, Denmark	20
La Pédicure (Jo Balfour) 1873 Essence on paper mounted on canvas 24 x 18 ⅛ inches Musée d'Orsay, Paris	26
A Cotton Office in New Orleans *(Portraits in a Cotton Office)* 1873 Oil on canvas 28 ¾ x 36 ¼ inches Musée des Beaux-Arts, Pau	30, 33
Cotton Merchants in New Orleans 1873 Oil on canvas 23 ⅝ x 28 ¾ inches Harvard University Art Museums (Fogg) Cambridge, Massachusetts	30

Acknowledgments

This story would not exist if my husband, Vince, had not begun teaching classes on fiction writing several years ago. I had never written fiction before, and his coaching helped me and many others to write in a style that was for many of us a completely new experience. Vince's support of my creative efforts has been invaluable, and I thank him for turning me into an author.

I owe a special vote of thanks to my stepmother, Neena Stewart. She read an early draft, encouraged me to publish, and kept asking not if, but when I would do so. But for her, I would have given up trying, and I persevered.

Professional editor Jessica de Bruyn read part of my manuscript when I submitted it to an *Ink and Insights* contest. As one of the judges, she gave me valuable initial feedback and then followed up with full critiques. I needed these, and have her to thank for pulling me out of many pitfalls. Later, Ellen Notbohm assisted with deep edits and made wise suggestions for improving the final draft.

Other friends deserve mention also. Several of these kindly read early drafts, put up with my obsessive ramblings about the book, and offered encouragement: Sue Adams, Tina Brown, Jo Critchfield, Audrey Van Cleve Dickson, Marie-Claire Dole, Maggie Fisher, Liz Jozniak Glickman, Laura Hamilton, Aleli

Howell, Robyn Kruse, Carol Masters, Martha Burck Shackelford, Gail Sheridan, Susan Lavell Warm, Jean Wharton, and my brother Jonathan Stewart.

I relied heavily for my research on the New Orleans Museum of Art publication *Degas and New Orleans: A French Impressionist in America* by Gail Feigenbaum and Jean Sutherland Boggs which was published in 1999 to accompany the Museum's exhibit of Degas's work in May–August 1999. The same exhibit was presented in Ordrupgaard, Copenhagen, in September–November, also in 1999. The paintings mentioned in the novel were all included as part of these exhibitions.

Thanks are due also to my publicist, Caitlin Hamilton Summie, who managed to make a publicity process that I dreaded into a worthwhile adventure, and to Libby Jordan, for her help with social media.

My adult children, Jenny and James Keul, followed the passage of the book with interest and gave me hope along the way. Other special friends fall into this category, too many to name. I thank you all.

I'm grateful to everyone at She Writes Press: the community of writers, including Ashley Sweeney, and especially Brooke Warner for accepting the story and Lauren Wise for helping bring it to print. I hope many women writers will be encouraged to publish using the outstanding services offered by this distinctive publisher.

About the Author

L inda Henley, an English-born American, moved to the United States with her family when she was sixteen. She is a graduate of Newcomb College of Tulane University in New Orleans. She currently lives with her husband in Anacortes, Washington. This is her first novel.

Author photo © Mark Gardner

SELECTED TITLES FROM SHE WRITES PRESS

She Writes Press is an independent publishing company founded to serve women writers everywhere. Visit us at www.shewritespress.com.

The Black Velvet Coat by Jill G. Hall. $16.95, 978-1-63152-009-9. When the current owner of a black velvet coat—a San Francisco artist in search of inspiration—and the original owner, a 1960s heiress who fled her affluent life fifty years earlier, cross paths, their lives are forever changed . . . for the better.

Portrait of a Woman in White by Susan Winkler. $16.95, 978-1-938314-83-4. When the Nazis steal a Matisse portrait from the eccentric, art-loving Rosenswigs, the Parisian family is thrust into the tumult of war and separation, their fates intertwined with that of their beloved portrait.

Peregrine Island by Diane B. Saxton. $16.95, 978-1-63152-151-5. The Peregrine family's lives are turned upside-down one summer when so-called "art experts" appear on the doorstep of their Connecticut island home to appraise a favorite heirloom painting—and incriminating papers are discovered behind the painting in question.

Hysterical: Anna Freud's Story by Rebecca Coffey. $18.95, 978-1-938314-42-1. An irreverent, fictionalized exploration of the seemingly contradictory life of Anna Freud—told from her point of view.

The Vintner's Daughter by Kristen Harnisch. $16.95, 978-163152-929-0. Set against the sweeping canvas of French and California vineyard life in the late 1890s, this is the compelling tale of one woman's struggle to reclaim her family's Loire Valley vineyard—and her life.

The Sweetness by Sande Boritz Berger. $16.95, 978-1-63152-907-8. A compelling and powerful story of two girls—cousins living on separate continents—whose strikingly different lives are forever changed when the Nazis invade Vilna, Lithuania.